A CHILD UPON THE THRONE

A CHILD UPON THE THRONE

THE KNIGHTS OF ENGLAND SERIES, BOOK FOUR

MARY ELLEN JOHNSON

Book and cover design by eBook Prep
www.ebookprep.com

February 2020
ISBN: 978-1-64457-020-3

ePublishing Works!
644 Shrewsbury Commons Ave
Ste 249
Shrewsbury PA 17361
United States of America

www.epublishingworks.com
Phone: 866-846-5123

Fourteenth
Century
England

Scotland

North Sea

Newcastle upon Tyne
Durham
Carlisle
County Cumbria
Lake Winandermere

Isle of Man

Blackpool
Pontefract Castle
York
Liverpool
Spurn Head

Irish Sea

Ireland

England

Nottingham

Birmingham
Kenilworth
Swaffham Manor
Bury St Edmunds
Oxford
Ipswich

Celtic Sea

Bristol
Bath
London
Tonbridge
Canterbury
Stonehenge
Dover

New Forest
Exmouth
Isle of Wight

Pensans

0   60   120 Km
0   60 Miles
All Distances Approximate

The Channel

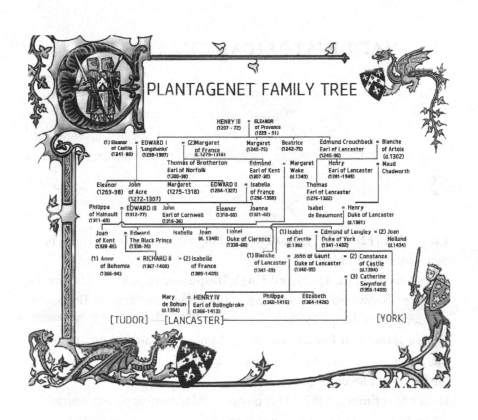

MAIN HISTORICAL CHARACTERS

Edward II (1284-1327): first English king since the Conqueror to be deposed; later murdered.

Piers Gaveston (d. 1312) and Hugh Despenser (d. 1327): Edward II's favorites. Showered them with lands, titles and other honors. Both murdered by unhappy lords.

Queen Isabella of France: (1296-1358) bore Edward II four children, including Edward III. In 1326 invades England to overthrow her husband with lover Roger Mortimer.

Roger Mortimer: (1287-1330) powerful Marcher baron and warrior. After deposing and possibly murdering Edward II, Mortimer and Isabella repeated Edward II's mistakes by rewarding themselves with riches. Killed by Edward III in 1330.

Edward III: (1312-1377) Edward of Windsor: Oldest son of Edward II. Reign often compared to that of the mythical King Arthur; ranked among England's greatest monarchs.

Philippa of Hainault: (1311-1369) King Edward's wife. Bears thirteen children. Happy marriage.

Edward of Woodstock, Prince of Wales and Aquitaine (later known to history as the Black Prince) (1330-1376) King Edward's oldest son and heir to England's throne. He wins his spurs at Crecy at age 16 and overcomes the far superior French in the Battle of Poitiers. Even enemies call him the "flower of chivalry of all the world."

Joan of Kent: (1328-1385) Black Prince's wife. Married twice before the prince, and mother to five previous children.

Richard II/Richard of Bordeaux: (1367-1400) Son of the Black Prince and Joan of Kent. Ascends England's throne at age 10. Hero during the Peasants' Rebellion of 1381, he reneges on promises to commons.

John of Gaunt, Duke of Lancaster (1340-1399) King Edward's third son. Richest man in England. Hated by many of the commons.

Henry of Bolingbroke: (1366-1413) John of Gaunt's oldest son. Born within three months of Richard II. In 1399 he will depose Richard II and become Henry IV.

John Ball: (1338-1381) a hedge-priest—priest without a parish—who wanders England for more than two decades, decrying the plight of the common man and pushing for a better life. The spark that ignites the Peasant's Rebellion/Great Rising.

FICTIONAL CHARACTERS:

Maria d'Arderne/Rendell (1300-1380): woman who starts it all!
Marries the knight, Phillip Rendell, and has an affair with Richard,
Earl of Sussex, which helps change the course of Edward II's kingdom.
Phillip Rendell: Maria's moon. Black-haired blue-eyed husband who
is inflicted with a discontent and wanderlust that forever frustrates his
wife.
Richard of Sussex: Maria's sun. Edward II's illegitimate half-brother,
who is torn between loyalty to his vassal and friend, Phillip Rendell
and his love for Maria.

CHARACTERS IN A KNIGHT THERE WAS, WITHIN A FOREST DARK, AND A CHILD UPON THE THRONE:

Margery Watson: daughter of Maria Rendell's oldest son, Thomas Rendell, and peasant woman, Alice Watson, who is murdered during the Black Death.

Matthew Hart: Earl of Cumbria. Margery's lover. Matthew has fought in most of the major battles of Edward III's reign—Poitiers, Najera, Limoges, The Great *Chevauchée*—which have turned him from eager warrior to weary survivor.

Thurold Watson: Margery's radical stepbrother who, along with John Ball, seeks a more just England. He vows revenge against Lawrence Ravenne, who was their lord during the time of the Black Death and who murdered Thurold and Margery's mother.

William Hart: Matthew's beloved father. Dies in 1373, after Matthew returns from the Great Chevauchée.

Elizabeth Ravenne nee Hart: Matthew Hart's sister. Marries Lawrence Ravenne. Mother of eight sons, all with names from the Arthurian romances.

Harry Hart: Matthew's younger brother. Indifferent knight. Marries Matthew's former lover, Desiderata Cecy, and dies during John of Gaunt's Great Chevauchee of 1373.

Sosanna Hart: Matthew's mother.

Thomas Rendell: oldest son of Maria and her husband, Phillip. Margery's father as the result of a dalliance with peasant woman Alice Watson.

Lawrence Ravenne: Matthew Hart's brutal brother-in-law. During the time of the Black Death, Ravenne murders Margery Watson's mother, (Thurold Watson's stepmother), which earns Thurold's lifelong enmity and quest for revenge.

Serill Hart: Margery and Matthew's illegitimate son.

Simon Crull: influential goldsmith who tricks a young Margery into marrying him. Margery mistakenly believes that Matthew Hart, who even then is her lover, betrayed her by not stopping the marriage. This leads to six years' separation and lingering distrust between Margery and Matthew.

Desiderata Cecy: Matthew Hart's former lover who marries Harry Hart in order to punish Matthew, who she'd tricked into leaving Margery Watson and becoming her lover. Only to fall in love with Harry and mourn his death following John of Gaunt's Great Chevauchee in 1373.

Ralph Hart: Desiderata Cecy and Harry's son.

PREFACE

I like to think of my five-part series, *Knights of England*, as the book-ends that encompass fourteenth century England. (At least my version!) *The Lion and the Leopard* begins with the disastrous reign of a king, Edward II, who is deposed and murdered. My final installment ends with the disastrous reign of a king, Richard II, Edward II's great grandson, who is deposed and murdered. Between that we have one of the most accomplished of England's kings, Edward III, who guides his kingdom through a golden age—at least for himself and his fellow members of the nobility, if not always for his less favored subjects—before it all crumbles into ruin. I always think of Edward of Windsor as the King-Who-Ruled-Too-Long. Like so many, he was not blessed enough to exit the stage when he would be lamented, but after he'd outlived most of his contemporaries, several of his children, and his beloved wife. As he'd outlived his health, his capacity to rule, and his faculties. But, while so many leap over the fourteenth century to dig around in the War of the Roses and dear God, the Tudors forever and ever, the roots of many of those conflicts begin here in the kingdoms of these Edwards. (And before of course. We could trace some things, such as the vagaries of human nature, back to the beginning of time.)

In 1348, the Black Death descended upon England, as it descended upon much of the rest of the world, with devastating results that directly led to the Peasants' Revolt of 1381. (A revolt that has been referenced throughout history, including during our own American Revolution.) Grand and doomed it was, as was the French *Jacquerie* of 1358. As is so often the outcome for the poor and powerless. But the oppressed keep fighting, in fits and starts, and will continue their quest for a just world, however they define it.

Mid-century marks the beginning of the Hundred Years' War, of so many grand and glorious campaigns when Edward III and his son, later known to history as the Black Prince, were the colossi who straddled the European continent. When England was burning its way through France, claiming that Edward III was rightful sovereign of both France and England. When the merchant class was expanding, often to the lamentations of their superiors, for what good was a society when merchants were sometimes richer than their lords and sometimes their lords were reduced to making a tradesman's living—or just as inappropriately—marrying into that lower class?

It goes without saying that everyone has a favorite period of history and can make an impassioned argument for their choice. Revolutionary... Most important... Most brutal... Most enlightened... I don't make any such claims to my tiny slice of the fourteenth century, other than to say that knights, castles, chevauchées, courtly love and all the rest ignite my passion. And, when researching kings and queens and political intrigues, I don't find much difference between their behavior and that of today's newsmakers. Regardless of what century, human nature doesn't change. We can pretty it up in the telling, but whether you're contemplating Edward II's favorites or Richard II's vindictiveness, so much seems to come down to the quest for power. Material goods. Titles. Prestige. More. More. You could transplant Roger Mortimer, ambitious lover to Edward II's Queen, into the twenty-first century, dress him up in an expensive suit and he would fit flawlessly into many corporate boardrooms or government cabinets. So, even when I'm writing about the demands of John Ball and his yeomen followers, the devastation of war, the depositions of Edward II and Richard II, I see parallels in the contemporary world. ("Of course," you say. "For man ever searches for meaning." And you're right.)

When creating the *Knights of England* series, my primary goal has always been to tell an interesting story. While I tried to be historically accurate and true to what we know about kings and knights, battles and politics, religious beliefs and cultural assumptions, I chose to create fictional main characters primarily because there are actual scholars out there who have already revealed everything that is known about the Kings' Edward and their satellites. I always feel presumptuous when putting thoughts into the heads of actual people. I have no such problems with my fictional characters and hope that the occasional expert who picks up my books might find something universally relatable— while simultaneously glimpsing themselves in the distant mirror that is fourteenth century England—via the lives of Maria d'Arderne, Phillip Rendell and Richard of Sussex in *The Lion and the Leopard* and Matthew Hart, Margery Watson and Thurold Watson in *A Knight There Was, Within a Forest Dark*, and *A Child Upon the Throne*. A theme that runs through all my work is the transitoriness of life, an echoing of the saying, "Life though pleasant is transitory, even as is the Cherry Fair." (Needless to say, I've tried unsuccessfully to name at least one of my books *The Cherry Fair*.) Fortune's wheel is another. Inequality, the discontent of the common folk. It reaches its crescendo in the Peasants' Revolt, which closes *A Child Upon the Throne*. Also, my lord Matthew Hart's transformation from a callow youth to a disillusioned warrior is addressed and resolved. As is Margery Watson's conflict over the matter of her "blood" and her loyalties. While my favorite parts of writing historical fiction always involve chevauchées and battles—the courage, stupidity, insanity and brutality that comprise England and France's "war of a long season"—I also enjoyed writing about the Great Rising/Peasants' Revolt. I only wish it had a happier ending.

Some notes on accuracy: I appreciate having mistakes pointed out to me for future correction. However, research is as frustrating as it is fascinating, for there isn't universal agreement on a whole host of things, including something as basic as how many legitimate children were sired by Edward III. Often, as in the death of Edward II, which was most likely murder but maybe not, I chose the most dramatic narratives. (Many thanks to Ian Mortimer, whose knowledge of the period is matched by his ability to make the reading of it such fun!) The extent of John Ball's participation in the Peasants' Revolt. Or the Black Prince's siege at Limoges. There is some evidence that there was NO slaughter of townsfolk, certainly not one of sickening proportions. (Many apologies to one of my forever crushes, Edward the Black Prince, who, yes, I know was only referred to by that appellation from Tudor times.) Bottomline, I'm trying to give the *feel* of the times, and since so much information is contradictory I'm simply choosing what I believe works best for the story.

Also, a few words on "words." While there is no way I can be accurate in my use of language that was common in that time period, I've tried to be as true once again to the feel as possible. Words like fuck and cunt were used but not as curse words. If a word, such as bloody, was used as a pejorative within a few centuries, I might use it. For references to such things as the tales of Robin Hood, oral forms had been around for centuries so I felt comfortable including them. Medieval man, unfortunately, had not invented the internet, so much original documentation may be forever lost.

Now we come, specifically, to *A Child Upon the Throne*: In a series it is always difficult to create a compelling narrative that can be read apart from other related books, while inserting enough background information to make the story comprehensible without boring those who have read the previous installments. Now here I am presenting my fourth book with more than sixty years of characters and events and a thousand preceding pages. I hope the addition of a map, the Planta-genet lineage and a list of recurring characters, both historical and fictional, will help with those who are picking up my work for the first time.

To summarize:

Had my knight, Matthew Hart, been a veteran of World War I's horrors, he would have been described as "shell-shocked." Today we speak of Post-Traumatic Stress Disorder. Did medieval man just call this shattering of the psyche madness? Weakness? I don't know. But whatever the label, Matthew retreats into the wilds of Cumbria to come to terms with the atrocities he's committed. His relationship with long-time love, Margery Watson, has ended more in sadness than acrimony, though she is determined to forget him. Thus her very fun-for-me-to-write tryst with Fulco the Smithy. But of course Margery and Matthew are reconciled, just as England lurches toward full-blown rebellion. The boy king, Richard II, and his counselors have overseen French raids along the coasts of England and watched vast tracts of land won by his grandfather, Edward III, being returned to their ancient enemy. Commoners long for the good old days of Crecy, Poitiers, Najera—when England was winning and English soldiers returned home with all manner of booty, which in turn increased their prosperity. Why should Englishmen (women did not count) now have their taxes raised to finance wars that bring no profit and a government that cannot govern? Just as Margery and Matthew are riding north to the earldom of Cumbria and their wedding, the Great Rising begins. John Ball, who Margery has always considered her lodestar, leads the rebellion, along with her stepbrother, Thurold Watson. During the final hours of the Rising, Thurold finally achieves revenge against Lawrence Ravenne, the hated knight who murdered their mother. But as is so often the case events end with the oppressed being slaughtered by their oppressors. And with the oppressed slinking back into their individual miseries... until enough time passes and enough injustices are heaped upon them that they rise up and try once again.

As far as my hero and heroine, will these tragedies finally doom Matthew and Margery and their love?

If not, what future awaits them in a kingdom ruled by a narcissist (a contemporary diagnosis), who seems doomed by fate (and temperament) to repeat the errors of his great-grandfather, Edward II?

Which leads me to my final question, which is also a persistent theme throughout, and is embodied in the haunting refrain from "Where Have all the Flowers Gone?"

"When will they ever learn? When will they ever learn??"

When will we?

CHAPTER 1

London, 1377

"*L*ook behind you to All Hallows-by-the-Tower," said the wayward priest, John Ball, addressing a surprisingly large audience. "'Tis a fine church, dating back to the time before the Normans, and grand enough to impress the noblest worshipper. But who constructed it? Not a king or his ministers or his knights or his bishops."

Margery Watson stood in All Hallows-by-the-Tower's precincts next to her stepbrother, Thurold, who appeared as enraptured by the Lollard priest's jeremiad as if he'd not been hearing similar versions these past two decades.

Margery simply enjoyed being in John's presence—never mind his political views—for the big man was her guardian angel, albeit minus wings and arrayed in a russet cassock. John Ball had rescued her from a life of drudgery tucked away as she had been in a village decimated by the Great Pestilence. And throughout Margery's life, John had a way of appearing when she most needed him, whether to provide her with a lawyer who'd repeatedly argued to the Consistory Court that her marriage to Simon Crull *must* be annulled, or before giving birth to her son while her lover had been chasing the French around Limousin.

"*You* constructed this church, as well as every church the length of England." John Ball's dark eyes flashed; he extended his massive arms as if bestowing benediction upon the crowd. "From the meanest to St. Paul's Cathedral, all were built from naught save the rocks of the earth, the timbers of the forest, and the honest sweat of men such as you."

John's manner of preaching was both seductive and powerful. Margery could not help but be stirred. For, no matter how seditious, the hedge-priest spoke truth. All could not be right in England until there was equality, when lord must remove his boot from the throat of the peasant, when the king's ministers no longer bled commoners via taxation, when bishops ceased residing in palaces that even John of Gaunt might envy.

Yet here I am, Margery often thought, *astraddle two worlds*. Daughter of a peasant mother and a noble father, Thomas Rendell, who had recently acknowledged her as his own. A widow made wealthy via the goldsmith's trade; a woman made privileged by being the mistress of Lord Matthew Hart, Earl of Cumbria.

"All Hallows-by-the-Tower is a testament to each of you, for your brothers created it." John's impassioned gaze swept the green-garbed yeomen, the somberly dressed merchants, the household servants paused in their duties to have a listen, the beggars still clutching their begging bowls. "Masons dug a foundation, just as you are the foundation of society. And just as broken stone is pitched into the holes, so are you discarded when your usefulness ends, or when your masters are displeased."

Margery raised her eyes to the nearby Tower of London, both prison and royal residence, where a conspiracy of ravens perched upon its battlements, as if overseeing the activities below.

Harbingers of death, ill omens, minions of the devil.

Margery crossed herself, pulled her cloak closer as much to ward off her sudden uneasiness as the January chill, and dragged her attention back to the hedge priest.

"It has been too long forgotten that though we are dependent on our

2

lords, they are also dependent on us." John Ball's voice rose and fell like a smithy's hammer. "Our entire society needs the priest and knight and peasant, and none can stand alone."

"'Tis so," said Thurold, his narrow face aglow. He shouted, "You speak truth, John Ball."

"You speak blasphemy," a tradesman countered, though others turned to glower at him. England of 1377 was a kingdom in crisis— bedeviled by an ailing monarch incapable of tending to any matter beyond the cosseting of his mistress; swarming with discontented laborers lamenting rising prices and stagnant wages; wearied of endless wars that no longer guaranteed victory; and mourning the recent loss of England's talisman, Edward the Black Prince.

"London could not survive without the bakers who bring their bread carts from Stratford. Or those who carry Kentish coal to Croydon. Look about you. The houses of the rich are being turned into tenements for workers to spin and weave and dye, and their masters are as dishonest as the lords they serve."

Was John Ball referring to last year's Good Parliament when the House of Commons had found members of the Royal Council guilty of financial fraud and high interest moneylending? Might Richard Lyons, former Warden of the Mint, at this very moment be gazing down upon them from slits in the Tower of London? Observing with eyes as cold and watchful as the Tower ravens'? Surely Richard Lyons was aware that All-Hallows-by-the-Tower was the temporary repository for prisoners after they were beheaded on Tower Hill. From his prison rooms, could Lyons view the disturbed earth or the shrouded torsos with their heads tucked... where? Upon their chests? Positioned within an arm, as if cradling a market basket? Did Richard Lyons awaken sweating from nightmares in which he himself was being led to the executioner's block?

How transitory is life and power.

Margery remembered how the financier, who she'd known from her days as wife to Simon Crull the Goldsmith, used to swagger about, how supplicants had trembled before him, how he had bent the rules of God and man to his purpose. As the Black Prince lay dying, Lyons had made a gift to him of a barrel supposedly filled with fish, only to have its contents revealed to contain £1000 of gold. Prince Edward had indignantly returned the bribe, though his father, who'd been sent a similar barrel and kept it, had merely shrugged and said, "He has offered us nothing which is not our own."

And now this same Richard Lyons found himself buried in the Tower, no doubt filled with the same fears and regrets as a thousand prisoners before him. A great Marcher lord, Roger Mortimer, who'd deposed the old, bad king, Edward II, and become lover to the old, bad king's consort, Isabella, had been literally walled up in the Tower while awaiting his trial (and execution, of course). Death followed arrest as regularly as night followed day. Had Richard Lyons also been walled away? No matter. The White Tower, so beautiful and so forbidding, was simply an enormous gravestone for all the men and women who had reached too high.

Margery felt a sudden urge to rush back to Warrick Inn, to hug her son close and to nestle in the protective embrace of her lover. Matthew Hart would protect her. He always had.

John Ball was winding up his speech, pacing and gesticulating as he did so. "Remember this! There would be no church bells, cathedrals, food, fine silver plate, nor even the meanest vessel without you. *You* are England's backbone. Someday all must come to realize the least is necessary for the greatest."

A pair of merchants, vintners from the look of them, began muttering and shaking their heads. One walked away, and Margery caught the word "treason."

As if John Ball, who had been preaching for decades, cared about the opprobrium of a few! John had been ignored, mocked, imprisoned, excommunicated—and still he persisted. Margery loved him for the man he was apart from his dangerous beliefs, and privately *because* of them.

With the waning afternoon, shadows from All-Hallows-by-the-Tower crawled across the crowd. Darkness came early and the season's cold had already begun settling in their bones. Margery nodded to her maid, Cicily, signaling it was time to depart. While she had inherited the Shop of the Unicorn, located on Goldsmith's Row, following the death of her husband, Margery, her son and Matthew Hart lived at Warrick Inn, a brisk walk east of the Tower.

Somehow, while Margery had been woolgathering, John Ball had veered from his usual closing statements to lambast their ailing king and his mistress, Alice Perrers, who had been banished following the Good Parliament. Or more precisely, the new woman who warmed Edward III's bed. Lady Desiderata Cecy.

"Ah, the shame, when our king tends to the needs of his leman rather than the needs of his kingdom."

At mention of Lady Cecy, Margery's spine stiffened and her eyes narrowed, as if the object of her hatred stood before her. She felt as if she were engaged in the metaphorical version of the biblical "weeping and gnashing of teeth." Scheming, unprincipled Desiderata "Desire" Cecy, mistress to King Edward, widow of Matthew's younger brother, Harry—and one time lover of Matthew Hart himself.

"Curse 'em all," someone growled. Others tsk-tsked or muttered darkly about the disrespect shown to the memory of their good Queen Philippa.

As if that strumpet would care, Margery thought, hands clenched inside kidskin gloves.

True, it had been nearly a decade since Desiderata Cecy and Matthew had been involved, and only following Margery's forced marriage to Simon Crull. But Matthew and Desire had been lovers for six years, during Matthew's entire service at the Bordelais court under his liege lord, Edward the Black Prince. The harlot, the whore—for she had surely earned those epithets with her careless promiscuity—had long conspired to woo Matthew Hart into her bed. And Margery was convinced, though she could never prove it, that Desiderata Cecy had been responsible for orchestrating Margery's marriage to Simon Crull in the first place.

If Satan were female, she would bear that woman's face and form.

Matthew, Margery and Desire shared a long, complicated history and now the slut had come round again, using her body and her wiles to have her way. Not to mention the disgrace Desire was bringing upon the Hart name for she was supposed to remain in mourning over the loss of Harry Hart, dead three years past.

I do not even have to ask whether the creature has any shame, for obviously she does not.

Eager to be off, Margery touched her stepbrother's arm and nodded in the direction of the street.

"Aye, Stick Legs." Thurold followed her and Cicily away from the bystanders.

Despite their attempts to remain friendly, Thurold and Margery's relationship was strained. Her stepbrother was well aware of her illicit relationship with one of those he held responsible for all the world's ills, yet they managed an uneasy truce. Meaning they both pretended her "arrangement" with Matthew Hart was an innocent one. And that Margery's son, Serill, had not been sired by Matthew but by her legitimate husband.

"Where are you and John Ball bound next?" Margery asked, following a quick parting kiss on the lips in the customary fashion.

"We'll stay in London for a time. Parliament is in session next week and mischief be afoot. Wi' the cursed duke in charge, anything can 'appen."

John of Gaunt, Duke of Lancaster, was Matthew Hart's lord. Margery did not respond to Thurold's veiled jab. Nor ask, "What mischief?" She tiptoed around so many subjects, as if they were sleeping children she feared awakening. Or something much more dreadful might be slumbering, something she must make certain was never let loose upon the day.

Margery had long ago decided it was better not to question her stepbrother, her lover, or anyone else about a whole host of matters. She knew enough of political events to understand that, with the death of the Black Prince and with a monarch who could scarce sit astride a horse let alone upon his throne at Westminster Palace, England resembled a rudderless ship drifting about the harbor. But so much was wrong in these dying days of Edward III's reign, where would one even begin to set things right?

After exiting All Hallows' precincts, Margery and Cicily walked

6

briskly in the direction of Warrick Inn. London seemed in a sullen mood, perhaps because of the forthcoming parliament. Or mayhap its inhabitants were merely tired of a winter barely begun and that had already kept them too long huddled in their dank, drafty rooms.

"Why has your stepbrother never married?" asked Cicily. "Too many campaigns? Too wedded to the hedge-priest and his insurrections?"

Cicily was middle aged and matronly with grown children and no desire for a second marriage, certainly not with some treason-spouting vagabond. Rather she asked out of mild curiosity.

"'Tis odd, is it not?" Margery said, with a smile. "I doubt Thurold could sit still long enough to court a woman. Can you imagine him being scolded by some ill-tempered wife or surrounded by a passel of wee ones? Though he is always kind to Serill," she added loyally.

They walked along in companionable silence. To the south flowed the River Thames, its current gleaming like silver-bellied fish. An occasional small boat or barge slipped past, gliding noiselessly into the gathering shadows. On Watling Street they detoured around a whore bickering with two drunks over the price of her favors and a pack of mongrel dogs searching for scraps amidst the kennels. Then to the better part of London where wealthy merchants, clergy and the nobility resided. As did Margery.

Once at Warrick Inn, Margery found Matthew and Serill in the small stable to the back of the residence. They'd obviously returned from a ride on the new dapple grey Matthew had recently presented their seven-year-old son.

"Maman, we rode all around Smithfield. Slayer nearly kept pace with Behrt," Serill said, his eyes shining.

"So you call your pony Slayer? What a fierce name!" Margery smiled so that he wouldn't misinterpret her comment as criticism. But, by the rood, she wanted Serill to be a merchant, not a knight. Why not christen the animal Adorable or Little Jewel or Grey? In Latin, Adorandus or Gemmula or Glaucus would sound masculine enough.

"Our son has the makings of a fine horseman," Matthew commented, patting Slayer's hindquarters before handing the pony's

7

reins to a waiting groom. Was that a challenge? Matthew's way of saying, "Our son, by-blow or not, will follow in my footsteps, and you have no say in the matter?"

But when Margery looked into her lover's eyes, she could decipher no hidden message. His hair, darkened over the years to a sun-streaked brown, was tousled, his cheeks bright from the ride and his smile seemed so genuine and so intimate that she felt her heart increase its rhythm, as it had in the old days of their courtship.

"I am pleased to hear it," she said, returning his smile.

A second groom appeared to lead Behrt away. Other horses in their stalls shifted restlessly or nickered, reminding stable boys that their evening feed was due.

"My two favorite men," Margery said, linking her left arm through Matthew's and looping her right across Serill's narrow shoulders. They retreated from the stables to stroll the garden pathway ending at Warrick Inn. Matthew slipped an arm around her waist, drawing her closer until their thighs brushed with each step. While Serill chattered about Slayer, about the adventures he and his father had enjoyed during their ride, Margery thought, *Now, at this moment, life is good.*

Though who knew what tomorrow would bring?

CHAPTER 2

London, February, 1377

 here was a spectre that forever haunted Edward III, as it would haunt his grandson, Richard of Bordeaux, the boy who would soon be crowned Richard II. Perhaps the spectre not only haunted regents, but the century as a whole. For it seemed that the phantasm's good and bad decisions, his enemies and those who championed him, the consequences of his abdication—the first in England's history—as well as his brutal demise and its bloody aftermath, reverberated across many decades.

The spectre's name was Edward of Caernarvon. England's first Prince of Wales. Known to history as Edward II.

Of His Grace, contemporaries wrote, "God had endowed him with every gift." Edward II was big and blond and handsome, as were most Plantagenets, and was said to be the strongest man in the kingdom. He delighted in physical activity of all kinds, from digging ditches and building walls to rowing, driving carts, thatching cottages, fishing, swimming in icy rivers, and shoeing horses. Sometimes he would sail his barge along the River Thames where he would buy cabbages and

9

other vegetables from those along the banks in order to make his version of a royal soup.

While such activities might be proper for a country knight, Edward's barons criticized them as being unworthy pursuits of a regent. They complained that Edward II was common, that he preferred the company of peasants to theirs. Which, considering their many grievances, feuds, and rebellions against him, might have been true. The irony was that when Edward was in need of his subjects to rally for him as he was being chased by his traitorous consort and her lover, they declined.

Edward Caernarvon enjoyed a good laugh—though his jokes tended toward the bawdy—but overall his tastes were refined. He loved music to the extent that he often had Italian musicians following him about. He enjoyed dancing, watching plays—even acting—reading and listening to Romances. He was loyal to his friends and, as a king, did his duty by giving his kingdom four children, including a son destined to become one of England's greatest sovereigns.

Edward II was loyal to his friends, generally a positive trait, though his critics complained that he was loyal beyond all reason, at least regarding his two male favorites. Was the opposition unusually incensed because His Grace was rumored to harbor unnatural affections for Piers Gaveston and Hugh Despenser? Or because it was Gaveston and Despenser, rather than they themselves, who were the recipients of Edward's largesse? Did his barons complain from principle or pique?

Edward II's father, Edward Longshanks, had been feared and respected if not loved by his subjects. He had been possessed of such a fierce temper that a clergyman, thinking to confront the king over high levels of taxation but terrified of his reaction, had collapsed and died in his presence. When his son demanded an earldom for his first male favorite, Edward I had been so enraged that he'd torn out handfuls of young Edward's hair. But Edward I was also known, rightly or wrongly, as a successful warrior king, where Edward II was not—though in fairness, 'twas difficult to war when England's coffers had been emptied by his sire and when many of Edward II's barons would rather complain and conspire against him than to serve him.

Edward Caernarvon was the spectre who ever stood at his royal son's shoulder, whispered in his ear and, at least at the end of Edward of Windsor's long reign, tormented his increasingly confused thoughts.

Edward III had been fourteen years old when he'd ascended to a throne that had been wrested from his father by his mother the Queen and her lover, Roger Mortimer, the most powerful lord of the Marches--that borderland between England and Wales. Isabella and Edward II's marriage had been arranged when he was sixteen and she five and was hardly a love match. But all such marriages were business transactions and those who saw them together often witnessed mutual respect and sometimes even tenderness. While Edward II's mismanagement of the kingdom and his personal misbehaviors were clearly wrong, it was nearly unheard of for a queen to take a lover, and certainly not to ride by her lover's side at the front of an invading army. Then to have the deposed monarch, who at the age of forty-three remained strong as an ox, so conveniently expire from a vague sickness of the lungs?

No.

How must young Edward III have felt, in the presence of his mother and Mortimer in the aftermath of their treason? To stand by and watch his father deposed, to observe Roger Mortimer lavishing titles and lands upon himself, his sons and minions in the exact same fashion Edward II had upon his favorites?

Why were such actions right and proper for Roger Mortimer when he'd cited them as the very reason Edward II must be overthrown?

Did no one ever learn?

Young Edward did. He studied everything. Said little. And stored it away in his agile mind, all the while honing acting skills his father would have applauded.

The young king watched his beloved mother, Isabella, enrich herself beyond all propriety. Watched her shovel honors and properties in Roger Mortimer's direction at an alarming rate, including one that had belonged to Edward II's favorite, Hugh Despenser.

How very peculiar.

Isabella and Mortimer behaved as if they were somehow exempt from consequences because they had deposed—and quite possibly murdered—an unpopular king.

They'd forgotten the truth of fortune's wheel, that nothing could cease its turning.

Already, common folk were declaring that miracles were being performed in Edward Caernarvon's name.

That he should be declared a saint.

That nothing good could come from deposing God's chosen ruler.

That Roger Mortimer and his she-wolf had cursed the kingdom.

Mortimer and Isabella ignored every criticism. They acted as if they existed outside the past, outside history, and that if they themselves pretended not to mark the rapaciousness of their actions, neither would anyone else. As if England's lords would put aside their ambitions because a boy king they all knew to be king in name only sat upon the throne. As if being Roger Mortimer rather than Hugh Despenser and Piers Gaveston, being lover to a queen instead a king, made all the difference.

How could such a shrewd, intelligent, ambitious and accomplished warrior as Roger Mortimer be so blind? How could he so miscalculate his youthful sovereign's nature? Was it because Mortimer was so contemptuous of Edward II that he disregarded the royal blood coursing through the son's veins and chose to believe that Edward III comprised only the worst parts of his father?

If so, it was a fatal miscalculation.

Though not yet eighteen, Edward Windsor had already married and his queen, Philippa, was carrying the future Edward the Black Prince. The young king had a family to protect. In addition, he possessed an innate understanding of what was necessary to make a great monarch. While remaining outwardly polite in Mortimer's presence, with little more than a tightening of the lips or a narrowing of the eyes to betray his feelings, King Edward continued weighing his options, feeling his way toward the moment when the Marcher lord would be openly disrespectful, or publicly challenged his authority.

Which happened in the fall of 1330, after Roger Mortimer had dared to order the execution of the young king's uncle, Edmund, Earl of Kent, for an aborted coup.

On a bone-deep level, Edward III understood that should he fail to smash Roger Mortimer, he himself risked deposition and death.

In October, young Edward surprised the lord-who-reached-too-high in a nighttime raid on Nottingham Castle, where Mortimer and Queen Isabella were ensconced. Was it because of Isabella's entreaty to her son, "Have pity on gentle Mortimer," that her lover was conveyed to the Tower rather than executed on the spot as Edward III had originally planned?

When Roger Mortimer was in power he'd refused his enemies the right to speak at their trials. Now King Edward returned the insult, gagging the Marcher lord in addition to binding him with ropes and chains. Roger Mortimer was found guilty of a long list of crimes, some by "notoriety," meaning his offenses were 'notorious and known for their truth to you and all the realm.' Afterward, Mortimer was stripped naked and dragged behind two horses to Tyburn. While noblemen were generally beheaded, Mortimer was denied that courtesy. Rather he became the first lord to be hanged like a common criminal on Tyburn Tree.

Thus ended the tyranny of the "King of Folly," (so later nicknamed by his very own son), and unofficially ushered in the reign of Edward III.

And what a glorious reign it was!

The Order of the Garter. Gallant knights and fair maidens. Chivalry. Courtly love. Magnificent tournaments, all consciously modeled after the legends of Arthur. King Edward created many new peerages and maintained his lords' loyalty with his generosity and martial prowess, but it was the ideal of Arthur and his fabled knights that bound everything together. Edward adopted Arthurian symbols and encouraged pilgrimages to holy places such as Glastonbury, the burial place of Arthur and Guinevere. Among his many tourneys was a Round Table Festival that took place inside a circular building within Windsor Castle. The Arthurian legends even provided justification for Edward's invasions of Wales and Scotland, and of course, for his conquest of France. His military victories only added to the belief, at least among the noble classes, that they were living in England's golden time.

But now, disasters, tragedies and simply time's passing had piled up like rocks in a foundation, one atop the other, leaving the radiant legend in tatters.

Now Edward III was a querulous old man, quaking at the possible resurrection of ancient ghosts. A handful of the opposition, more enemies of his son, John of Gaunt's, than his, terrified him with their oblique references to Edward II's strange passing in the bowels of Berkeley Castle. Easy to ignore political chatterings when you are young and strong and can stride the continent like a colossus.

No longer.

Oddly, as Edward slid toward the grave, it seemed that events from his father's last year were indeed being replayed. With the same players, or the sons and grandsons of those who had shaped and then shattered Edward II's reign. No wonder, as His Grace's mind grew increasingly wayward, that he must have wondered which Lancaster was being referred to, what Mortimer, what plots and intrigues. And whether he was rooted here in 1377 or had tumbled back in time to 1327.

When the Good Parliament had been called in the spring of 1376, the king had felt as if he were beset by enemies or the children of ancient enemies; it was so hard to keep them all straight. Even his son the Black Prince had seemed on the side of the Commons, though that was mainly to ensure Richard of Bordeaux's succession to the throne for Edward III's favorite son, the child of his heart, had been so very, very ill...

Sixty serious charges of corruption had been brought against those closest to Edward III. Richard Stury, one of the knights of the king's chamber and one of those accused of corruption, gave voice to Edward's most secret fear. He whispered into the old man's ear that some were saying he should be removed from England's throne.

"What must I do to prevent such a thing?" Edward had asked the treacherous Stury, who told him to immediately cease all parliamentary proceedings. Would that end the horrible talk? Reverse all the terrible things the Commons were doing? And where was his mistress, Alice Perrers? What had the opposition said about her? That she was as corrupt and greedy as his ministers and must be banished?

How can it be that I have a mistress when I am a faithful husband? But why have I not seen Philippa? Aye, she's gone. Where is she? How can I be charged with grasping favorites when I would never... when I know how such people destroyed my father? Such unspeakable things they did to him when he is at heart a good man...

Edward leaned back upon his throne and closed his weary eyes. *'Tis all so very... vague.*

In June of 1376, the business of the Good Parliament had been mercifully—or tragically—halted, depending on one's outlook, by momentous news. England's beloved Edward the Black Prince, so long plagued with illness, had dictated his will, a signal that he knew his death was at hand.

And now, a year later, with the Prince entombed in Canterbury Cathedral, it was King Edward himself whose life was staggering to its close.

CHAPTER 3

London, 1377

$\mathcal{A}$s Margery Watson lay beside her lover in their great canopied bed with draperies closed to keep out winter's chill, she was thinking about dead people. Some she'd known and some she'd never met.

Matthew's breathing was blessedly rhythmic, unlike most nights when he tossed and turned, thus allowing her uninterrupted time for contemplation. Though Warrick Inn was a bustling household by day, the only sound beyond the velvet darkness was the crackle of logs in the chamber's fire. If Margery strained her ears she could hear a watchman in the street outside calling the hour, or the occasional rumble from a passing carriage.

The dead marched across Margery's consciousness, starting with those from plague times—her mother, Alice; her half-sister Giddy; and her stepfather, Alf, all of whom, truth be told, she could scarce remember. Her husband, who she largely visualized in bits and pieces—tiny hands and feet, a bald, egg-shaped pate, broken veins alongside his nose. It only took a whiff of peppermint, which Simon Crull had used to disguise the odor of his rotting teeth, to tie her stomach in knots. Orabel, her faithful maid, who'd been murdered by the aforementioned husband and his band of cutthroats. Harry Hart, Matthew's younger brother, who had been so ineffectual and unreliable and kind and guileless.

There were others, of course, for death was as commonplace as the calling of the hours, but those had been the ones who had most affected Margery.

Should I include Prince Edward? she wondered. She'd largely known him through Matthew's eyes, but 'twas impossible not to mourn him all the same.

As she mourned two men she'd never met; well, mayhap "mourn" was too strong a word, for three months past she'd barely registered their existence. Yet now they consumed much of her imaginings.

Richard of Sussex and Phillip Rendell.

The sun and the moon.

At least that's how Margery's grandmother, Maria Rendell, had referred to them during their private meeting in her tower rooms.

Maria Rendell's lover and Maria Rendell's husband.

'Twas a stirring of ghosts, like a stirring of leftover ashes in an ancient hearth. Nothing but puffs of grey, rising startled into the air. And yet, in her nocturnal imaginings, Margery had reshaped those dusty particles into vivid life.

Since both men were historical figures she knew some basic facts. Richard, Earl of Sussex, was Edward II's illegitimate half-brother, one of the few who'd remained loyal to the king following the invasion of Isabella and her lover.

Phillip Rendell had become the subject of minstrel's tales after saving his lord Sussex's life at the Battle of Bannockburn early in Edward II's doomed reign. Margery had heard the story, and a heroic one it was, but she'd never connected an event sixty years past to real people. Never connected *that* Phillip Rendell to her grandfather.

How her life had expanded since reuniting with her father, Thomas, in the precincts outside Canterbury Cathedral. It had been following Edward the Black Prince's final entombment and... well, 'twas something to take out on long nights when she couldn't sleep, like a child hoarding a secret treat.

The sun and the moon.

Maria Rendell's husband, so darkly handsome and so unapproachable.

Margery imagined a bone-white winter moon frozen in a cloudless, starless midnight sky. Distant and alone. No wonder Phillip's reserve had driven Maria near to madness.

Or so her grandmother had shared. No matter how Maria had tried to reach Phillip with her body, to make herself indispensable by being the perfect wife, mother and mistress, she'd always ended up frustrated. So she would try harder, ever seeking the key that would finally, finally unlock that aloof exterior and open up his heart. Maria *knew* the fault was in herself no matter how often Phillip assured her otherwise. His restlessness was his curse—that ever present nagging that there were sights and adventures he simply *must* experience somewhere beyond the sea, *somewhere.*

"I wish it were otherwise," he'd said so often that Maria imagined those words chiseled on his tomb chest.

Phillip had tried to do what was expected of him as lord and husband, but it had been as inevitable that he would succumb to adventure's siren song as it had been for Maria to turn to their liege lord, Richard of Sussex, afterward.

Foolish maids might call such a love triangle romantic, after the fashion of Lancelot and Guinevere or Tristan and Iseault *("Apart the lovers could neither live nor die, for it was life and death together.")*. But there had been nothing save pain for all involved. That much Maria Rendell had also told her.

Margery heard the pad of feet upon the rushes beyond the draperies, then the dull thud of fresh logs being thrust inside the massive fireplace. A crackling and roar as the flames took hold.

At one time I would have been the maid tending the fire, she thought, clasping her hands across her stomach. *How odd life is.*

Matthew sighed in his sleep. Or was that a moan? Margery tensed until his breathing resumed its regular rhythm. Hopefully, this night he would be spared his usual troubling dreams.

Margery's thoughts returned to the men Maria Rendell had loved. *What sort of man were you, Grandfather?*

Phillip Rendell had certainly been a great warrior. Epic poems were not penned about just any man. But he must also have been honorable in his own fashion. Tender. Selfless. For what ordinary man cares for his wife's wounds after she's been publicly flogged? After he's been publicly cuckolded? Phillip had even forgiven Richard, rescuing his liege from Roger Mortimer, then later riding beside him and the very young king Edward III during a border campaign against the Scots.

Had Phillip considered those acts appropriate penance for abandoning his wife?

If a bard wished to compose something to make maidens swoon, he might have written about what happened after that night raid in which Richard had been killed and Phillip so horribly disfigured by a Scotsman's claymore. Now Phillip Rendell was the stuff of nightmares, travelling by night and hiding his ravaged face in the depths of a hooded cloak rather than risk the frightened wails of children or the shocked stares of even battle-hardened warriors.

As if Maria would care how he looked!

"It is enough that you came home to me," she'd said, when she'd met him in the darkness, among the cherry trees.

They'd fashioned a silver half-mask to cover the ruined portion of his face.

And gone on together.

Margery wondered whether Phillip had been bitter about his fate. *I must ask my lady Grandmother when we attend this year's Cherry Fair.*

Had her grandfather been embarrassed when people pointed and stared and whispered behind their hands? Grateful that God had granted him more years so that he could hug his children and guide them into adulthood? Thankful that he'd sired another son and daughter? Had he and Maria lain in the darkness of Fordwich's solar, with the moonlight gleaming softly upon his mask and Maria whispering, "Remove it, my love"? Had she caressed the scars and hollows coursing from eye to chin with her fingertips, then ever so gently with her lips?

Most certainly she would have thanked the saints that her beloved could yet embrace her and make love to her. That they could laugh and discuss the settling of accounts or harvest yields or their children's latest antics; that Phillip could reach out and entwine her fingers with his while they read to each other in front of the fireplace or strolled among the cherry trees.

How would I feel if my lord returned to me so disfigured? Margery wondered. She reached across to run her fingers lightly along Matthew's naked thigh with its downy covering of hair.

He did return to you disfigured, a voice whispered. *Only those wounds you cannot see.*

Matthew sighed and shifted his muscular leg closer, as if he were a cat seeking to be stroked. Banishing that troublesome inner voice, Margery kept her hand resting upon his thigh, knowing, like her grandmother, that it would not have mattered.

The sun and the moon.

But here is where fate's skeins grew tangled. For upon first seeing Matthew Hart in Fordwich Castle's great hall, Maria Rendell had said, "He reminds me of someone," and, soon, pleading her great age, had fled to her tower rooms.

Later when she and Margery were alone, Maria had confessed how the sight of Matthew Hart had shaken her.

"I thought he was my Richard, come to life, and I asked myself, How can this be? Though when I looked more closely the similarities faded." She'd added with a chuckle, "No one would mistake your knight for a holy man. Which is a good thing. For what woman can compete with God?" Then she'd grown serious. "Still it's passing strange, is it not?"

Passing strange, indeed.

"My sister... I had a twin, you know, who was gifted with the sight. Eleanora used to dream, long before I ever met Richard, of 'a golden knight who shines like the sun.'"

At those words Margery had felt the most peculiar prickling. For hadn't she always considered Matthew to be *her* golden knight?

Gazing at the canopy overhead, she could almost visually replay scenes from certain long ago dreams. Matthew, his hair an amber halo, armored and astride a white stallion with golden bridle bells that tinkled with each step as it picked its way across a moon-dappled field. To her. Matthew would reach out his hand and beckon Margery to him and she would gaze into that shining face and know she would follow him anywhere...

Only Margery had christened Matthew her faerie knight.

What did all this mean? Was there some sort of invisible threads connecting them all?

Even now, cocooned in the darkness, the possible implications raised goosebumps. Margery felt as if the warp and woof of their fates was being mysteriously woven. She imagined one of the mythological *moirae* spinning the thread of life, while another measured it to see how long they all would live while the third chose the manner each would die with a snip, snipping of her shears.

What will happen to us?

Margery moved to snuggle against Matthew's chest, reassuring herself with the rhythmic beating of his heart. He looped an arm around her and murmured her name in his sleep. She pressed her lips against him, in the exact spot where his heart pulsed, and felt a sudden pricking of tears.

Had Maria Rendell known, when making her choices, that they would lead to tragedy? Of course not. For if her grandmother had seen such a pathway, she would have simply chosen another. Wouldn't she?

But what if I am on a similar path, Margery thought, with Matthew's heart whispering against her ear. *And I don't realize it either?*

MATTHEW RESTED QUIETLY next to his leman. Trying not to think about dead people. Or dream about them, both of which were impossible. He thought of his old king, whom he loved, as he'd loved Edward's son the Black Prince, and wondered what it might be like when Edward III lay in *his* bed surrounded by *his* shadows? His dead queen, his eight dead children, John Chandos and so many of the advisors who had served him into middle age, so many original members of the Order of the Garter... How could one count them all? Did Edward of Windsor search fearfully among the shadows and scan that ghostly parade of spectres for the ultimate shade, Death itself?

Matthew forced himself to stay still in the great canopied bed rather than flop about like a caught fish, as he was wont to do.

What is it about kings? he wondered. *Does greatness skip a generation?* It would seem so if one simply calculated the reigns of this century begun by Edward I, maker of laws and molder of institutions and scourge of England's northern neighbors. To be followed by his feckless son. And then Edward of Windsor.

So if our king, even in his dotage, is compared to Arthur, doesn't that bode ill for his grandson? Will Richard of Bordeaux's reign be as doomed as his great-grandfather's?

Matthew willed his breathing to remain even, his hands to remain unclenched, his body relaxed. When he could not feign stillness, Margery's lovely countenance filled with worry and she would say, "Oh, sweeting. Might I mix you a sleeping potion?"

Sleep was the last thing Matthew needed. In that state he had no control over what dreams might come. Dreams of his brother as Harry had been during the march that chroniclers and Englishmen had begun to call the "Great Chevauchée" and which Matthew privately nicknamed the "March to Oblivion."

They were deep in the mountains of Auvergne, bedeviled by howling winds and endless snows and of course the enemy who tracked them like hounds following the scent of a fox.

Dead littered the trail, macabre sign posts marking the passage of their liege lord's army. Harry, with his wild hair and beard, his face as ancient as that of Jack Frost, with deep grooves running from nose to mouth and around his eyes, and cheeks so hollowed that his face would sometimes turn into that of a skeleton even as Matthew's dream self looked on.

And sometimes 'twas not flesh and blood Frenchmen who shadowed them, but children carrying their heads. Or mothers. Or townsmen. Banshees, screaming in concert with the incessant wind, flew around them, red eyes blazing as brightly as the fire leaking from the windows and doors of a dilapidated hut positioned along the trail. Matthew would approach the hut with trepidation, fearing what he would find inside but helpless to stop. When he opened the door, his father, William Hart, was seated before a small table with an empty chair positioned opposite him. A draught board covered the surface of the table with all the pieces laid out on its checkered surface.

William Hart would look up, gesture to the board, and say, "Are you ready, son?"

And Matthew would reply, "But you can't be here. You're dead..."

No, I will not think of it.

Matthew would force his heart to slow and distract himself by filling his head with mundanities. A passage from a book he'd read or a letter he'd received from his mother or sister, a forthcoming joust, lists of matters he must discuss with a particular bailiff or seneschal during a forthcoming visit to one of several Hart demesnes scattered throughout the south and midlands. Or he would turn on his side and pull Meg close to him, hugging her against him as if his very survival depended on it.

He felt an overall sense of doom. Though so much had already happened, he sensed something dreadful was making its way toward him, toward them all. When not distracted by duties and obligations, Matthew's focus had narrowed to Serill and Margery. They were who he must protect. Not his mother, tucked safely away in Cumbria, or his sister Elizabeth, who had her husband and her sons, or his nephew, Ralphie, who lived as luxuriously as any prince. They all seemed so distant, as if he might have conjured their very existence. So often they didn't seem *real*. Besides, they all had their champions. Margery and Serill were *his* responsibility and he must not fail them.

Yet, it was an odd thing. Matthew loved them so much, yet most of the time he remained outwardly detached. Inwardly, he was such a mass of fears, particularly about Serill, who, at age seven, remained so achingly vulnerable. When he and his friends played tag or hide and seek or went exploring along the Thames, Matthew had to stop himself from hovering about, urging them to be "Careful, careful!" It was imperative that Serill be a good horseman, for, despite Meg's meaningful silences whenever the subject was broached, Serill *would* be a knight. Yet each time they went out riding Matthew worried his son might be thrown or his pony step in a hole and pitch them both to their deaths. Or that Serill would break one or several of his limbs or fall upon his head and emerge an idiot.

Matthew was so beset by such worries that he found himself overcompensating by appearing indifferent, even cold, toward his son. And Meg, as well.

He tried to lose himself in physical activity by spending long days at the Savoy where he and the duke's other retainers would sword practice, tilt at the quintain, race their horses, and wrestle. They challenged each other to foot races—short distances inside the Savoy's great courtyard and longer runs beyond city walls, which Matthew especially enjoyed. The way his heart pumped as if it would burst through his chest, the sweat that chilled his body, the straining muscles that afterward would ache so badly he limped and groaned like an old man. And yet, he was gratified to mark his body's progress, every day becoming more fit and ready.

For what he did not know.

What a fine paradox! Because many days Matthew had to force himself to crawl from bed, to leave Warrick Inn's solar before he would do what he so wished, which was to settle himself in a chair before the fireplace and endlessly stare into its flames. To sit like a mute, acknowledging no one. To cease playing the part of lover, father, loyal knight and lord of his own demesnes. All the day. Or forever.

Increasingly it seemed to Matthew that he was damaged goods, that there was not enough left of him to give to anyone. No matter where he was or who he was with Matthew wished himself to be elsewhere. Or found himself only half in the room. He might be conversing with Meg when he would feel a part of himself wander off. As if he were populated by a legion of ghost men. Only it was becoming more difficult to know which were the ghosts and which the man of flesh and blood.

Matthew knew that the best parts of him had been buried in the graves alongside those he loved. He was not the man he had once been and that troubled him greatly, for he did not know where that man was.

Or even if he still existed.

CHAPTER 4

London, January-March, 1377

January 27, 1377, marked the opening of the parliament that would prove to be Edward III's last. In contrast to 1376's "Good Parliament," this parliament had almost immediately been dubbed the "Bad."

Under John of Gaunt's watchful eye and guiding hand, the Good Parliament was declared unconstitutional and its acts removed from the books. A cowed Commons acceded that a king could renege on political promises that had been forced upon him. Royal courtiers who'd been impeached were reinstated. A new form of royal taxation was introduced—a poll tax of four pennies for every person over the age of 14. The Commons approved, even suggested it in an attempt to expand taxation down the social scale. Perhaps, before proposing such drastic action they should have consulted soothsayers, had astrologers cast the appropriate charts, or merely pondered their actions based upon the mood of the kingdom. For this poll tax, as much as anything, would lead to the Peasants' Revolt of 1381.

The Commons met in Westminster Abbey's Chapter House. When Parliament was not in session, Benedictine monks gathered in the

House to read, contemplate, discuss monastic matters, and study the murals blanketing its walls. The dazzling paintings covered a range of subjects from biblical to fantastical and the monks spent hours deciphering them as if they were in the presence of an enormous picture book. What was the meaning of the Last Judgement painted upon the east wall, so subtly different from others of its kind? Christ and his apostles crowded into a pair of boats? Mythical beasts mixed with the commonplace? The different postures of Saints Thomas, Christopher, and Faith? And why was the tomb of Sebert, ancient king of the East Saxons, graced with the remains of vine leaves, a Catherine wheel and the head of a woman?

But for now, the Benedictines had been displaced by angry, frightened, beseeching knights, citizens and burgesses who, with their raging and pacing and comings and goings had managed, in the space of a month, to wear the Chapter House's carpeting down to its floor tiles. The atmosphere between the Commons and their lords was so toxic that, had Edward III been able to oversee the proceedings, he would have found the circumstances unpleasantly reminiscent of those preceding his father's abdication. The infighting and political factions seemed eerily similar. The characters might be different, for it was Edmund Mortimer, not the old queen's lover, Roger, leading the Marcher lords against another Lancaster, this time with the title of duke rather than earl. But the surnames and the blood lines were identical. Even had his mind not been clouded, King Edward might have wondered whether he'd been spirited back in time or if his entire reign had simply been a product of his imaginings.

While the Bad Parliament ground toward its ignominious conclusion, a troubling religious matter arose that must needs be attended to. Or so said the powerful William Courtenay, Bishop of London. John Wycliffe, Oxford scholar, theologian—and heretic, according to his enemies—was ordered to appear before a convocation of bishops to be interrogated regarding his preachments against Mother Church. An ecclesiastical trial, it was called. Bishop Courtenay had had enough of Master Wycliffe's blasphemies, particularly his assertion that the state must step in to right ecclesiastic abuses.

Of course John of Gaunt championed the Oxford scholar. He would! For the church's loss would somehow be the greedy duke's gain.

On a gloomy mid-February afternoon, John of Gaunt, Master Wycliffe, and Henry Percy, Marshal of England, along with a contingent of knights including Matthew Hart, approached St. Paul's precincts. Their task was to accompany John Wycliffe safely to the Lady Chapel, where his trial would be held.

But when Wycliffe's guard reached their destination they were in for an unpleasant surprise.

~

"OUT OF OUR WAY," bellowed Sir Henry Percy. Dressed in battle armor and spoiling for a fight, the hot-tempered Percy was having none of the Londoners clustered around the doors of St. Paul's and packed tight about cathedral precincts.

Matthew Hart and two dozen other retainers comprised John of Gaunt's flank—his honor guard of pikemen to the fore, Gaunt, Percy and the troublesome Oxford scholar in the middle, trailed by a foursome of mendicant friars and finally, Matthew and his fellow knights.

"We are warriors, not theologians," grumbled Matthew to Robert Knolles, the grizzled knight and famed freebooter. "Or nursemaids."

"Bloody hell, the depths we've sunk to," growled Knolles. "We should be ravaging Aquitaine, not following behind some mincing Black Robe."

Matthew would rather not be ravaging *anything*, but Robert Knolles was obviously cut from a different cloth. 'Twas no wonder he and his mercenaries had been nicknamed "the dogs of war." As for now, however, they need not travel across the channel to court danger for the threat of violence was unmistakable.

John of Gaunt's group reached the doors of St. Paul's, now creaking slowly open. John Wycliffe, with his blatherings about the Bible being translated to English—*for who really cared?*—and his condemnations of ecclesiastic wealth—*well, there he has a point*—was a troublesome piece of baggage. Though Matthew took a measure of comfort in one of Wycliffe's criticisms. Every church he had ever entered, including Cumbria's family chapel, possessed a mural of the Last Judgement with the same exact scene—paradise opening to receive the saved on one side and Satan and his executioners gleefully tormenting the naked souls entering hell on the other. Which Wycliffe asserted was sinful in its own right because confessors were exploiting folks' fears for coin. Matthew would like to think it so, that the threat of everlasting damnation was simply another moneymaking venture...

"Bloody hell," Robert Knolles repeated after they stepped inside St. Paul's and their eyes adjusted to the gloom.

Matthew silently echoed Knolles' oath. He was quite familiar with the cathedral for, like many others, he used its north-south transept as a shortcut from one part of London to the other. When clerics weren't preaching or offering mass, the nave would be commandeered by lads playing ball and other sports, with artisans hawking their products— indeed, with a cross-section of London as it existed beyond cathedral walls. Matthew sometimes imagined that, if viewed from St. Paul's vaulted ceiling, they must all look like a scurrying mess of bugs.

But not today.

Today St. Paul's nave, the longest in the world, was so chock-full of Londoners that no one could do much more than raise a hand or swivel a head.

Packed tight as fish in a barrel, Matthew thought, his worried gaze scanning the multitude. *Wall to wall.* Twelve enormous bays receding into an impossibly vast distance that they must traverse in order to reach their destination. And not a viable way forward.

Ahead, Matthew could see the pikes of the duke's honor guard still aloft. And stationary.

If we're going to reach the Lady Chapel, we had best sprout wings.

Matthew risked a glance behind to see whether the path through which they'd entered might be free but the crowd had flowed into the empty spaces.

Surrounded on all sides.

His eyes met Robert Knolles. If possible, the grizzled warrior's perpetual scowl had deepened. Master mercenary, head of one of the dreaded Free Companies that intermittently decimated the continent, he too was taking measure of the dangers and devising a strategy should the mob do more than point and stare and grumble.

The mood was definitely hostile, as it had been since the beginning of the Bad Parliament. Londoners accused John of Gaunt of being responsible for everything from the royal court's corruption to the murder of various family members—and even of being a foundling who was no true son to Edward III at all. Most galling, parliament had approved a payment of £6,000 to the duke, marking it as back salary. But wasn't John of Gaunt rich enough already, they groused, even richer than the king? Why further enrich himself when England's exchequer was nearly empty?

And now the hated duke stood before them. One man against hundreds, if not thousands. Would they fall upon him—upon them all —like ravening boars?

John of Gaunt and Henry Percy were speaking to each other over the head of the far shorter Wycliffe. Too far away for Matthew to hear. Behind the trio, the mendicant friars, in the grey, black, brown and dingy white cassocks of their orders, huddled together like terrified children. Odd that Wycliffe had chosen the mendicants as his champions for he'd long accused them of spewing heretical "garbage." Yet here they were and most assuredly wishing themselves far, far away.

"Master Wycliffe!" someone called. Others echoed his name but Wycliffe did not acknowledge them and the voices receded to an indistinguishable murmur.

Good. So far there seemed to be no leader to rouse the press.

Matthew inhaled deeply, noticing in a detached way that his head felt as if someone were beating it with a smithy's sledge. So many unwashed bodies, the air so thick it seemed a living thing invading his lungs...

Another anonymous man yelled at Henry Percy, whose recent appointment as Marshal of England obviously did not sit well. Londoners were a tetchy lot, always looking for real or imagined threats to their independence. "Why be ye bringing armed guards into God's holy house?"

Another joined in, hollering something about "taking away our rights."

Angered by the jibes, Henry Percy hollered, "Stand aside." He plunged forward. "Remove your vulgar carcasses," he ordered the clot of men before him. "Let us through."

Surprisingly, they gave way, though only momentarily.

Percy swore.

Matthew clutched the pommel of his sword as if it were a talisman. He would rather be anywhere than here, possibly facing off against his fellow countrymen. Soldiers, he knew, numbered among the throng, some who'd participated in Crecy, Poitiers, Najera, Limoges, even in the March to Oblivion. And as for the rest, no doubt all had recently stood with heads bowed to honor the Black Prince with the passing of his funeral cortege.

Englishmen should not be fighting Englishmen...

Townsfolk huddled on the banks of the River Vienne; Wailing women, screaming children, mothers begging, "Mercy, mercy, gentle knight..."

Matthew felt suddenly dizzy and his heart began that familiar racing whenever images from Limoges came to the fore. *Stop.* He tightened his grip on his sword, blinked hard and re-focused. *The end of the nave, far in the distance, the friars, the scholar, my liege lord, the pikemen...*

And then suddenly, the Bishop of London, William Courtenay, appeared before them. How had he so abruptly materialized?

The bishop looked angry enough that, had he been the Viking god, Thor, he would be hurling thunderbolts at them all.

Can this get any worse without a full blown riot?

Wearing a mitre to add to his middling height and carrying his crozier lest anyone forget he was their shepherd and they his flock, William Courtenay addressed Henry Percy in his public preaching voice. "I will not have my people mistreated!"

While Bishop Courtenay was in fact Edward I's great-grandson,

Matthew could see no resemblance between the horse-faced cleric and his regal cousin, the Duke of Lancaster.

"Like it or not we'll not allow you or anyone to stand in our way," retorted Henry Percy. And with that, the duke's honor guard pressed forward. Astonishingly, the crowd parted with little more than a protesting murmur.

Courtenay watched them brush past, metaphorical thunderbolts flashing from his eyes. *Now* he resembled a Plantagenet. It was there in the set of his mouth and in his bearing, which proclaimed quite clearly that *humilité* was as unfamiliar a concept to him as it was to his royal cousin.

Foot by foot, John of Gaunt's group made their way forward. Matthew stayed on the alert, looking for the glint of a weapon or an expression that appeared particularly crazed or murderous. Familiar faces, people he passed in the Strand or at Smithfield or strolling the Tower gardens—merchants, artisans, apprentices, the occasional cleric or dame. And of course yeomen, soldiers, veterans from the campaigns. He wondered suddenly whether Margery's stepbrother, Thurold, would number among them. Of course he would. Matthew was glad their residence was a safe distance away in case there was trouble, but the Shop of the Unicorn was nearby and hadn't Meg said something...

Stop!

Matthew willed all personal thoughts to go the way of his earlier images of Limoges.

Halfway there.

Almost there.

The doors of the Lady Chapel ahead.

Safe?

JOHN OF GAUNT'S honor guard stood outside the Lady Chapel, pikes crossed in front of the door, barring entrance. Inside, Matthew and the duke's other retainers had formed an iron ring against the back wall with booted feet firmly planted, gauntleted hands laced in front of them, silently observing the unfolding drama.

Bishop William Courtenay had slipped away from the crowd at the entrance of St. Paul's and into the chapel via a side door. Now John Wycliffe, flanked by the Duke of Lancaster and the Marshal of England, was slowly crossing the paving stones to Courtenay, who awaited the trio at the top of a three-tiered stair leading to the altar. Trailing behind were the four mendicant friars.

Several bishops, designated to pass judgment upon Wycliffe, sat to the back of William Courtenay. The only one Matthew recognized was Simon Sudbury, Archbishop of Canterbury, who'd officiated at the Black Prince's funeral and often supped with John of Gaunt at the Savoy. With bushy eyebrows and an over-large forehead that caused his features to look as if they'd all slid down to rest between cheeks and chin, Sudbury could best be described as homely. No matter. Privileged position was far more important than comeliness, which was fleeting in the best of circumstances. Still, while Simon Sudbury must be uncomfortable being caught between the Bishop of London and Duke of Lancaster, he, like most of those present, was a skilled actor. Sudbury's only show of nervousness was the continual twisting of the huge bishop's ring topped by an enormous amethyst that sat upon his middle finger.

So here we are with the players all in place.

Matthew had lived long enough to be familiar with the intrigue so omnipresent in English and Bordelais courts. And, though he disdained such intrigues, he was astute enough to at least sense the resultant undercurrents now swirling around him. The posturing and words were just parts in a play, with each of the actors jockeying for dominance over the other.

How to interpret today's characters and their motives? It was obvious that William Courtenay, Bishop of London, and Simon Sudbury, Archbishop of Canterbury, were engaged in a power struggle, beginning with who would control these proceedings. Sudbury was a proxy for his man, the Duke of Lancaster, while Courtenay championed the Commons who had taken away so much royal power during the Good Parliament. Though Courtenay's plebian sympathies did not mean he was a friend of John Wycliffe. Far from it, for Courtenay considered the theologian to be a mortal threat to the natural order of things. While heresies were common in other parts of Europe, no Englishman had ever before attacked the Church and yet here was Wycliffe demanding that it be taxed, its monasteries dissolved, its property returned to its original secular owners and that all clerics be excluded from government office. Heretical rubbish!

The air felt far too close for Matthew, who was already sweating beneath his gambeson. He had little use for bishops in general and these in particular with their scarlet robes pooling about them like grotesque splotches of blood—*Nay. Like bullfinches, with their bright red breasts and timid song,* he assured himself with a mental shake.

He refused to let his mind drift to all the blood that coursed through his nightmares. What with the hostile crowd beyond the Lady Chapel's walls, the current situation could spin out of hand and 'twas his duty to protect not only his liege lord but everyone involved in this unfolding drama.

He was glad Robert Knolles stood beside him. A tougher, more battle hardened knight did not exist in all of England, perhaps even on the continent. Knolles' mercenary activities had made him a wealthy man, though he'd recently been stripped of lands and fined 10,000 marks for leaving English troops stranded on hostile shores to be picked off by the French. The shortage of rescue ships had not been Knolles' fault but he'd accepted the setback as he did his victories, with a shrug and a scowl.

Fortunes wax and wane, his attitude seemed to say, and I'll survive it all.

How? Matthew wondered, before blinking hard and forcing his attention to the two prelates, Courtenay in his miter and Sudbury in robes that made him appear the size of a pavilion. What was it about bishops, nay, most of the religious above the rank of village priest? Every bit as ambitious as their civilian counterparts, they tried to hide their lust for power behind false piety, donning their sanctimony the same way they donned their palliums and finely worked chasubles. And as easily discarding it.

Matthew had to admit that, if he were a pondering sort, some of Wycliffe's complaints were worth a ponder. Two in particular nagged him. The first dated back to 1349 and the Great Plague. Wycliffe's native county was the West Riding of Yorkshire, where two-thirds of his fellow countrymen had perished during those bleak days. Wycliffe was not the only one who had noticed that it was the clergy, in West Riding and elsewhere, who had been hit hardest by the pestilence. Harder than the peasants and their lords, the elderly, pregnant women, even infants and children. The Oxford scholar's explanation had been that the Death had been a particular punishment for the corruption of the clergy. God had thus singled them out for their wickedness.

'Twould seem so. For what other reason could there be?

The second ponder dealt with the end of the world, not a surprising subject to turn one's mind to in the aftermath of an event that had annihilated so much of England. John Wycliffe preached that the end was imminent, or at least would visit itself upon mankind before this, the fourteenth century, drew to a close.

For Edward our prince the end of the world came with his death, Matthew thought. *And the end of the world will soon come for our king. And at times it does feel as if the rest of us are hurtling toward some horrific cataclysm.*

Matthew was familiar enough with Wycliffe's teachings, for his liege lord often expounded upon them, to know that the theologian also preached predestination. Which made a certain amount of sense for, judging by the trajectory of Matthew's life, he figured he could chart the inevitability of his damnation from his time in his mother's womb to Limoges... and beyond.

John of Gaunt, Henry Percy, and John Wycliffe halted at the beginning of the first stair. In his plain black gown, with his white beard, ascetic face and fragile build, John Wycliffe did not look like a mortal threat to anyone.

William Courtenay slowly descended the altar steps and halted a few feet in front of the trio, still on the bottom stair so he loomed above them. Matthew wondered whether Courtenay would be oblivious enough to extend his hand for his ring to be kissed, an act that would surely set Wycliffe on fire.

"Your Grace, Lord Percy," Courtenay said, formally acknowledging them. He kept one hand at his side, the other wrapped around his crozier. "Master Wycliffe," he finished with a nod.

Sunlight streamed from tracery windows upon the scarlet and white spill of the bishops on their benches, clearly etching their lined faces, all appropriately grave, and the grey or white hair rimming their zucchettos. In St. Paul's nave beyond, the humming of the crowd provided a constant reminder of potential danger. Beside Matthew, Robert Knolles shifted position and muttered something that Matthew didn't catch beyond "Bloody hell."

John of Gaunt and Henry Percy settled into a pair of nearby chairs that had been arranged for that purpose. The mendicant friars disappeared into the shadows.

John Wycliffe remained standing.

Gesturing toward a chair, Henry Percy addressed John Wycliffe. "Sit." When the scholar didn't immediately respond, the marshal favored him with a benevolent, though forced, smile. "You have much to reply to. You'll be in need of the softer seat."

"Aye, do ease yourself," chimed in Simon Sudbury, speaking for the first time. "We have many questions—which I am sure you will most ably answer." He smiled benignly though his fingers continued worrying his ring.

William Courtenay frowned. "This is impertinence. The accused must stand to give answers."

"I think not." John of Gaunt sat straight as an arrow, his gaze sharp upon Courtenay, who returned his glare. "Master Wycliffe's examination might take several days. He is old and frail. He needs his own chair."

Here was a second play of power, among Courtenay, the duke, the marshal, and the scholar. Or more accurately between two men— Bishop William Courtenay and John of Gaunt.

Ostensibly about whether a man should stand or sit.

"You have no authority in my church," said Courtenay, unaware that his possessive use of "my" perfectly illustrated one of Wycliffe's complaints. For surely St. Paul's Cathedral belonged, not to the Bishop of London, but to all God's children.

"There is no need—" Simon Sudbury began, seeking to act as peacemaker, only to be interrupted by John of Gaunt.

"I do not intend to bow to your dictates, Your Excellency," the duke said, making the customary form of address sound an insult. He then turned his head and *sotto voce* addressed Percy. "If needs be I might just drag Courtenay from St. Paul's by that straggling mess he calls his hair. What think ye?"

Hearing John of Gaunt's threat all too well, Courtenay's face flushed. But since holy men were not supposed to succumb to the sin of vanity and they were in the Lady Chapel to uncover Master Wycliffe's heresies, he stayed focused.

"You have proven yourself a loyal patron to Master Wycliffe, Your Grace. Does that mean you support his attacks upon our church? His call for the dissolution of monasteries? His diatribes against our monks, who he has labeled pests of society and enemies of religion?"

The drone beyond the Lady Chapel had grown to a roar, like that of the avalanches that had plagued Matthew and the rest of the duke's army during their March to Oblivion. Inwardly, he shuddered and thought once again of Margery, who he was sworn to protect—as he had been sworn to protect his dead brother. Had Meg mentioned that she was returning to the Shop of the Unicorn to go over accounts? Matthew couldn't remember. He should have paid more attention; he should have ordered her to stay off the streets.

Jesu, what is wrong with me? Can I not properly perform my duties on behalf of anyone?

Bringing the quarrel back round to its beginning, John Wycliffe finally spoke. "I do not mind standing. And I am eager to speak God's truth, no matter how long it takes. In fact, I welcome the debate."

Matthew expelled his breath on a weary sigh. If the ecclesiastical trial went forward this was bound to be a long day. Part of many long days. It was not as if the Oxford scholar had been chary in his writings or pronouncements. Why the need for further debate when Margery might be in danger and William Courtenay considered John Wycliffe a threat to the church while John of Gaunt touted him as a needed reformer?

That's the crux of it, isn't it? And whether there is any room for compromise?

Courtenay's gaze bore into the duke's. "Do you deny as Master Wycliffe does, the validity of purgatory? His contempt for pilgrimages and the granting of indulgences and his ridicule of the efficacy of prayers to our saints?"

Matthew's attention, which had once again drifted to Margery's potential whereabouts, snapped back to the present.

To the rising cacophony from outside the Lady Chapel.

To Simon Sudbury twisting, twisting his bishop's ring while his eyes shifted repeatedly from Courtenay to the duke and back again.

To William Courtenay and the bench of bishops who billowed on either side behind him so that by a trick of distance he appeared to have sprouted enormous red wings.

"Do you agree, Your Grace, with Master Wycliffe's interpretation of the doctrine of transubstantiation—"

John of Gaunt leapt to his feet. "Enough, Bishop. Let me speak!"

The shouting beyond had reached fever pitch. Matthew listened for the pounding on the doors which would signal that Gaunt's pikemen had been overcome. He looked around to see if there was an exit other than the one through which they'd entered.

Catching Robert Knolles' eye, he nodded toward a narrow door, barely noticeable in a shadowy corner at the far end of the chapel.

"Aye," breathed Knolles, then caught the attention of the knight next to him as did Matthew to the man on his right.

"I have listened long enough," shouted John of Gaunt. "You seem to be relying overmuch on your noble birth to advance your quarrel." Readying to respond, Courtenay drew himself up to his full height but the duke rushed on. "You are exactly what Master Wycliffe preaches against."

"How dare—"

Lancaster bellowed, "Do not speak!"

And then the reason for John of Gaunt's own personal anger against William Courtenay was laid bare. The Good Parliament. For nearly a year, John had nursed his grievances against those who had hurt his family. As became obvious with his next words.

"When my brother the prince lay dying, you and the rest of those traitorous Commons terrified my father by threatening him with losing his throne. You well know his history, the history of *his* sire and yet you dared stir up ancient ghosts—"

"We merely wished to remove King Edward's greedy harlot and his corrupt councilors—"

"How convenient for you, and how proud you must be to bully a man who has done more good in one day—even in his present unfortunate state—than you in your entire duplicitous lifetime."

Crash!

Matthew flinched for he'd thought the crowd had breached the Lady Chapel. But William Courtenay had simply slammed his crozier upon the stair.

Ignoring the bishop's attempt at regaining control, Lancaster rushed on. "I will never forget nor forgive what you did to my brother and my father."

Despite the outside din, the Lady Chapel suddenly stilled.

There it was.

Bishop Courtenay had disrespected, humiliated and terrified those who John of Gaunt held most dear.

Matthew unsheathed his sword and looked to Robert Knolles and the others, who were also in the process of removing their weapons.

With his next words, the duke took what might have begun as a personal quarrel to the next level, the level that exposed the private fears of each of the bishops who'd thought to stand in judgment of one errant scholar.

"I will make you bend," said John of Gaunt, his voice now menacingly soft. "You and all the rest of England's bishops."

A collective gasp emerged from the scarlet sea. Simon Sudbury ceased fiddling with his signet ring and gazed at the duke with open-mouthed horror. William Courtney clutched the pectoral cross around his neck, which contained a relic of the true cross, as if that might protect him from the duke's implied threat.

"By the rood," Matthew breathed, finally understanding. Here it was, the heart of a political quarrel he'd only dimly grasped. Two of England's greatest, one a member of the church, one of the nobility, were engaged in a primal struggle. One in which Thomas Becket and Henry II had also been engaged. As had many Matthew had never heard of, going back into the mists of time.

Today's quarrel was about one thing.

Power.

Spiritual vs. temporal.

And who—church or state—would wield the ultimate power?

A howling from beyond the doors.

Matthew recalled certain intimate supper conversations when John of Gaunt, who was both knight and scholar, had felt free to expound upon his complaints. What had the duke said? That Christ had never given temporal lordship to the Pope and had certainly never granted him supremacy over the king? That it was wrong for the Pope in Avignon, a *Frenchman* residing in a country with which England remained at war, to receive five times more revenue than his own father, the king?

Matthew had heard all that and more, though he'd largely listened with half an ear. *I should have paid attention.* His fingers squeezed the grip of his sword. *Another mistake.*

The noise from the nave was deafening. While the mob had not breached the doors, the banging on the walls was an indication that the moment was at hand.

Matthew, Robert Knolles and the other knights stepped forward.

Our turn: to protect.

Which meant getting them all, priest and lord alike, out of the Lady Chapel alive.

~

SO THERE IT WAS. There would be no hearing against John Wycliffe, not at this time. Following Wycliffe and the other's escape, William Courtenay had lost his hold over the remaining bishops and the matter of an ecclesiastical trial was pushed into the background.

There were more immediate problems to attend to.

The day after the incident at the Lady Chapel, London's rabble ransacked Henry Percy's residence and released a prisoner whom Percy had kept in the stocks for uttering words against John of Gaunt. A black monk, also friendly to Gaunt, was labeled a traitor and murdered on the spot.

Afterward, the mob headed for the duke's Savoy Palace, where he and Percy, oblivious of the danger, were dining with a wealthy Flemish wool merchant. Hearing the mob, the trio had to hurriedly exit through the back, toward the Thames, where the duke's luxuriously appointed barge was docked. There John of Gaunt, increasingly concerned for the safety of England's heir, made for Kennington, the residence of Joan of Kent, his dead brother's widow, and where young Richard was in residence.

Trembling for the safety of the city—one misplaced torch could set London ablaze—even Bishop William Courtenay pleaded for his parishioners to disperse. Various attempts were made to patch up the quarrel and resultant riots. Finally, a deputation of London officials travelled to Edward III's residence at Sheen. There a city spokesman, fearing business would suffer if the king, the duke, and other powerful lords sought revenge, profusely apologized to His Grace.

Although Edward III's health was poor, he tried to concentrate on the barrage of explanations, but, in actuality, all he wanted to do was return to his leman, Desiderata Cecy, his hawks and his hounds and pleasant reminiscences of long-past times.

A few words detached themselves from the official's mumblings.

What is he saying? Edward wondered. *That neither my son John nor his men has suffered any material damage from these insurrections? God's bones, how brazen my subjects can be!*

He blinked and sat up straighter in his chair, trying to follow what seemed to be very convoluted, and self-serving, reasoning.

Surely, Henry Percy would argue that the ransacking of his residence qualifies as "damage." And had not that poor Scottish knight, Sir John Swynton, who'd had John's badge torn from his very neck by the mob, also suffered several broken ribs? And what about that Benedictine priest who was beaten to death?

But King Edward was growing weary, his lower back ached, and he did not want to quarrel. When city leaders promised that all those who had insulted the duke's name would be found and punished, His Grace pretended to believe them, dismissed them all and returned to more pleasant matters.

Throughout the city, the atmosphere remained explosive. The business of Parliament effectively ceased, though that did not divert Londoners' attention—or their hatred. The duke's men dared not venture out without being heavily armed. John of Gaunt himself prudently exited the city, though he demanded that the anonymous authors of vicious lampoons, impugning everything from his morality to his birthright, be immediately excommunicated.

When peace and order were sufficiently restored, the duke proceeded to undo every last remaining act of the Good Parliament.

CHAPTER 5

London, June 1377

$\mathcal{D}$esiderata Cecy sat beside King Edward's royal couch in his palace at Sheen, along the River Thames. From a strategically placed window she could look out upon the most beautiful gardens. Today, Sunday, June 21, 1377, had been blessed with a dazzling sky and plump clouds. Too bad Edward's sight had failed him. He'd always so loved the views.

Reaching out, Desire ran her fingers over the rings glutting the king's thin, heavily-veined hands. For the past few days His Grace had been in a semi-comatose state, only occasionally rousing himself. Today would be his last; Desire was certain of that.

And I will be sorry.

She did love Edward III, not just because of the legends and because he was KING, with all that title entailed. How much higher could a woman reach than to be companion to a monarch? No, she loved Edward because, while he might be more a sixty-five-year-old child than a man, he was always pleasant and possessed an optimism that might now border on delusion, but which she found touching. She loved him as a fellow human being who was in need of her and who looked at her with such a guilelessness. As her son, Ralphie, yet did. In an old man some might feel revulsion, but Desire felt... compassion.

What has become of me? she wondered. *I am not the woman I once was.*

She wished she were as ambitious and heedless of other's needs as she'd once been, as certain that what Desiderata Cecy wanted she must have simply because she wanted it. Because she willed it. But that woman was a stranger. Her ladies and the royal courtiers around her made sly comments—for one must never come outright and say how much one despises a king's mistress—about parties, feasts, and the material possessions lavished upon her, implying that was the only reason she was with Edward. And behind her back counting the days until her power ended and she would plummet to well-deserved disgrace.

Desire knew what they said and went along with the pretense, prattling about matters of no consequence as if she were interchangeable with Alice Perrers, who'd been so intent on furthering her own and her family's fortunes.

I have more wealth than the treasury, which means little since we are virtually bankrupt. And so many demesnes I have not visited them all. What I need, what I want... Desire sighed. For what she wanted she could never have.

The truth was so very different than what others believed. But let them think what they would. The end had arrived, at least *one* end had arrived, and she must complete her performance.

On St. George's Day, April 23, Edward had managed to hold his last feast of the Garter, where he'd bestowed knighthood on ten-year-old Richard of Bordeaux and his cousin, John of Gaunt's son and heir, Henry of Bolingbroke. Desire had told herself then that the king was improved, that many years yet remained to his life, even though daily events reminded them all otherwise. One of the most humiliating had been when Edward had been forced to greet a group of Londoners swaddled like an infant in cloth of gold and muslin and nailed to his throne so that he would not fall from his perch. He'd been unable to speak at the time, which was just as well for so often his words made little sense, though Desire struggled very hard to decipher their meaning in order to please him.

Our Arthur, she'd thought following the meeting where the hero of Crecy had been held upright by expensive swaddling bands. She'd wept when she was completely alone, away from him, her maids, everyone. She wanted no one, *no one* to view her sorrow.

Now Edward's moment was at hand. And afterward? Desire knew well enough what her future would hold after His Grace's death.

Such fools you all are, thinking, hoping that I will miss the power. Her fingers absently kneaded the counterpane covering the king's wasted body as she addressed her invisible audience. *You say that is what I want—to have bishops and lords and even the Duke of Lancaster coming to me, pleading for me to intercede. If you only knew.*

What Desire really wanted, what she demanded, was their hatred— all of them, from the meanest villein behind a plough in the farthest reaches of Northumbria to John of Gaunt himself. To spit out her name, to attribute all the world's wickedness to her, to look upon her with loathing, to recoil from her presence as if she were a leper.

It was only what she deserved.

"Ah, Harry," she whispered, addressing her dead husband, and her eyes brightened with tears.

When King Edward bestirred himself, his confessor and a dozen other priests entered the room. Though they were intent on hearing his confession and preparing his soul for death, Edward would not cooperate. He muttered about his hawks and hunting and his plans for the future, which did not include dying. So strange that while 'twas common practice for folks, from the ordinary to the most exalted, to have premonitions of their deaths so far in advance that they would insist upon funeral preparations even while appearing outwardly healthy, the most important person in the kingdom—if not the entire world—had not the slightest inkling.

King Edward turned his head on the pillow, toward Desire. "Look at them, so solemn-faced," he said weakly. "How silly they are!"

"Aye, sire." Desire smoothed a strand of hair away from his brow. "By the morrow you will be up and enjoying the hunt, just as always."

She was no Alice Perrers, who Edward truly loved, but what hold she had over him lay in her ability to pretend that he remained young and virile. *'Tis a small enough fiction*, she thought, smiling down at him. *To make a man happy as he lies dying.* Desire took a deep breath, shuddered, and continued her vigil.

King Edward again lost consciousness. His breathing slowed until his alarmed confessor, fearing it had stopped altogether, bent over his chest.

His Grace's eyes fluttered open. "*Jesu Miserere*," he whispered.

The priest thrust a crucifix in the king's hands, then raised it to his lips. Another priest left to send for his four remaining children. Now everyone knew Death would not grant another reprieve.

Edward's household servants and courtiers stood on the opposite side of the chamber, watching the drama unfold, waiting for the moment when their king would die. The end had been predicted for so long that much of the grieving had passed, though it was still difficult to imagine a world in which Edward III had not existed. He had outlived five of the six earls he'd created, six Archbishops of Canterbury, five popes, his two great adversaries, Phillip and Jean of France, and eight of his thirteen children.

Finally, Edward III's breathing ceased. His servants began weeping; courtiers hurried away to relate the news; priests performed the necessary ablutions upon his body.

Desire waited until she was alone with the king. She found herself crying silent tears for she'd become soft-hearted about loss of any kind, from one of Ralphie's toys to that of late summer when she glimpsed the first turning of a leaf, to this, the most enormous loss of all.

Nay, not the most enormous loss. There was one other...

She stared down at Edward's face, taking note of the slackness in the mouth, the relaxing of his knobbled hands on the coverlet.

How had Harry looked when his life had slipped from him? Since Harry's brother, Matthew Hart, fled at the very sight of her, she was left to her imaginings, each one more terrifying than the last. Actually,

Desire knew very little about her husband's death beyond the fact that he was referred to as a hero, as were so many who had participated in the Great Chevauchée. But what had been the manner of his passing? Swift? Slow and painful? Had he called for her and Ralphie? What were his final words? She'd learned little more than that Matthew had been with him, meaning that Harry would not have died alone...

Desire smoothed Edward's brow, which was as warm to the touch as if he were only sleeping. This was a portentous moment. It would be discussed, every nuance, for years, perhaps generations to come. Priests and chroniclers would put quill to parchment and relay the minutest of details—the date of his demise, who attended, Edward's final words, his dress, the size and shape of the chamber in which he expired, the final dispersements of his largesse, any evil portents preceding his death or subsequent miracles. The scribes would also shape opinions of those yet to be born.

Which meant there was only one thing to do.

Desire bent over to lift Edward's head from the pillow and remove a thick gold chain from around his neck. Then she stripped the rings from his fingers and thrust the jewelry inside her purse. Meaningless, all of it. She had coffers, rooms full of similar. But her actions would surely cause tongues to wag and chroniclers to sharpen their feathers and bend over their writing desks, frowning their disapproval as they documented her scandalous behavior.

"I am sorry, sire," she said to the corpse. "But you know what is in my heart."

Desire turned and tiptoed from the room.

AT WARRICK INN, Matthew and Margery were just beginning a game of chess when his squire entered the room.

"Excuse me, my lord," Jerome said. "The duke has just announced that His Grace is dead."

Matthew picked up his king, squeezed it in his fist, and replaced it on the wooden board. "'Tis all over then."

London's bells began to ring, hesitantly at first, then seemingly in a rolling wave, relaying the news.

Margery reached out to place her hand over Matthew's.

He looked down at the slender fingers covering his own. "It is as it is," he whispered, quoting one of the dead king's mottoes. He did not speak for a long time. Then he said, "I am very tired," removed Margery's hand, stood and left the room.

CHAPTER 6

London, Summer to Fall, 1377

"*I* am so pleased to see you." Margery smiled at her father, Thomas Rendell, who sat beside her in Warrick Inn's small pleasance. Thomas and his wife, who was resting inside the Inn's guest chamber, had arrived for Richard of Bordeaux's coronation. Lords were attending the event from across the kingdom as if to remind jackals, both domestic and foreign, that, while the lion might have been downed, his cubs had converged to protect his pride.

"Who would miss our prince's coronation?" asked Thomas, his tone light. His wife Constance's psaltery rested against his knees. He'd been measuring lengths to replace two broken strings on its board but his attention was clearly elsewhere.

Margery wondered whether her father's remark about Richard's coronation might be sarcastic. In these emotional times, anything even hinting of the political had to be carefully treated.

They were nestled in a turf seat tucked into a wall topped by sweet-smelling herbs. Before Thomas's arrival she had been weaving a garland of periwinkles which rested half finished on her lap.

"They say 'twill be the most magnificent ceremony ever," Margery

49

said after a time. She did not add that Thurold and John Ball were wild at the expense of it when England was bankrupt, so many good Englishmen were out of work and foreign workers were flocking into the kingdom, undercutting wages and disrupting the normal balance of commerce.

"I am old enough to remember our Edward III's coronation," Thomas said without elaboration. Margery cocked her head to study him. Thomas Rendell must be sixty years of age or thereabouts and yet, where Edward of Windsor had become a doddering ancient, Thomas would still command a woman's attention and a man's respect. Had it been the same with his father, her grandfather? If so, 'twas no wonder Maria Rendell had been forever captivated.

"London is packed to the rooftops," she said aloud. "It reminds me of the Christmas stories about there being no room at the inn. My lord's family are all at Hart's Place. Some have even erected tents in the garden."

"Let us pray our young prince enjoys a reign as prosperous as his grandfather's."

Everyone is pretending, are they not? thought Thomas. *Mouthing platitudes and hoping for the best when the enemy raids our coasts and the kingdom trembles for its future. Our king had barely drawn his last breath when we were terrorized by swarms of French ships disgorging thousands of troops who sacked Rye, burned Lewes, which should have been safely inland, and then set fire to Plymouth. Atrocities more suited to Nordic sagas than these civilized times.*

Thomas picked up the psaltery, placed it across his knees, removed the broken strings and carefully replaced them with new ones. Constance plucked her psaltery like an angel but the accompanying singing could most charitably be described as determined.

"I do know one thing," he said. "No matter what, England will survive." He remembered the abdication of the second king Edward— as well as the resultant scandal regarding Thomas's mother, Maria, and her lover, Richard of Sussex, (which to this day Thomas had never mentioned). The kingdom had been just as torn in 1327. And then been raised to mythical heights by Edward III and his son, the Black Prince. 'Twas simply fortune's ever turning wheel.

Thomas leaned the psaltery on the turf seat next to him and sighed deeply. He was too fixated on the past, a sure sign of age. Soon he'd be an old fool sitting in a corner, mumbling to himself and wondering why everyone, even his wife and children, avoided him.

"I do not harbor much fondness for London," he said suddenly. His gaze fashioned upon the gold and orange flash of minnows circling the pond directly across the pebbled pathway. "But then I've never been much of a traveler. If it weren't for campaigns and attending to our other manors, I would ne'er leave Fordwich Castle." He stretched his booted legs before him until the heels were planted upon the pathway.

"I am grateful you chose to travel to Cambridge one particular year," Margery said with a shy smile. "Else I would not be here."

Thomas laughed. "Aye, Sturbridge Fair. How I balked and complained about traveling five days with pack horses and carts and instructions as to what must be purchased and brought back home. The barges and wherries cramming the River Cam, from as far away as Italy and beyond, were loaded with so many goods the like of which I'd never seen. It did not matter. I was instructed to bring back a little, and sometimes a lot, of everything." He paused, and his voice softened. "But after meeting Alice, I counted the days from one year to the next."

Ah, Margery's mother. Somehow their private conversations always meandered back to Alice.

"Sometimes I think I remember Sturbridge but I'm not sure whether I'm confusing it with more recent fairs," she said. "There must have been plays, of course, and puppet shows and acrobats and stilt-walkers and jugglers. I can almost see Thurold handing me a cryspe powdered with sugar, which I'd ne'er tasted before. And it seems Giddy once got lost..." Margery's voice trailed away. In truth her half-sister had long ago become just a name. She might have dreamt chasing that tiny copper-haired hoyden around stalls and among a sea of kirtles and chausses, for Margery would have been too small herself to easily view anyone from much above the waist.

Thomas and Alice: the past sat between them. So many questions

Margery might ask. She knew her father would be eager to answer them all.

She wasn't even sure what her mother looked like anymore. Thomas always remarked on their resemblance, save for Alice's hair, he said, which had been much lighter. Margery remembered, didn't she, her mother combing her luxuriant tresses in front of a shaft of sunshine? Would the light have come from the window opening in the Watson cottage, which, thanks to Thomas Rendell's largesse, had been the finest in all of Ravennesfield?

Margery wanted to question her father about so many things—the timbre of Alice's voice; whether she was quiet or laughed often; whether she was clever or slow, vulnerable or haughty; whether she accepted the attentions of a great lord with awe or as her due? Did they speak of love and of shared dreams, all the while knowing such were impossible? Or did both just accept it for what it was, a dalliance with a by-blow as a result?

But Margery would probably start off by asking something simple like, "How did you meet?"

She had a vague memory of sitting on a stool with Alice plaiting her hair while recounting the details, but it was impossible to sort truth from embellishments. Or Margery might have created something out of whole cloth and then built upon those imaginings.

One thing was certain: Sturbridge Fair was the largest fair in the world. So how, among those many thousands, would Thomas have ever noticed a peasant woman dressed so nondescriptly in a cheap woolen dress? But Margery seemed to recall that contrary to custom Alice always allowed her hair to fall free rather than wear a wimple. That alone would have drawn attention. And the most shapeless shift could not completely hide a curvaceous young woman with a seductive bearing, for that her mother must have had. Something... to set her apart, to pique the interest of a lord like Thomas Rendell.

So many questions. But Margery would not disrespect Thomas's wife, sleeping so innocently nearby in Warrick Inn's guest chamber, by voicing them. Instead she busied her hands weaving more periwinkles into her half-finished garland and allowed the silence to stretch between them.

Thomas sighed, as if shaking off memories. "One becomes maudlin with time," he said cryptically and traced circles in the pebbled path with the toe of his boot.

Margery continued shaping the stems of her garland. Settling on a safer topic, she said, "I hear that London has been transformed for the coronation. That when His Grace makes his way to Westminster the surrounding streets will have been turned into places of enchantment."

Thomas laughed. "Enchantment is hardly a word I would use when describing *any* part of this city."

Margery returned the garland to her lap. "'Tis more a word I would use for your Cherry Fair." She placed her hand atop his. "I am so pleased my lord Hart and I attended this year. So often during those days I would find myself thinking that paradise could not be lovelier. Only in paradise the trees will never lose their blossoms."

"But isn't that what makes them so bewitching, the fact that we know they are transitory?"

While Thomas was touched by Margery's enthusiasm, a pall had hung over this year's festivities as persistently as mist off the River Stour. Knowing that King Edward's death was imminent, many lords and ladies had stayed away, calculating that they'd soon have to make a second trek in order to attend a royal funeral. And with all those raids and rumors of raids...

"Have you ever considered leaving London for somewhere safer?" he blurted. "And for a political atmosphere less... poisoned? I worry about you and Serill. Lord Hart speaks so fondly of Cumbria. Why not retire there? Save for an occasional summons to Parliament, the lords of the north are largely left alone to do as they please."

"Lords of the north." Margery tried the unfamiliar phrase upon her tongue. She hadn't often heard that expression or if she had she'd not connected it to her beloved.

Is that what you are, a lord of the north?

It sounded dangerous, uncivilized. She imagined giants with great matted beards and hair, fashioned more in the mold of Viking marauders than English knights, sweeping out of the darkness on howling winds and hammering snows with ice clinging to the great muscled flanks of their destriers as they galloped southward until they reached London where they would upend the natural order of things.

The image made her smile. *I must remember to share it with Matthew.* Aloud she said, "Lord Hart hasn't returned to Cumbria since his father's death."

Thomas's hand tightened in hers, as if he understood the deeper meaning.

Margery watched a pair of robins hopping about a filigreed cage; bees and butterflies dipped among the gillyflowers, primroses, and periwinkles edging the pathway and pond.

Holding on to the image of the lords of the north, she thought, *Will you smile when I tell you? And... when was the last time I've even seen you really, truly smile?*

She knew exactly. It had been at the Cherry Fair, or more precisely, at Chilham Castle and the jousting that always accompanied the Cherry Fair.

The day had been perfect; the bluest of blue skies with just a hint of breeze, enough to lift the parade of banners and provide a measure of relief for those on the field and in the stands. The emerald carpet of grass surrounding Chilham Castle, so newly whitewashed it hurt the eyes. Garishly colored shields and pennons and caparisoned horses and riders.

How handsome Matthew had looked, sitting so confidently atop his prancing destrier, his jupon, crest, heraldic shield and horse's coverings all bearing the red, white and yellow of the Hart family coat of arms.

How proud Margery had been when he'd worn her garter upon his lance and a tippet from her sleeve atop his crest.

How excited when he'd so effortlessly knocked four opponents from their perches.

How filled with love afterward when, along with a handful of other knights, he'd approached the stands to claim his prize. His gaze had swept the crowd, seeking her out and when he'd found her, his smile had been as if it were just they two in all the world.

How she'd thrown him a kiss, pressed a hand over her heart, and mouthed, "Forever."

Not caring whether she was being publicly brazen or betraying Thurold and John Ball...

"Mayhap Cumbria is too far away," Thomas said, interrupting her reverie. "For how would I ever see you? So we will simply convince Lord Hart to find a townhouse in Canterbury. Do you not think so?"

Before she could respond they heard voices and the crunch of footsteps upon gravel. Matthew and Thomas's wife appeared arm in arm.

"Did you sleep well, dear wife?" Thomas asked, rising to greet her. "I fixed your psaltery." He handed it to Constance, kissed her on the cheek and they stood a distance away conversing in the intimate manner of married couples.

Matthew sat down beside her on the bench. "It pleases me to see you with your father." He picked up the unfinished garland from her lap, placed it at a cockeyed angle so it dipped forward upon her brow, and smiled into her eyes.

Only this smile, Margery thought, suppressing a twinge of sadness, *is nothing like the smile you gave me at Chilham Castle.*

RICHARD OF BORDEAUX was crowned king of England on the eve of the feast of Saint Kenelm. Saint Kenelm was a boy king in ancient times who had been murdered by his elder sister and buried in a pass in the Cotswolds. His body had been uncovered, so went the legend, after a mysterious dove laid a parchment detailing the crime on Rome's altar of St. Peter. Though coronations were customarily held on Sundays, Richard's ceremony was scheduled for that Thursday, July 16, 1377.

England might be nearly bankrupt and the French openly raiding her southern coast, but the magnates, led by John of Gaunt and Joan of Kent, now the Queen Mother, were determined to make Richard's coronation the most elaborate ever. John hoped that his nephew's reign would mark a positive turning point for the kingdom itself. He prayed

Richard, who was already being heralded as a new Arthur, would evolve into a similar idyllic sovereign.

On the day preceding Richard's coronation, the peers of the realm, along with London's mayor and sheriffs, had assembled at the gates of the Tower of London, awaiting the ten-year-old heir's arrival. Matthew Hart stood among the lords dressed, as were they all, in their finest. Around him the crowd, aided by the free wine flowing from city fountains, shouted and jested and elbowed each other, vying for better positions from which to view the boy king. Jugglers, dancing bears and monkeys entertained, while the many carts, tents, horses and barking dogs jammed amidst the celebration added to the merry chaos.

Unlike those around him, Matthew could summon forth no joy or even curiosity—though he dutifully went through the motions. Edward III, their warrior king, was dead; it was inconceivable to Matthew that people could so glibly transfer their allegiance to a mere babe. They might see the boy king, even now coming into view wearing a dazzling robe of white satin, but Matthew saw their true king, his embalmed body placed upon a bier and covered, save for his wasted face. Edward's sons and twenty-four black-garbed knights, including Matthew himself, had borne their monarch at a slow march to Westminster where he had been laid to rest beside his queen. That day, less than a month past, Englishmen had wept as loudly as they cheered today. Matthew could not reconcile himself to the shallowness of their emotions. Edward had reigned for fifty years, had led England through a golden age.

How can you call a child "Arthur," Matthew wondered, *when we already lived our Camelot?* Yet, judging from the fickle populace screaming for Richard of Bordeaux, Edward's entire reign was of no more consequence than dandelion spores drifting upon the wind.

England's magnates conducted the boy king, perched gracefully atop a handsomely accoutered charger, down Cheapside and Fleet Street toward Westminster Palace. All along the route houses were decorated with cloth of gold and silver or bold colored hangings. A huge floral castle with four towers, each containing an exquisite girl, had been erected and as Richard rode past, they showered him with gold leaves. Spectators shouted their joy; even the hated Duke of Lancaster and Henry Percy, who headed the cortege, were cheered.

"'Tis truly a new era," commented Matthew's brother-in-law (and murderer of Margery's mother), Lawrence Ravenne. Ravenne walked carefully, favoring his right leg, for he was oft plagued by gout brought on by too much easy living and inactivity.

"I would prefer the old era," Matthew responded, but his words were lost in the tumult.

At noon the following day the coronation began. Richard, dressed in white robes to symbolize his innocence, looked ethereally beautiful. Spectators maintained that he was as "fair among men as another Absalom."

Though the king tried manfully to stay alert, the rituals were numbingly long and complex, and his jewel-encrusted coronation robe was as stiff and heavy as armor. The bishops hid Richard behind a gold cloth and removed his outer garments, including his royal shirt which had been cut in two pieces and was held together by silver links. He was then anointed with chrism. Obediently Richard intoned all the prayers and hymns, striving for perfection in his every word and movement, for even the smallest mistake might be construed as an ill omen. Then the crown was placed upon his head and the ring upon his finger, and he was invested with the scepter, orb, and sword of his office.

Throughout the ceremony, the king's face grew whiter; his eyes showed huge and round. Richard's helplessness, his youth and innocence touched all those packed into Westminster's nave. Even the most embittered barons privately vowed to put away their quarrels and willingly serve their king, who so obviously had need of them.

Near the ceremony's end each of England's greatest lords came forward to touch their sovereign's crown. The act symbolized the barons' service and support, as well as their cooperation in helping to ease the burdens of the royal office.

When Matthew reached down to touch the golden circlet he gazed into Richard's drawn face. The king smiled up at him, and Matthew noted there the delicate, yet unspoiled beauty that had been his mother's trademark. Richard's namesake was the Lionheart, and his father had been the greatest of all warriors. Yet Matthew could see nothing save an exquisite, exhausted child. Impossible not to feel protective toward him; but a king's duty was to lead, not arouse paternal instincts.

'Twill be easy to love Richard II, Matthew thought, returning to his position among the other barons. *But how easy will it be to serve him?*

By the time the coronation ceremony was completed, Richard was so weary he could scarce hold up his head. Sir Simon Burley, who had been with the Black Prince at Limoges and was one of Richard's tutors, finally swept the king into his arms and carried him outside the Abbey to a waiting litter. One of the boy's slippers, first fashioned for Edward the Confessor more than three hundred years past, fell off, and as the litter moved off toward Westminster Palace, the mob swarmed around it.

Standing just beyond the west door of the Abbey, Matthew watched the mob fight for possession of Richard's slipper. Was it the coolness of evening emanating from the cathedral stones, or the scene itself, which caused a shudder of foreboding?

Matthew wondered what it might mean—the king who had lost a shoe.

IN THE MONTHS following Richard's coronation, his lost slipper did seem a harbinger of troubled times. Peace negotiations with France completely collapsed. The Scots swept down to burn Roxburgh. Henry Percy, who Richard had bestowed the title, Earl of Northumberland, perhaps to keep him far away from London, gathered ten thousand men and burned and pillaged in revenge. The French overran the Isle of Wight and put the inhabitants to ransom for a thousand marks. They then assaulted Winchelsea, burned Rye, Hastings, and Rottingdean, killing all they could find and hauling off livestock and valuables. By the time All Hallows Eve 1377 arrived, the French had inflicted more damage on England than during the last forty years.

CHAPTER 7

London, August, 1378

In the year that had passed since Edward III's death and his grandson's ascension to the throne, Matthew was away more often than he was home. Always on campaign with his lord the duke. When ports in northern France and Brittany were being threatened, Lancaster's army travelled there, laid siege to Saint-Malo, and generally wreaked ineffectual havoc in places that all blurred together in Matthew's mind. He did as he was told. What more need be said?

Each time he returned to Warrick Inn, Matthew's mood worsened. Darkness cloaked him like a mantle. Merely being in his presence risked a return of Margery's own melancholia so she took to avoiding him. His drinking increased. What he did on campaigns she could not guess—and he would not have told her had she asked—but here he often shut himself away in the guest chamber with only himself and a flagon of wine. Matthew was not a mean drunk like her stepfather, or a happy, harmless one like his brother. He grew quieter, if that was possible, and even more intense.

But that was not what upset Margery. At those times, when she looked into her lover's eyes, 'twas not Matthew Hart who looked back at her. Or any human for that matter. She could not even compare his eyes to an animal's, for they seemed as lifeless as a statue's. Margery couldn't explain it. She only knew that, at such times he frightened her.

Increasingly, Margery contemplated returning to the Shop of the Unicorn, simply removing her few things when he was on campaign and be gone when he returned. Or opening a second shop in Canterbury, where she could be close to her father and grandmother. She hated the campaigns for how they'd scarred Matthew and resented his loyalty to the Duke of Lancaster, who was so universally hated and who he so fiercely defended, no matter the charge.

Mayhap I should strap on armor and wave a sword around like a madwoman, slice off a few random limbs and you would champion me for a change.

When they were together they quarreled about matters large and small. What time to attend morning mass, *whether* to attend morning mass, play chess or draughts, visit the Tower menagerie or the Tower garden, hire two new chambermaids or three? Should Margery go over accounts at the Shop of the Unicorn, Matthew would intimate that she was too friendly with Nicholas Norlong, who ran the goldsmithing business. Upon Matthew's return from his latest sortie, Margery would accuse him of bedding camp followers or, more bizarrely, she would imagine something straight out of a fantastical tale. A beautiful damoiselle locked away in a crumbling castle that Matthew would rescue after stumbling upon it during one of his sieges. A bewitching creature who would cast a spell upon his heart, which explained why he'd become so distant. Margery even brought up Desiderata Cecy, who'd been banished from court following King Edward's death and who her lover had not seen in years.

Or had he?

'Twas all so ridiculous. Even while hurling her accusations Margery wondered where they came from, how she'd degenerated into such a sharp-tongued shrew.

Their most serious quarrels revolved around Serill. Increasingly, every conversation seemed to end with some reference to his future.

Matthew hadn't been returned from the duke's latest campaign a sennight before that particular quarrel was resurrected.

He'd been hawking with some lords (he said), no ladies (he swore), beyond London's walls and was returning his favorite peregrine to its perch inside Warrick Inn's solar.

"We canna put off Serill's leaving any longer."

Situated in the window seat where the light was strongest so she could work her sewing, Margery pressed her lips together in annoyance. "Is that what you were doing on campaign, stewing about my care of our son? Or were you discussing me, us, Serill, today when you were supposed to be hawking?"

She imagined Matthew with his "companions," all gossiping about her shortcomings in between oohing and aahing over the weapons of death they'd unleashed upon helpless mice, rabbits, and kits cowering in the tall grass.

The hooded hawk flapped her wings, then curled her wicked talons around the perch's dowel.

"'Tis past time that Serill began fulfilling his obligations."

Matthew carefully wrapped his falcon's leather jesses around the bar and watched until she'd properly settled. He kept a trio of hawks in their solar—which Margery immediately banished to the mews upon his departure.

"Serill is doing very well with his studies," she said aloud. "Brother Udo tells me he is quite clever, that he can read—"

"Learning Latin and the rest is all fine and good, but Serill is eight years old now. He has duties and obligations for which he must prepare."

Margery put aside the pillow slip on which she'd been working. The afternoon sun highlighted the vines and leaping harts chiseled into the room's oak paneling. A beautiful solar with its great mahogany bed swathed in royal blue curtains and a black coverlet of martens' fur embroidered with multi-colored birds, beasts, and flowers. From the pleasance below, Serill's voice drifted upward as he called to his latest menagerie of puppies and hounds.

"Our son has plenty of time to begin an apprenticeship." Margery pretended to misunderstand Matthew's meaning. Or simply to prick him into a quarrel. But over what? Sometimes she had no idea. "Serill does spend some time at the Shop and he seems to enjoy working with Master Norlong and—"

"No son of mine will be a goldsmith. Serill will be a knight, like his father." Matthew carefully eased the hood from his peregrine, who once again flapped her wings and stretched her neck, seeking a treat which he retrieved from a covered container.

While Matthew fed his bird, Margery looked away. She hated the way the carrion stank up the solar. Despite the room's beauty, she'd also begun to hate the solar itself. "The Shop of the Unicorn is a worthy legacy. Serill will be heir to a thriving business. But he is still so young."

"I was already a year into my service at his age. 'Twas not pleasant but 'tis necessary, lest you would have our son killed his first time in battle."

"For all the world knows, Serill is Simon Crull's issue. No one would question his choice to become a tradesman."

Matthew snorted. "Really, Meg? Who do you think you fool with such nonsense? Serill looks just like a Hart, he looks like *me* and his interest is in the sword. Furthermore, since we have lived together these past many years do you not think people have guessed his heritage? This might be a pretense you need to maintain for whatever reason, but I have already talked to my lord Duke and Serill will begin his training in the Lancaster household on Michaelmas."

Margery gasped. "With John of Gaunt?" She rose, then thought better of it and sat down again, clutching her suddenly trembling hands together. "Is that wise? And so soon? Why did you not consult me?"

"Because then I'd have to listen to your cavilling." Matthew tossed his jeweled hawking glove on one of several iron-bound chests, crossed to a small table, and poured himself a goblet of wine which he downed in one long gulp.

"You are mistaken if you think you have a voice in this matter," he said, turning back to her. "That just because you are Margery Watson you can write society's rules as you please."

She felt her face flush, as if he'd slapped her. They were in danger of veering into uncharted territory from which they might not be able to return. "I just do not want our son involved in war," she said carefully. *You lost your brother to war. You lost your soul to war.*

Matthew waved a hand dismissively. "We are all involved in war— goldsmith or villein, king or abbot, it makes no difference. And Serill is my heir, whether we wed or not. And he *will* be a knight."

Margery once again picked up the pillow slip to busy her shaking hands. She smoothed the fabric as if she were smoothing away her frustration and bit back the words she wanted to hurl at him, which were, "*So that he can kill innocent women and children?*"

"Serill would be so far from home, and pages are treated so very harshly," she said, her manner as reasonable as she could make it. "He is such a gentle boy, so sensitive—"

"Serill? He is as rough and tumble as any lad. He doesn't need his mother hovering about turning him into a girl."

"I've seen what knighthood does," Margery snapped, feeling her temper slip. There were certain wounds that must not be re-opened, certain subjects that must not be broached. Yet they were there on the tip of her tongue, readying to explode like those cannon balls about which she'd been hearing.

"And what precisely is it that knighthood does? Enlighten me, Margery Watson." Matthew drew himself up to his full height. Even in ordinary dress, he looked every bit a warrior; his expression was fierce enough to chill her heart.

How many more have you killed on this campaign? She wanted to taunt. *How much more bloodletting*? But Matthew had killed women and children without a qualm, hadn't he? *What might you do to me?*

"I just want to protect Serill," she said, her tone placating. "Allow him to be carefree... and innocent... for a while longer."

"As do I." That look left Matthew's eyes. More softly, he said, "I would not quarrel with you. I wish we could keep Serill cosseted and close but that is not the way of the world, *my* world."

"Why does it have to be so? Why—"

"I am doing what is best for our son and for the family name."

"I would prefer—"

Matthew cut her off with a look of ice. "No more, Meg. 'Tis done. Serill will be serving as a page in my lord's house. And if you further complain, I'll send him off tomorrow." He slammed his goblet down on the table, strode to the solar door, and as a parting dig, tossed over his shoulder, "Who would have thought that you would become such a nag?"

Margery stared at the closing door. *And you, former light of my heart, what have you become?*

IN THE FIRST month Margery and Matthew had moved into Warrick Inn, she had painted a calendar on the wall above the fireplace which detailed all the days and seasons until the end of the decade. Important dates had been circled in red—birth days and death days, political events, saints' days and celebrations. Had the lovers known, they surely would have marked today's date, August 15, 1378, for this was the day their relationship ended.

The morning began auspiciously enough with no hint of what was to come. As Matthew and Margery had settled back into long-established routine, forced politeness had gradually given way to more relaxed conversation. In the night when Matthew reached for her she went willingly, and entwined as they were in each other's arms, the hurts fell away. At least until dawn.

Margery, Matthew, and Serill walked to Smithfield to view the weekly horse racing. Serill chatted about the last time they'd enjoyed a similar outing, which had been on Easter Sunday. London's churches had been adorned with lilies, and Londoners, in high spirits after six weeks of fasting, had been arrayed in their finest. Serill had joined other children wrestling, foot racing, and rolling hard-boiled eggs on the grass.

Margery remembered that day for another reason. Matthew had needled her once too often for her reluctance to wed and they'd publicly quarreled. He would have been within his rights to backhand her for her disrespect so today she vowed she would be the perfect helpmeet, as unruffled as the female saints that forever gazed upon worshippers from chapel, church and cathedral stained glass windows. Of course the women were all martyrs. But what was it about Catherine, Cecilia, Agnes, Perpetua and the rest? How could they bear such placid expressions while being stuck full of arrows, decapitated, boiled in water or burned alive, or even when they gouged out their own eyes, as did Saint Lucia, who was oft depicted carrying them around upon a plate? Virginity, or the fear of losing it, seemed to be the reason so many had cheerfully undergone torture, disfigurement and death.

Which is one of the many reasons I will never be a saint.

Once at Smithfield they made their way slowly toward the crowds surrounding the racing paths. Excited as a pup, Serill pestered his father to purchase treats from various vendors and a kite in the shape of a dragon which Matthew then taught him to fly.

What a fine day with the sun warm on Margery's back, the cheerful cries of hawkers; children's shouts and laughter; strolling lords and ladies looking like brilliant flowers, and in the distance racing horses with their necks stretched taut, their legs a blur as they thundered toward a finish line.

Suddenly, Margery heard someone call Matthew's name. She felt an unpleasant prickling along her spine for she well recognized that voice. Turning, she watched Desiderata Cecy, her son, and a pair of her ladies-in-waiting approach.

"I thought your duke banished that creature from court following His Grace's death," Margery mumbled to Matthew, who had returned Serill's kite, which he'd maneuvered high enough to catch an air current, to his son.

"Smithfield is hardly Westminster, more's the pity." Matthew did not appear to be any happier seeing his former sister-in-law than Margery felt, though Serill, with his kite bobbing and jerking like a great red snake, ran to greet his cousin, Ralphie.

"We'd best have a care to our fingers, lest she strip off all our rings," Margery said nastily. She noted that Lady Cecy was dressed quite demurely, all in black, with gold piping, as if in mourning.

Who do you pretend to mourn? she wondered. *The king? Harry still? Your banishment from court? Or simply do you wear black because it flatters you?*

"My lord, God you keep!" Desire stopped before them, curtsied to Matthew and favored them both with a friendly smile.

Did you plan this? Margery wondered, responding with the barest acceptable curtsy.

Matthew echoed Desire's greeting. Regardless of their unfortunate history, she was his brother's widow and must be shown proper respect.

"Come along, Ralphie!" Serill grabbed his cousin's hand. "I'll teach you how to fly my kite."

"And then we'll watch the races," Ralphie said. "Mightn't we?" Serill nodded and they ran away, across the green, trailed by the rapidly descending dragon.

"How tall your son is," Desire observed, following the boys' retreating forms. "Near as tall as Ralphie."

Neither Margery nor Matthew commented, though Desire continued, seemingly oblivious to the tension-filled air. "I am so happy that our sons are friends as well as kin. Harry would be pleased."

At mention of his brother, Matthew stiffened while Margery could scarce hide her annoyance. If Desire had any sensitivity at all, which she did not, she would realize Matthew avoided all mention of Harry Hart.

"Blood is everything," Matthew agreed, keeping his gaze on Serill and Ralphie, who were running along the banks of the Fleet River trying to coax the dragon kite once again high into the air. 'Twas impossible to look his former sister-in-law in the eye. Throughout the March to Oblivion Harry had often spoken of his wife and son, but Matthew would not remember those conversations.

"'Tis only right that Serill and Ralphie be close growing up," he added, pushing down any stir of memory. "Which is why I arranged for both to serve my lord duke."

"I am so grateful for your intercession. Ralphie was so unhappy in the Gloucester household."

What? Margery's eyebrows shot up. *What are you talking about?*

She looked from one to the other. *When had Matthew talked to John of Gaunt about his nephew? How would he have known anything about Ralphie's plight unless Desire had told him?*

"...pleased to help," Matthew was saying.

"My son can be timid and, despite my differences with your lord, 'tis the best household for him."

Margery didn't know whether to roll her eyes or slap the woman. Desiderata Cecy never worried about anyone or anything beyond herself, and her doting mother act was as artificial as the paint on her face. She wanted something, of course, but what? Most probably Matthew.

You are using your son as an excuse and, being a man, my lord is stupid enough not to notice. Unless he still wishes to bed you himself.

Margery felt that old rush of jealousy. Somehow without her knowing, Matthew and his former leman had been in communication. How dare he? What other secrets was he keeping?

But to bed your brother's wife, that would be incestuous. Surely you would not so dishonor Harry...

While Margery thought her dark thoughts—for weren't Desire's ladies-in-waiting also eyeing her lover far too boldly?—Desire chatted about past travels to her numerous estates throughout France.

"I am leaving soon for Bordeaux," she said suddenly. "I will not return."

Matthew peered at Desire, trying to decipher the meaning behind her unexpected announcement. For the first time he noticed that she appeared weary and there was something about her, a certain vulnerability—could it possibly be so?—that he'd not previously noticed.

"God's speed on your journey." Margery's voice was heavy with sarcasm.

At that moment, Serill and Ralph came tearing back and Serill grabbed her hand. "Come along, Maman. 'Tis your turn to help us fly our dragon."

Reluctantly, Margery acquiesced, and after Desire gestured to one of her ladies to follow, she turned once more to Matthew, who'd been mulling his own exit.

"Would you walk with me, Lord Hart? One last time?"

Matthew hesitated. He had a lifetime of reasons he did not want to be alone with Desire. But she had been Harry's wife and she was Ralphie's mother, and despite her disgraceful behavior with King Edward, despite her many faults, that status granted her a certain courtesy.

"Please."

She seemed nervous and while he would once have said he knew her every expression, her every pretense, he could decipher nothing beyond a certain wistfulness.

Rather than speak, he offered his arm in the customary fashion. They walked in silence, her arm lightly atop his.

Desire cleared her throat. "Remember how it was in Bordeaux? What grand amusements we enjoyed? The banquets, with lakes of real water that Prince Edward's artificers used to bring into the dining hall? Remember how skilled they were, how they made boats row up and down, and lions appear? And the night they caused an actual stone castle to vanish right before our eyes?" She gestured broadly with her free arm, as if brandishing a magic wand. "Those were golden days, were they not?"

Matthew tensed. If she thought to tread the well-worn path of their relationship, he would walk away. "'Tis past," he said bluntly. "I never think on it."

She sighed. "England was never my home. And now... well, 'tis best."

They strolled past merchants selling trinkets and toys; a group of carolers singing and dancing in a circle, horses being cooled down by their handlers. Matthew craned his neck to see if he could spot Margery and the boys. Being alone with Desire was definitely uncomfortable.

"I really learned to love him, you know," Desire said, her voice barely a whisper.

Matthew's vision darkened, and for an instant he could see nothing at all. It was as if he was caught up in a thunder cloud, and he felt a roaring in his ears. He knew well enough who Desire was speaking of and he would not, could not speak of Harry.

He opened his mouth to reply, but no words emerged. His instinct was to race back across the grass to his family, scoop Serill up in his arms and hurry away from Desire and whatever it was she thought she needed to confess.

"I know I wasn't the most understanding of wives. I have always had such a wayward tongue... When I canna sleep I run back and forth in my mind the cruel things I said to him."

Matthew turned to study her. Was she sincere? Was this some sort of trap? He'd never been able to keep up with her mental machinations. But so many years had passed since they'd been lovers, since she'd married Harry, since he'd spent any time in her presence. He was certainly not the same person. Could it also be so with Desire?

"I know how it must have appeared to others, but when your brother and I were alone..." Tears pooled in her dark eyes. He'd seen those before as well, copious tears no more to be trusted than her rages or gentleness. Was this too for effect?

"I miss him more than I can bear at times." The tears slipped down Desire's cheeks, tracing tracks upon the white powder of her makeup. "So many regrets," she sighed.

Matthew felt his own eyes burn. He could not say what was in his heart, which was that Desiderata Cecy was not the only one who lay awake nights. That he dreaded sleep and its resultant nightmares just as he dreaded sleep's absence. For then his head would be crowded with so many images that he grew dizzy trying to sort through them all...

"Your brother was always kind and gentle to me."

"That was Harry's nature." His voice was gruff. *I really do not want to speak of this.* If he could just disappear. Drift away upon the wind...

She cast him a glance. "You were never kind or gentle."

He managed a smile. "Nay."

Desire paused and faced him. In her expression, he saw nothing but pain, and his chest tightened. What did she seek from him? Whatever it was, he was incapable of granting it. If it had to do with his brother, they could not alter the past, which meant this conversation served absolutely no purpose.

"I ask you one final kindness before I depart."

"And what is that?" *Here we are, when she'll reveal what is really in that scheming mind of hers*. Or worse. He would prefer manipulations to genuine sorrow.

Desire looked into Matthew's eyes. "Tell me how my husband died. Please. Tell me everything."

MATTHEW HAD NOT RETURNED to Smithfield. Where was he? Soon it would be Vespers. Margery and Serill and Ralphie and Desire's maid had passed the afternoon flying the dragon kite until it got caught and torn in one of the trees along Fleet River. Ralphie had eaten so much that he complained of a stomach ache and both boys had to be repeatedly reprimanded for getting too close to galloping horses. While Margery would like to have subtly (she hoped) question Desire's ladies-in-waiting about whether their mistress had been sincere about departing England, the women spoke very little English and Margery's French was abysmal. So as soon as possible she'd returned to Warrick Inn.

And waited for Matthew's return.

And waited.

Settled in the window seat, she absently wrapped around her hand a streamer of knots of ophreys from her sewing box. She had been planning to use the gold lace to border the sleeves of one of her gowns. Instead, unable to concentrate, she rearranged the box's contents—her leather thimble, scissors, spools of thread and various-sized needles. She'd planned to knit Matthew a cloak...

Margery closed the lid, rose and crossed to one of the square wicker bird cages hanging in a nearby window. Darkness was inching across London's rooftops. So many times of a summer's night, after the rising moon, lads and maidens would dance upon the green, lay neath sheltering oaks, and make love. She sighed. It seemed so long since she and Matthew had done anything similar—at least with a merry heart.

The raven inside its wicker cage followed her with its sharp black eyes before turning its tail, as if in dismissal. She thought of Robin, of the night she'd killed Simon Crull, of so many things. It was not just her lover's leave-taking with Desire that was so troubling. What she was feeling was not jealousy. It was weariness.

I cannot do this anymore.

Margery leaned against the window frame, gazing into the twilight. How to parse the mysteries of love? In the early years, because their relationship had been so forbidden and their time so limited, their every moment had been as charged as lightning... The wasteland that was her heart, her life, following her marriage to Crull... Then, after she and Matthew had reunited, she'd been so immersed in thoughts of him when he was away that, whether on campaign or with the Black Prince or in the wilds of Cumbria, he'd been as ever-present as a shadow. If she could have created a magic potion to conjure him, she would have risked her soul for a few blissful hours together. Her golden knight, her faerie knight under the moon. As much a part of her as her blood, her breath, her bones. She would imagine Matthew hiding in storm clouds and riding on the wind and in sunrises and sunsets. Her force of nature. She'd see him everywhere—in a courtier's grin, a certain stance or gesture, the narrowing of the eyes, the shape of the hands, the cock of the head—and the longing would be as sharp as if she'd been pierced with a dagger. In dreams she would taste him and feel him and touch him and, even upon awakening, tingle with the after-blush of lovemaking. Had he been as obsessed, as in love? Odd that she'd never asked, but she'd never doubted, always just assumed... until now.

What is true? Margery wondered. *Can I be certain about anything?*

Of course the marker, the before and after of their demise, was Limoges. She'd assured herself they'd weathered that and all the other challenges when she'd simply been distracting herself with pretty tales in order to ignore the truth. Which was that they'd become strangers

71

who might still love each other but 'twas questionable whether they were happy sharing the same room.

A servant entered to light the candles, ready the hearth fire and turn down their bed.

"Thank you, Cicily."

Sometimes, when Margery saw a shepherd playing his pipe or passed a well-tended cottage with a heather-thatched roof and tidy garden to the side, or transacted business at the Shop with a prosperous merchant—perhaps someone in the wool trade—and his placid wife, she wished, oh, she wished, that her and Matthew's lives could have been different. Quieter. Simpler. Without all the obligations that came with noble blood. Of course everyone had obligations but it was easier to marry who one pleased and, so long as you gave your betters their due, be left alone. No dealing with political intrigues and weighty decisions that could affect an entire kingdom. Or going off to war; for there was always war. In her imaginings she chose to construct a sweet, simple, happy existence, rather than some of the more unpleasant realities she'd experienced and that Thurold and John Ball related. She fancied herself as an herbalist and Matthew a fletcher, or he a blacksmith and she a basketmaker or spinster or maybe both. Not too prosperous because there would be the demands of the business, as it was now with the Shop of the Unicorn. But enough so they would not want...

She heard a noise on the stairs and knew by the tread that Matthew had returned. *Did you bed Desiderata Cecy? Do I care?*

His steps stopped in the doorway. "I am returning to the Shop of the Unicorn," Margery said, without turning around. She'd expected that with the utterance she might cry or at the very least her voice would break. Neither happened.

"Ah, Meg."

She turned to face her lover. He had stepped into the room but made no move to approach her. Nor could she read anything in his expression other than sadness. Shouldn't he react more strongly— protest, demand an explanation, yell? Confess his indiscretion, plead for forgiveness?

"Are you upset about Harry's wife?" He offered no explanation, merely the question, but if she could read him at all—which perhaps she could not—he'd not bedded his former sister-in-law.

"Nay, not upset." Grateful perhaps. For Desiderata Cecy had been the catalyst that had forced her to focus, to strip back the yearning and the pretense and to clearly see their relationship. They'd been breathing life into a corpse, that was all.

Margery returned to the window seat where she placed a pair of sewing gloves back in the sewing box. Carefully she folded the knots of ophreys atop the gloves and closed the lid.

"Perhaps our love is not enough," she said quietly. "We are both unhappy and have been so for a very long time..." Her voice trailed away. How would he respond? Would he say something that could convince her to stay? If he told her he loved her, would that be enough? But love was such a hollow word, and, for certes, never an answer to a successful pairing.

Why am I not weeping? When we've known each other since children? When I can scarce remember a time when I did not at least know that someone named Matthew Hart walked this earth? Why don't I feel anything at all?

Matthew remained inside the door with his legs slightly apart, his hands at his side. He made no move to approach her, to protest, to deny their unhappiness and plead with her to reconsider.

Rather, he simply shook his head and said, "I am sorry, Meg. For the both of us."

CHAPTER 8

Christmas, 1378, Kenilworth Castle

After Matthew Hart relinquished his son to John of Gaunt's household, he left London. Margery had moved back to the Shop of the Unicorn, as she'd said she would, and the few times they met, they might have been strangers. "My lord" this and "Dame" that with little eye contact and nothing beyond formalities in speech or action. Had Matthew pondered the past, he might have mourned, but there seemed to be a mental wall separating all that from the present. As if it were a bottomless well and should he happen to peer over the edge he would encounter only blackness.

Over the next months, he and his squire, Jerome, travelled around the Midlands. While in Berkshire he stayed at Abingdon Abbey near one of the demesnes that had been part of his mother's dowry. He and Harry had sometimes wandered about the Benedictine Abbey in childhood, and Matthew hoped God might bestow upon him some special wisdom or guidance amid the tombs of nobles and abbots, or the holy relics of Abingdon's Church of St. Mary's. But God did not. Nor did He at the mill stream near the abbey where Matthew would sit for hours at a time, staring at the water coursing over the wheel.

After a few weeks in Abingdon, he and Jerome continued on, never staying more than a few days in any one place. While travelling, he found it easy to be distracted by the journey itself, and not think of much beyond the road, the scenery, and the night's lodging. But his restless odyssey was merely postponing the inevitable. His return to Cumbria. If Matthew were ever going to come to grips with the past, and how it had destroyed the present, he must go home.

On his way north, Matthew stopped at Kenilworth, where John of Gaunt was in residence. He planned to discuss his decision to retire to Cumbria, as well as to see his son.

Upon approaching Kenilworth, Matthew was struck by its beauty. When not on campaign, the duke increasingly bypassed London for the gentler countryside. And Kenilworth, situated in the middle of an artificial lake spanning more than 100 acres, was John of Gaunt's favorite residence. Now the water was glutted with ice, but in the summertime Kenilworth must look like a fairy palace.

Anticipating his reunion with Serill, which would be pleasant, and his conversation with his liege, which would be less so, Matthew and his squire dismounted near Swan Tower.

He was spotted by the duke's leman, Katherine Swynford, returning from a walk with her sister, Philippa, and Henry Bolingbroke, King Richard's cousin and the duke's first-born son. Henry and Richard had been born within a few months of each other, had been knighted together and would in the distant future—if anyone had cared to consult the stars—battle over England's crown.

Katherine smiled and curtsied to Matthew, as did her sister, Philippa, a fussy creature who was married to the poet, Geoffrey Chaucer.

"The duke is in the banqueting hall with Master Geoffrey," Katherine said. After grooms had appeared to take the travelers' horses and Jerome had followed, peppering them with instructions, Katherine said, "We'll show you the way, Lord Hart. My lord will be pleased to see you." Her hood of grey squirrel, which framed her face, reflected the warm grey of her eyes. While she might not be, as many asserted, the most beautiful woman in England, the duke's mistress was definitely comely.

"Serill is adjusting to his duties so quickly 'twill soon be time to allow him downstairs with the men."

Something about Katherine's smile and gentle manner reminded Matthew of Meg, and he found it difficult to meet her gaze.

"How is Dame Margery?" Lady Katherine asked, as if reading his thoughts. A light snow was just beginning to fall, this eve of Christmas Eve. Involved as he was in his own unhappiness, Matthew had nearly forgotten the time of year.

He murmured something non-committal. When was the last time he'd seen Margery? On the heels of his leaving. He'd just left an armorer's shop where he was having his armor repaired when he'd literally run into her. He'd been so preoccupied that at first he'd not recognized her until she addressed him by name. Dispassionately, he'd noted that Master Craftsman Nicholas Norlong was by her side so mayhap his suspicions had been correct. But what did it matter? Their brief conversation had been stilted, confined to the most perfunctory of pleasantries. He'd not mentioned that he'd be returning to Cumbria or shared anything else of substance. Nor had Margery, though if pressed he would have had to confess he couldn't even remember her part of their exchange.

Afterward, reminding himself he might never again see his former leman, Matthew had tried unsuccessfully to conjure up sorrow.

"You can both be proud of Serill," Katherine was saying. If she noticed anything amiss in his answer about Margery, she did not comment. "He is eager to follow in his father's steps and will someday become a great knight."

Matthew bit back a sarcastic rejoinder. But John of Gaunt would only have told his mistress the parts of campaigns he wanted her to hear, the parts that fit the propaganda.

Kenilworth's banqueting hall was the second largest in all of England, surpassed only by Westminster's. It possessed soaring windows and beautiful paneling, all decorated with pine boughs and ribbons for the Christmas season. The warmth from the four fireplaces caused the snowflakes dusting Matthew's mantle to melt and disappear into the fabric. He began to smell strongly of wet wool, and his face to tingle from the change in temperature.

Matthew spotted the Duke of Lancaster seated before the largest fireplace with his two-year-old son, Henry, on his lap, conversing with Geoffrey Chaucer. John was Chaucer's friend, as well as his patron. Matthew liked Geoffrey well enough, though he had always been leery of him. He did not want to end up the disguised subject of the poet's verse; nor had he ever been able to see any lasting merit in Chaucer's scribblings.

When the duke saw Matthew, he handed his son to Geoffrey, ladled Matthew a bowl of wassail from the cauldron above the fire, and met him halfway across the hall. Handing Matthew the steaming bowl, John said, "I have thought of you often since our return from Saint-Malo. Have things gone well for you?" He could already read the answer on his vassal's face.

Matthew's first swallow of wassail warmed his throat and chest. He cupped his benumbed fingers round the bowl, allowing its heat to warm his hands. "That is why I am here, my lord. I've come to a decision."

At that moment, Serill entered the room. Matthew noted with amusement that his son began running toward them before abruptly slowing to a dignified walk. He was struck by how much Serill looked like Meg. She had always remarked on their son's resemblance to him, but he could see her in the line of Serill's jaw, the shape of his eyes, the luxuriant thickness of his hair.

After greeting Matthew, Serill asked, "How is Maman? I receive letters and I will see her when we return to London, but I do miss her."

"She is very well," replied Matthew, patting the top of his son's head and placing his arm around his shoulder. "She misses you and speaks of you all the time."

The falsehoods came so smoothly that Serill did not even question them. As he'd not questioned when he and his mother had moved to the Shop of the Unicorn while his father had stayed at Warrick Inn.

Matthew could almost believe the lies himself. Like so many other lies and half-truths with which he'd deluded himself.

"How long will you be at Kenilworth, Father?" Serill asked.

"Not long. I am on my way home, back to Cumbria."

"I would like to see Cumbria. Ralphie said 'tis a fearful place with jagged mountains and steep cliffs and cold winds that howl through the castle, but it sounds most interesting."

After Serill retreated, Matthew returned to the duke. Sensitive to his mood, John left Chaucer and they drifted off to themselves, away from the servants beginning to set up tables for the even meal, the bustling pages, the lords and ladies who had just returned from a ride along the crest of Kenilworth's dam.

"I have done a bit of traveling these past few months," Matthew said, "trying to settle my problems, but I have not succeeded. 'Twas like when the French shadowed us during the... Great Chevauchée but never directly engaged. I fear I can no longer shadow the problem. I have made up my mind. I would ask from you my leave. I think now I must return to Cumbria."

"Why do you not just go on pilgrimage? There is peace to be found there. And salvation too, I think."

Matthew winced, but did not respond.

The light from a huge half-octagonal oriel window played over Matthew's face, highlighting every feature. John saw the same expression in his eyes that he'd seen in other knights just before they bequeathed all their land to the church and retired to a monastic cell, or forsook all to become hermits. Some even ended up at London's St. Bartholomew's Hospital or Bethlem. He was surprised. Of all his vassals he would not have thought Matthew Hart would number among the flawed.

Throughout their campaigns, John had relied on the earl's steady presence and wisdom more than most. He was comforted simply by seeing Matthew's face among his war council.

"I understand some of your unhappiness," said John tactfully, thinking of Matthew's brother, who'd died almost within sight of

Bordeaux. But they'd lost so many during the Great Chevauchée. "Events weigh heavy on all of us."

"When your father died, I think then 'twas the very end for me, though I tried to continue. Sometimes I feel as if I am surrounded by so many ghosts, and I cannot face the future until I properly exorcise them."

"I have need of you yet. I am beset by enemies. And they are not all from across the channel." John dropped his voice as if fearing they might have followed him to Kenilworth. "You well know King Richard's council consists largely of my adversaries. They challenge my actions on every front and twist my motives until I myself would hate the Duke of Lancaster if I did not know better. The time must come when I will be forced to respond. I will need your support. I have too few men I can truly count on."

"I would never forsake you, my lord. You know I have always championed your quarrels at home and followed your banner into battle. But I fear now I would not be much good to you or anyone."

"King Richard needs you also. 'Twould mean much to have lords of the north besides myself and Henry Percy he can trust."

"I have been thinking on that also." Matthew's voice dropped, and he moved closer. "I know what others say, what the laws say, but I no longer care. Tell me true, sire, why you should not be king of England?" Though the duke recoiled as if he'd been pricked by a dagger, Matthew rushed on. "You are King Edward's second son. There is precedent for passing to the second son rather than the first-born's son. John Softsword—"

"God's Blood! Do not even think such a thing!" John looked around to see if someone might have heard. "Listen to me, and listen well. By the grace of God, I have many titles, but King of England will never be added to that list. Nor should it. I promised my brother I would support his son, and unto death I will keep my word."

"But England needs a man like you, not a child who can be torn every way by his advisors. What does *Ecclesiastes* say, 'Woe to thee, O land, when thy king is a child?'"

"Do not speak thus!"

Matthew rushed on. "I look into Richard's face and I see not the merest trace of my prince. Where is our Edward of Woodstock? If only Richard were more like his father. How can England prosper with an eleven-year-old on the throne?"

"You forget, Lord Hart. Father became king when he was fourteen. And my brother was sixteen when he won his spurs at Crecy."

"They were *warriors*. Richard was raised in Bordeaux among courtiers and sycophants. He will be a diplomat, not a fighter."

"But my brother's blood runs through him all the same. And mayhap at this juncture England needs diplomats."

Matthew shook his head. "John Softsword was not a fighter, and he was reviled by both his own and common Englishmen. His brother, the Lionheart, was a warrior. Whom do we revere? Softsword or the Lionheart?"

"I have never heard you talk so. You must not even think such thoughts. If Richard is young, loyal friends like us will guide him toward what is proper. You well served my father, my brother, and myself. Do not now forsake my brother's son."

Matthew did not answer for a long time. He felt so cold, so tired, so... defeated. "I will be of no purpose to anyone if I canna get straight my thoughts." He sighed heavily. "I would that I could go back twenty years, to the good times. When England was proud and victorious and filled with sunshine instead of fear and uncertainty."

"Mayhap those grand days never were," John said. "Mayhap we were just young enough to think 'twas so." He placed his arm around Matthew's shoulder. "How much time do you crave?"

"I canna say."

"If events decree that I must call on you, will you fulfill your obligation?"

"I have always fulfilled it, sire. But I hope you will not call."

Matthew gazed past the duke, to Katherine Swynford, laughing with her sister as they worked a tapestry, at the people bustling about the hall. The pages knew this night they would serve the duke at table, Geoffrey Chaucer knew he would orate his latest poem, Katherine knew she would serve her master in bed, his barons that they would serve him with their sword arm and loyalty. As Matthew himself had once known. But now he doubted, and his doubts frightened him.

If I cut myself off from my lord and my obligations, where do I then belong? What purpose does my existence serve?

But the demons whispered relentlessly in his ear. *What purpose did you ever serve? What purpose had even the most glorious campaigns, what meant loyalty and honor when your suzerains died all the same and ordinary Englishmen term your kind oppressors rather than protectors?*

Matthew knew. How glibly he had hidden behind his talk of honor when he deliberately broke his promise to his brother, when he'd let Harry die, when he'd disgraced the Hart name at Limoges. When he had been weighed and found wanting.

"My lord—" He wanted to say to his liege that he'd once viewed knighthood, with every sentiment that word embodied, shining like the grail. And that he was now beginning to believe that the grail did not even exist. But he could not utter the words; rather he stood mute. *Like a dog,* he thought in disgust. *What is wrong with me?*

John squeezed Matthew's shoulder. "I give you leave, and I will offer prayers for you during your struggle. But I must warn you, I will not wait forever."

Matthew forced the corners of his mouth up in a smile. "I hope you will not have to, my lord."

CHAPTER 9

February, 1379, Canterbury

argery Watson entered Canterbury Cathedral through huge wooden doors opened to accommodate the usual press. Privately, Margery was skeptical of the business of pilgrimages, for that's what she'd come to consider them. A business. Where abbots and abbeys and bishops and their bishoprics grew rich off the misery of others. Of course she was not intemperate enough to voice her disillusionment. She left that to John Ball and Thurold.

However, Margery, who had only been on one extended pilgrimage following her marriage to Simon Crull, knew from bitter experience that saints answered prayers on a whim. "I will cure you;" "I will bring you low;" "I will make your life even more cursed." They granted or rejected the pleas of desperate multitudes as if they were pagan gods rather than Christian. For if the saints and their relics had truly listened to Margery, her goldsmith husband would have been dead ere they'd bent their knees before the first reliquary.

How long ago that had been—nearly twenty years! And yet, when Margery remembered, the rush of feelings were a reminder that sometimes it took more than time's passing to fully heal.

On the heels of a "frustrating" wedding night, Crull had dragged Margery around to a seemingly endless round of shrines—for England possessed more holy places than its fields had wildflowers—in an effort to cure his impotency. They had visited Saint Swithun, whose remains were housed at Winchester Cathedral; little Saint Hugh who'd been found in a well at Lincoln Cathedral; and Oxford's Saint Frideswide. They'd travelled as far north as Durham Cathedral to worship before the remains of Saint Cuthbert, the Anglo-Saxon monk, bishop, hermit and patron saint of Northumbria.

Margery and her husband—how she hated Simon Crull, which might account for why, even now, she could muster little regret for having poisoned him—had also prostrated themselves before count-less relics. After gazing upon Saint Swithun's bones Simon had purchased clay replicas so that he could pray over them in order to prod a centuries' dead bishop to stiffen his privates. Then on to crowns of thorns, fragments of the true cross and rags from saints' clothing, all of which, when added up, were surely more numerous than starlings in springtime. They had watched caretakers open saints' crypts in order to cut their nails and gather the leavings to be sold. Simon had purchased a pouch full. Margery had touched a hair from the head of St. John the Evangelist, the foot of St. Blaise, and such a variety of extremities that a heavenly army might have been constructed from their whole.

Yet still her husband lived. As did Matthew Hart, whom she'd also implored God and his minions to strike down in order to avenge his seeming betrayal of her and their love. For she'd sent Lord Hart letters —intercepted, she'd later discovered—warning him of her pending marriage and begging him to rescue her. (Here Margery was thankful that heaven had ignored her imprecations. For both she and Matthew had been tricked by Desiderata Cecy. Which meant her lover would have expired because of a mistake).

Margery stepped inside Canterbury Cathedral, its painted interior and stained glass so dazzling 'twas as if she'd entered paradise. Here it didn't matter about the capriciousness of saints, the mysterious reasoning of God or religious imponderables such as the nature of evil or the problem of free will. This building, its very essence, provided all the answers she, at least, would ever need.

At this early hour crowds were sparse. In the cavernous interior the usual chattering pilgrims, bantering merchants and peddlers, lords and ladies with squawking falcons on gloves or yapping hounds on leash provided little more than background noise.

While approaching the first rise of stairs and the choir screen, Margery contemplated, as she always did, a more personal history. For it had been here, five decades past, that her grandmother, Maria Rendell, had publicly paid for her adulterous liaison with Richard, Earl of Sussex, Edward II's illegitimate half-brother.

Over time Margery had coaxed the horrific details from her grandmother. First the flogging in the precincts after Maria's hair had been shorn and her hair shirt cut away, revealing her naked torso to the gawking, snickering crowd. Then her tortured journey, sometimes crawling, sometimes on hands and knees to the tomb of Saint Thomas Becket, where her cuckolded husband had been waiting to care for her wounds. Despite Phillip Rendell's humiliation. Despite his public repudiation of the wife and liege lord who'd so betrayed him.

The story always brought tears to Margery's eyes. Because of the loyalty of a grandfather she'd never known and because of a woman who had loved without apology and who had willingly accepted the consequences of that forbidden love.

Thomas Becket's shrine was located near the back of Canterbury Cathedral in Trinity Chapel, as was the tomb of Edward the Black Prince. Veering past the martyr's bejeweled and gilded shrine, Margery stopped before Edward's tomb. During these semi-regular visits, Margery allowed herself—as she seldom did otherwise—to ponder Matthew Hart. Neutrally, as if he were just another person. Without judgment.

Studying the gilded bronze effigy, she thought, *So many memories.*

Prince Edward's eyes were seemingly fixed upon the Throne of Mercy painted on the underside of the wooden canopy above his tomb chest. Edward's fingers were tented more in contemplation than prayer; his poulained feet rested upon a creature that resembled a friendly gargoyle rather than one of his dogs, as had been detailed in his funeral instructions.

In the fall of 1376 Margery and Matthew had been part of the miles-long procession wending its way from London in order to put England's prince to rest. The entire kingdom had been in mourning, nay, all of Europe, for the Black Prince was considered the flower of chivalry. Even Margery's stepbrother had bemoaned his loss, saying Edward was one of the few who'd had a care for the average soldier.

Margery had only actually seen Edward of Woodstock a handful of times. First, following his stunning victory at Poitiers, when England's vastly outnumbered army had annihilated the French and captured their king, Jean le Bon. Upon the troops return home, Prince Edward and the French monarch, who was being held for ransom, had been welcomed by ecstatic Londoners. Edward had made an unforgettable sight. More than two decades later, Margery could still remember how his golden hair had gleamed in the sunlight, how he'd nodded so graciously in acknowledgement of the thunderous cheers, how magnificent he'd looked astride a plain black hobby and dressed as simple as a yeoman. Even now, the memory made Margery's breath catch in her throat.

No wonder my lord Hart loved you so.

The second time had been in 1361 at Prince Edward and Joan of Kent's wedding banquet, held in Kennington Palace. As wife to London's mayor, Margery and her husband had been seated at the same dais as the royal family. There she'd enjoyed an unobstructed view of the prince and his bride. While some called Joan of Kent the fairest maid in England and others carped that she was past her prime and running to fat like a poorly exercised horse, there was no doubt as to Edward's opinion. A bachelor until the age of thirty-one, he had eyes only for the woman who shared his loving cup.

It was nearly unheard of—even considered improper—for a royal prince to marry for love. Yet here was Edward, in the thrall of a twice married cousin two years his senior, mother to five children not his own and to whom marriage was actually forbidden because of their shared blood line. No matter. Edward had even braved the displeasure of his royal parents to secretly marry his beloved a year before the official ceremony.

How bold! How chivalrous!

Or Margery might have thought so if she, newly wed herself and seated next to her troll of a husband, had not been awash in cynicism— or more accurately, heartbreak.

Edward of Woodstock, in the prime of life and flush with happiness, had been so handsome, even handsomer than his younger brother, John of Gaunt, also sharing Kennington's dais.

Though not so handsome as my lord Hart, Margery had thought even that night, even in the midst of her misery. Or perhaps a more accurate adjective to describe Matthew might have been "irresistible." For that's how she'd always regarded him. With his restless energy, his cocksureness about the rightness of life and his place in it, and his larger than life persona.

Irresistible.

Until you lost your way...

Margery reached out to touch the gauntleted hands of Prince Edward, unaware that her lover had done the exact same thing during his final visit to the tomb.

Margery blinked back tears. Such a loss for them all. She closed her fingers over the cold, sharply appointed gloves as if expecting England's prince to awaken, lace his fingers through her own and murmur, "There, there, Dame Margery, do not fret. I will always watch over you."

Like England's Saint George? Like our King Arthur?

But that could not be. Edward of Woodstock, Prince of Wales, dead on the eve of his forty-sixth birthday, had proven himself all too mortal.

Margery removed her hand to trace her fingertips along part of the inscription that had been chiseled around the outside of the prince's tomb. King Richard had recently ordered its completion, obeying yet another directive from his father's will.

"...Such as you are, so once was I." Margery laboriously translated from Norman French.

"You will be like me;
To death I never gave a thought,
I lived delightfully.
On earth I had such riches great,
They made a noble show—
Land and mansions, clothes and gold,
Horses, here below.
But now I am poor and despised,
Beneath the earth I lie;
My lovely form is all away,
In flesh I putrefy."

Before the end Matthew had been so bowed down by all the deaths. His prince. His father. His brother. All the French in all the chevauchées, all those "wars of a long season." All the brave English knights and yeomen. Friends and companions. For those who lived long enough, death would shadow them as relentlessly as French soldiers had shadowed John of Gaunt's army across the mountains of Auvergne in the Great Chevauchée.

Odd that a man so steeped in war had been shattered by it.

Margery continued to caress the letters. Perhaps, because she'd known death, despair, and deprivation at an early age, she'd learned to be more accepting of loss.

"A narrow house I live in now;
The truth only is here.
And surely if you saw my face,
It hardly would appear
That I was once like you a man,
For Death has changed me whole.
In mercy pray to Heaven's King
That he may save my soul."

Even as children, when their lives had first intersected, Matthew had overflowed with self-confidence. As if believing that his life was charmed might actually make it so. And for a long time he seemed correct. During the days of Crecy and Poitiers when Edward III had been strong and manly and Edward of Woodstock would have been more properly nicknamed "Golden One" than "Black Prince." Then 'twas easy to believe they all would remain invincible...

Margery eased herself down on the paving stones—every visit more brutally attacked her knees—to recite a *Pater Noster* and *Ave Maria.* Her thoughts wandered for she still had much to do today. Her stepbrother was helping her set up Aurum, a second goldsmithing shop on High Street. With John Ball preaching in Canterbury and its surrounds, Thurold could more easily oversee the equipment, new apprentices, and the hiring of a competent goldsmith for the times when Master Goldsmith Nicholas Norlong remained in London.

A big undertaking, thought Margery, *though already a profitable one.*

After making the sign of the cross, Margery gingerly rose from the stones, feeling every day of her thirty-eight years. When turning to leave, she noticed another woman off to her side. Otherwise the area was unusually empty.

"Dame Margery," the woman said in a low, melodious voice.

Margery looked more closely and found herself staring into the eyes of Lady Elizabeth Ravenne.

Margery's heart plummeted. She did not need another reminder of her past, particularly when she was healing so nicely. Certainly she did not need to be confronted by Matthew Hart's sister.

After quickly looking around to make certain Lady Ravenne wasn't accompanied by her murdering husband, Margery considered her options. She couldn't recall ever being formally introduced to Lady Ravenne, so perhaps she could deny her identity.

"It is Dame Margery, isn't it?" Elizabeth persisted.

Well, not exactly for now that her father, Thomas Rendell, had recognized her, might Margery not be addressed as "lady"? That was the problem, wasn't it, not precisely knowing one's place?

"Aye, I am Margery Watson." She executed an awkward curtsy.

Lady Elizabeth's gaze was intelligent and friendly enough, though something in her eyes warned she would brook no nonsense. Probably out of necessity. Margery knew she was mother to a great pack of sons.

"Walk with me, will you not, Dame Margery?"

Margery reluctantly acceded. Without speaking they retraced their steps down cathedral stairs, past Canterbury's transept and through the bustling knave. Surreptitiously, she studied her companion. Even in youth, Elizabeth Ravenne would never have been considered a beauty. Matthew sometimes jested that Harry was the prettier sibling. But Lady Ravenne possessed an arresting dignity and solidity, as well as a natural warmth that attracted people. Though not Margery, at least not in these circumstances.

What exactly do you want?

She tried to remember what she knew about Elizabeth Ravenne, other than the fact that her husband had murdered Margery's mother. Lots of children, all boys named after knights in the Arthurian romances. Dabbled in verse; loved pilgrimages with Glastonbury being a favorite because of its ties to Arthur and Guinevere.

Once outside, Lady Ravenne turned to Margery. "It seems I spend most of my days traveling from shrine to shrine. Now that my children are largely grown... and with so many dead to pray for. Are you also on pilgrimage?"

"Nay, my lady." Margery didn't want to reveal anything of her habits. Nor would she ask about Matthew, whom she'd not heard from in more than six months. Which was as it should be.

"I thought you resided in London," said Elizabeth.

"We've opened a goldsmithing shop here. And I sometimes stay in a cottage on the road to Fordwich."

Too much information. She didn't want Lady Ravenne carrying tales to her brother. Which was foolish. Matthew need only make a few enquiries or visit their son to know the truth. If he'd cared...

Feeling oddly panicked, Margery suppressed the urge to wipe her suddenly damp palms on her gown in a most unladylike fashion and push past Lady Ravenne in order to seek out John Ball, who was ministering to prisoners at nearby Canterbury Castle. John need not say a word to be able to calm her. And she was in need of calming.

"I saw your son at Kenilworth a fortnight past," Elizabeth said.

Margery raised her eyebrows in surprise. "Serill?"

"Aye. Two of my boys, Lancelot and Perceval, are also in the duke's service."

"I did not know, my lady."

"Serill looks very much like his father. He had just received a letter from you and was most pleased. "

Margery nodded. Was this why Lady Ravenne had wanted to speak to her? Not because of Matthew at all?

Good. I do not care about him anyway.

"We plan to meet this summer when his lord Lancaster's household moves to the Savoy," she said aloud.

Lady Ravenne's shrewd eyes remained on her. Willing her to say something about her brother?

I'll not.

"How fares my lord Hart?" Margery blurted, as if the words had somehow just bubbled forth out of nowhere.

A shadow crossed Elizabeth's face. She did not speak for a long time.

Then she simply answered, "Alone."

MARGERY HANDED John Ball a meat pie and mazer of ale she'd purchased from a nearby vendor. They'd stretched out beneath an ancient oak in full view of Canterbury Castle, where she'd caught up with the hedge-priest as he'd strode away from the royal prison with his arms crossed and hands tucked into opposite sleeves, head bowed in contemplation.

Canterbury Castle, its flint and sandstone rubble walls rising more than eighty feet above the town, cast its hulking shadow beyond their oak and the green to the jumble of narrow shops on Castle Street.

'Twas a rare mellow day and the ground beneath the oak was dry, though the branches overhead remained winter bare.

"Tell me the future, hedge-priest."

John Ball laughed and pinched off a piece of crust from his pie. "If only I were in possession of special spectacles through which I could view such matters!"

"You intuit so many things others cannot," Margery pressed. "And we've known each other for—how long has it been?"

"More than two decades. An entire lifetime." John Ball drank from his mazer and wiped his mouth with the back of a hairy hand.

A Benedictine nun passed, swathed in black scapula and white wimple and flanked by male guardians hurrying her back to the safety of the nearby Priory of St. Selpuchre. A knight and his lady, with the knight wearing the flowing robes of the newly popular houppelande. A wayward greyhound dragging its leash. Margery didn't want to say anything about Matthew Hart or to discuss things that were past, that didn't matter, that could not be changed. Yet she felt a vague panic, an inexplicable need for comforting.

What am I seeking from you, old friend?

After placing his mazer upon the grass, John turned his penetrating gaze upon her, trying to discern the real purpose of Margery's conversation.

Alone. My lord is alone.

She cleared her throat. "Remember, before Serill was born, when you were still allowed in my bedchamber?"

"Aye."

"When you read to me from Roger Bacon?"

John nodded. He finished his meat pie and brushed his hands together, dusting off crumbs. His gaze drifted from her to a matron in a patched kirtle calling, "Hot peascods."

"Remind me once more of Brother Bacon's prognostications."

Again, that gaze. Rather than face her friend, Margery pretended an interest in passing merchants with their wide sleeves and jaunty hats, pilgrims with their saints' badges and walking sticks and urchins peddling last season's costards.

"What is troubling you, daughter?"

She shook her head. *I will not utter Matthew Hart's name.* She would not allow her former lover to intrude on this unseasonably warm day when her life was fine enough, when circumstances had decreed that their paths would nevermore cross.

Alone... Alone...

"Speak to me of things that will happen long after we're gone. I would ponder a better time and place."

John Ball doubted whether any time or place could be improved so long as man remained hostage to his fallen nature. However he obliged, knowing that if they conversed long enough he would discern Margery's need and address it.

"The *Epistola de Secretis Operibus*. I remember Bacon's exact quote. 'Instruments of flying may be formed in which a man, sitting at his ease and meditating on any subject, may beat the air with his artificial wings after the manner of birds.'"

Margery gazed up at a sky dotted with puffy clouds and tried to imagine manmade birds laboring across its surface.

"And machines with blades that move so quickly they can lift the machine off the ground and high into the air."

Like some sort of dust whirlwind? Blades shaped like a horizontal windmill that could spin in the manner of a child's top? She couldn't fix such images in her mind.

"What else did Bacon say?"

"That we'll possess special instruments through which we'll be able to bring the stars so close we can see every detail."

Stars had always seemed little more than pinpricks in a veil of darkness. Up close would they look like enormous diamonds? Or blocks of ice similar to those she'd seen glutting the Thames in winter? Learned men lectured that stars were divine creatures which consumed earth and water drawn up through the atmosphere to heaven's purer realm. When she'd first heard that, she'd tried to imagine giant icy maws inhaling the earth and chewing upon it, but the image had been too troubling to contemplate...

"He wrote of ships that can be moved without oars and of men able to descend into the depths of the sea wearing special suits that will allow them to easily walk around on its bottom."

Margery imagined something akin to a sea monster, or walking upon a bottom *inhabited* by sea monsters. Perhaps a world similar to that of the Lady of the Lake, with thousands of underwater faerie lights and with the arms of the lady's nymphs waving like seaweed caught in the current to knights watching from the shore...

"Bacon described bridges that can span great distances with only wires to hold them, and cages that will replace stairs and will move up and down tall buildings."

Margery eyed the cathedral. Much of the Norman work was being pulled down and a magnificent new nave and transept were being built under the direction of King Richard's master mason. She tried to imagine a cage crawling up the side of Canterbury Cathedral's bell tower the way a bug scuttles up a wall.

"Carts driven by machines rather than horses. They will be able to cross great distances faster than a hawk can swoop and soar."

"'Tis hard to believe England will not always be as it is today."

"Aye," agreed John Ball. "Though the good friar maintained such things have already been invented, that he was simply uncovering ancient secrets. Regardless, should the time come round again let us hope that advancements in the human heart will match scientific progress."

He turned his gaze to her, yet probing past the outer to lay bare the inner. Margery refused to look at him, to utter Matthew's name or even think it lest the hedge-priest snag it in his thoughts.

It doesna matter.

Before Roger Bacon's predictions came to pass they would be less than the bones of the saints, crumbled to dust. Most likely Thomas Becket's shrine, Canterbury Cathedral or even the whole of Canterbury itself would have long since vanished.

"We, all of us, end up in only one fashion, do we not?" she said, leaning her back against the rough bark of the giant oak. "Like the inscription on Prince Edward's tomb, 'Beneath the earth I lie, my lovely form is all away, in flesh I putrefy.'"

John Ball's gaze again, weighing and measuring the meaning behind her words. "Some believe we actually never die but rather return again and again. That our souls enter a multitude of bodies in an endless cycle of birth and rebirth."

Margery contemplated this. Might she and Matthew have lived and loved before? Had she and John Ball resided in Canterbury during Thomas Becket's days? Or in the time of the Vikings? She remembered the ancient saying, 'Preserve us from the Vikings and their terrible dogs,' and wondered what it would have been like to be terrorized by those slavering marauders with their dogs the size of ponies. Or perhaps she had been? The original Canterbury Castle had been built soon after the Battle of Hastings, in the time of the Conqueror. Might William the Bastard have ridden these very streets, passed within a hand span of this oak tree under which Margery and her companion were now lounging? Had she and the hedge-priest been among those sullenly watching the usurper's triumphant procession?

Impossible. I would have remembered, at least on some level. Suddenly she wondered whether her long ago visions of the faerie knight might have been some peculiar flash of memory regarding Matthew. *Nay. Those were the conjurings of a foolish girl.*

Besides it would be horrifying to struggle forever with the same sins and desires and relationships, to be ever trapped upon fortune's pitiless wheel.

As if reading her thoughts, John Ball said, "Rebirth is heresy, of course. The ravings of inflamed minds for which many like the Cathari were put to the stake. Mother Church is ever a jealous parent."

"What do you predict for your future, hedge-priest?"

John's generous mouth lifted at the corners. "Recently, I've had this image before my eyes. I see the great lion of England coming upon this hapless rabbit that he thinks to enjoy as a tasty morsel. Yet when the lion opens his mouth he finds he's faced with a badger not of a mind to be anyone's meal."

Margery laughed. "And you will be that badger?"

Rather than respond, John Ball struggled to his feet and held out his hand to her. He drew her up beside him until they faced each other.

"What would you have chroniclers say of you, old friend?" Margery asked. "Far, far into Roger Bacon's future?"

94

John Ball's unfocused gaze rested upon the rubbled walls of Canterbury Castle. "That I was someone who started a revolution," he said finally. "That in the time of those carts and flying machines and men walking under water our ancestors will trace the beginnings of a better life to one tired old man standing beneath an oak tree in a place called Canterbury."

CHAPTER 10

Winter-Spring, 1379, Lake Winandermere

Matthew Hart sat cross-legged in his tiny hut, feeding kindling into the fire. His residence, barely long enough to accommodate his length, consisted of stone on three sides, a roof of birch boughs thatched with heather, and was fronted by more boughs and a makeshift door. Upon arrival he had erected the hut, which was positioned flush against one of the mountains overlooking Lake Winandermere. Besides his cooking stone and other related implements, it contained a bed of deer skins and a tiercel peregrine strapped to a perch. Matthew had happened across the injured falcon near Scafill Pike, nursed it to health and taught it to hunt. Oft times it supplied his only meat.

Winter's snow fell, silent and deep, as it had these past several days. It was March, 1379, and Cumberland's weather raged at its fiercest. But Matt's hut was snug, and his woodpile high enough so he did not fear the storm. *I have naught I must do and no place I must be,* he thought, tossing a handful of dried kale leaves into the pottage bubbling in an iron pot above the blaze. In the days before the storm he had snared two rabbits, but now he had not even enough meat to flavor the barley.

The smell of smoke, birch kindling, and pottage filled the hut. Outside the snow drifted down to rest atop the roof, layer after layer, like brushstrokes upon a painting.

Thirteen years past, Matthew's father had stood overlooking Lake Winandermere, and declared, "My day is past." The ghosts were strongest here, particularly the ghost of William Hart. Weather permitting, when Matt meandered around the lake's banks, or fished its depth for perch, trout, pike, or char he would raise his gaze to the spot where his father had stood, and imagine William watching him. Strong, invincible, as timeless as the land itself. Or so it had seemed. But that was a false notion, of course, for William was gone, and as unrecapturable as the rest of Matthew's past.

I can look into the depths of the sun, stare at it until I am blind, wait a million days and nights, but never once will I see you again. Where are you? What good does it do when you remain as invisible as the wind rippling across the water?

After constructing his hut, Matthew would sit outside gazing endlessly across the lake. During a mizzling rain its surface reflected the grey of drooping clouds, on fair days the sapphire sky. When the sun set between the twin peaks of the Langdales it turned black as the jet of paternoster beads. And occasionally, when misty fingers rose from the water, Matthew fancied them to be the spirits of all those he'd killed, or of Harry or his father or his Prince or King Edward.

No doubt that Winandermere was a living thing and in the beginning it had unnerved him. He would watch the moon break upon its waves as if some great beast were stirring and imagine the monster Grendel lurching from the lake's depths, as well as Beowulf's dragon circling overhead, leathery wings flapping and causing the surrounding air to shimmer as it was stirred in passing. Or could it be Satan in the guise of a dragon? Might Winandermere be Lucifer's lair? Matthew could believe it so. At such times, his mind danced with images he'd long forgotten, such as a diagram of the universe from his Book of

Hours which depicted demons streaming like enormous bats toward the Prince of Darkness, bound in chains below the cosmos.

How still the nights could be. What disturbing turns his thoughts would take! He remembered the Berwick vampire—Berwick was not so very far away—whose corpse had long haunted locals until its body had been dug up and destroyed. That was not conjecture but chronicled fact. And stories of other corpses, whose ghoulish wanderings had only been halted when their heads were cut off and placed between their legs. Or their hearts cut open. But that could be a dangerous business for sometimes ravens flew out, screeching and terrifying assembled villagers. Matthew was also familiar with evil sorcerers who created werewolves which they then sent out to stalk and rob and destroy. Of course he'd witnessed the human version in France—bands of beggars and brigands covered in wolf skins. Those wolf packs had been dispatched easily enough, but then again, they'd not been shapeshifters conjured from the dark arts.

Matthew chastised himself for his unease, but his mind continued to wander where it shouldn't. He was unused to being alone with his musings—being alone, period—but now he had only his tiercel for a companion. Twice his mother, surprisingly spry for her years, had ridden to visit, while Jerome, his squire, made semi-regular treks with supplies and news of the outside world.

Two Popes now, one in Rome and one in Avignon; more war in France; more defeats; more restlessness among the populace; more unpopular poll taxes. Matthew could no more grasp his squire's gossip than capture a waterfall between his fingers. True enough his thoughts raced about like skuttering mice, but not with concerns about whether Pope Urban or Pope Clement be the true head of the Church, or the corruption of King Richard's ministers, the dangers of John Ball's increasing influence, or the bishops' unease regarding John Wycliffe's determination to translate the Bible into English. Matthew had far more personal matters to contemplate, such as how black and endless were Winandermere's skies. Like being lost in heaven's maw...

At such times he found himself cowering—at least inwardly—like a frightened child.

So this is how Harry used to feel.

Now he understood. Nights were meant to be passed safely within doors or, when on campaign, the darkness would be broken by camp-fires and the comforting presence of others. But not now.

Alone.

On one of those nights when he'd been trying not to remember the content of a years-old sermon about mankind living in the sixth and final age in which the world's end would be heralded by the walking dead, Matthew suddenly realized that his heart was hammering. And that he was experiencing fear... when for so long he had known only numbness.

Fear. That was something. And he preferred feeling *something* to nothing at all. Subsequently, he would take fear out and examine it from every angle. Only to find that, rather than grow in magnitude as he had once believed, it would dissipate. More than that, Matthew was fascinated by its impact upon his body. He wanted to experience more and mentally chronicle it. As if he were re-learning the most basic of emotions. *So this is my body's reaction to fear. This is joy. This is love. This is sadness. This is anger. This is longing.* Or at least a simulacrum of them all.

With the waxing and waning of the moon, winter slipping into spring, Matthew increasingly embraced his solitude. When the weather was mild he would lie outside his hut, pull the darkness around him like a cloak, listen and simply... be. He learned to decipher the night's moods as easily as he'd once deciphered the mood in a banquet hall. By the calling of the birds who might be hungry or frightened or staking out their territory. He marked the whisper of wings and determined the distance of owls or divers seeking their prey, the abundance of food by the number of each flying creature's passes.

Sometimes, he heard the howling of wolves—even though wolves had supposedly been eradicated from the kingdom. No matter. He recognized them well enough from when they'd shadowed him and Harry and all the dying across Auvergne. Matthew rather admired wolves for their intelligence and their loyalty to their pack. It was only when they lamented their empty bellies that he would fortify his door, heap more wood upon the fire, and force his mind to blankness.

With the gentler weather Matthew took long walks where he would glimpse Cumbria's common animals—a herd of upland sheep, rabbits, foxes, and deer. Nothing peculiar, nothing like the creatures he'd studied in bestiaries—crocodiles, elephants and dromedaries; bitterns and bonnacons and boas. And of course the more fantastical. He remembered explaining the manticore to Harry, tracing its outline on the page of their father's elaborately illustrated bestiary. Matthew's fingertips would move from the manticore's face, which was that of a man, over its lion's body and follow the curve of its scorpion's tail.

"Its voice sounds like that of a flute," he'd said, paraphrasing the description, for Harry was yet too young to read.

"Why? I like flutes, don't you?" Harry was very careful and precise with his enunciation, as if speaking more quickly might cause him to lose control of his tongue.

"It represents the siren song of temptation as our souls make their way through our earthly existence."

Harry frowned, trying to sort through all the big words, but merely said, "I like to sing, don't you?"

Harry would point to other drawings which Matthew patiently explained. The centaur, whose chief characteristic was that it was hopelessly lustful—he glided over that part—but sensitive enough to cry when saddened. The unicorn, which represented the Savior; the kingfisher, whose talent was calming stormy seas; the heron, known to be the wisest of birds. And ignore his brother's queries about such creatures as the basilisk, which was similar to the devil and could kill by its smell, a sideways glance, or via a hissing sound. No sense in filling Harry's mind with scary details for then he and Harry's nurse would be up until the wee hours calming his night terrors.

Such strange things Matthew found himself pondering or that would suddenly pop into his head. And just as odd that they all seemed to come from his childhood. As if his life had stopped then. Or that it consisted of nothing more than disjointed flashes, like fish in a stream. Playing marbles or knucklebones or hide and seek; he and Elizabeth kicking leaves while walking along a narrow lane flanked by oaks flaming like torches; William lifting him onto his first pony, a sorrel with a white blaze; following his mother as she carried a sleeping Harry up a narrow staircase; he and his siblings skipping stones across a lake; sneaking a treat from Cook. Matthew wished he could pull out the defining moments of his life rather than insignificant fragments... and find... something...

I am an old man, older than many who die, certainly older than many who expired in the campaigns. Why can I not make sense of my life? Why can I not accept such conditions as death and loss, when those are common to all men?

Plague, famine, God's judgment, war, the natural order, as it was with cows or hawks or their prey, or the flock of sheep he sometimes saw drinking at Winandermere's edge while a nearby shepherd serenaded with his pipe.

All born to die.

All reminders that all of life is change.

During his squire's last visit, Matthew had told Jerome to return for him on the first of May. As Earl of Cumbria, Matthew could not ever neglect his duties. But as he marked off the days until his leaving, Matthew wondered whether he had resolved anything at all.

CHAPTER 11

Spring, 1379, Canterbury

Margery did not see it coming, the event that would once again re-order her life. Aurum, her second gold-smithing business, was already prospering, and she'd leased a small cottage on the road from Canterbury to Fordwich. From her recently planted garden she could see the outer curtain of Fordwich Castle and the tower where her grandmother spent most of her time. During the day Margery could hear the noise of sailors and merchants loading and unloading cargo from as far afield as the Low Countries and Italy on Fordwich's nearest quay. At night when her shutters were open she fancied she could detect the whisper of the River Stour which was only a few chains away.

This part of Kent was so quiet and peaceful and lovely with its many orchards and water meadows where cattle, sheep and horses grazed; its hay fields and woods blanketed by delicate flowers she'd never seen before. Though London was an easy three day journey, the local climate was far gentler, the rains softer and the sun unmarred by a persistent haze. Margery had already decided she would spend most of spring and summer in Fordwich, only returning to London full-time when the roads became muddied and rutted and travel uncomfortable. With each visit she found the city dirtier and fouler smelling. The people were ruder, particularly the foreigners, who seemed to be everywhere. Londoners smiled less frequently than she remembered and had a tendency to cheat more when they measured out their products. And the quality of their ale and bread and meat and even ordinary things like cloth, footwear, and candles, had deteriorated.

Margery tried to put a name to her feeling about her new surroundings, but the best she could say was that she felt... contentment. Perhaps it was simply because her cottage was so charming and her frequent visits with her grandmother so delightful, while London, if she allowed herself to think on it—which she pointedly did *not*—contained too many memories of... him.

Before the Death of 1348, Canterbury had been a city of ten thousand, though so many had been wiped out that only during the day did the current population swell to anything approaching one-third that number. Like ants marching to their food source, pilgrims streamed to Thomas Becket's shrine. The sickest were borne in litters while others were carried or led or hobbled on makeshift crutches or shuffled past precinct gates and then into Canterbury Cathedral itself. But with dusk, the closing of shops and departing tourists, Canterbury became so quiet you could hear the wind sighing through the River Oaks or pushing bits of trash along deserted lanes; the dip of oars as a rowing boat slipped along the Stour; the coughs, moans, and murmurs emanating from pilgrims bedded down inside St. Thomas the Martyr of Eastbridge and other hospitals.

Since Margery visited her grandmother as frequently as Maria's health allowed, she often felt as if she were reliving the area through the older woman's memories. Beyond her cottage was the quay where a seventeen-year-old Maria had met her black-haired, blue-eyed knight, Phillip Rendell, and braved a public scandal in order to wed; Sturry's Leopard's Head which had been sold to St. Augustine's Abbey and which Richard of Sussex had re-purchased thinking to please Maria—and which had triggered a long dead abbot's revenge; King Street where, during the twelve days of Christmas, Maria, little Thomas and the Rendells' other three children would go a'mumming; ice skating with bones tied to their feet on the frozen River Stour; treks to Tancrey Island to purchase its famous honey. And of course, Canterbury Cathedral, like some colossal watchdog, guarding the town houses and manor houses, the woods, fields and St. Augustine's Abbey, Canterbury, Chilham and Fordwich Castles, and the forever undulating river.

Margery knew exactly when it happened, when her life yet again veered off its predictable course. It was the week following the annual Cherry Fair. While it was in the middle of the Lenten season, the mood had been festive and with the many fish and related dishes, there had been little feeling of deprivation. Margery had attended all four days, as had her grandmother, whose health had been perfect. Her father and his family had returned from another of the Rendell holdings for the event. Everyone remarked that the cherry blossoms had been unusually lovely; some commented they were more pink than normal and the fragrance more intoxicating. One of the lords of the north, Henry Percy, had even put in an appearance. (Though some wondered what mischief he was up to because King Richard had made Percy Earl of Northumbria in order to keep him far enough removed so that he'd cease meddling in political affairs).

All in all, the consensus was that 1379's Cherry Fair had been another success.

This day Margery was walking to Aurum, which was located inside Canterbury's walls, with her stepbrother, Thurold. Halfway to the city's north gate, a large retinue approached.

"Make way," shouted a knight riding in the lead. By the dress of the others it was immediately apparent that they were clerics and that Simon Sudbury, Archbishop of Canterbury, drew near. Pedestrians stepped to the side of the road. Women genuflected while men doffed their hats and also knelt—all save Thurold, who remained defiantly upright.

In passing, Simon Sudbury absently bestowed blessings with sloppily executed signs of the cross. As Archbishop of Canterbury, Sudbury—and his power--covered all the city the way a great bird covered its prey with its wings.

When the archbishop spotted Thurold, he reined in his jennet and considered questioning him. Lent was always a sensitive time, for the preaching friars ratcheted up their chitterings, bordering on heresy, about how Christ had died for all men, which caused some to incorrectly interpret their message. And then there was the business of Maundy Thursday when he and all the other high clergy and royals would ritually wash the feet of the poor, some of those who might even now be genuflecting before him. Mayhap even the malcontent glaring at him, though he was too well dressed to be a candidate. In these uncertain days it was better not to risk stirring the populace, so Sudbury donned his most pious expression and executed a very deliberate sign of the cross, bestowing a personal blessing upon the peasant before moving on.

"John of Gaunt's fool," Thurold muttered, after Sudbury murmured something to the priest riding next to him, who also turned to frown at Thurold. "He'll be the first to have his head chopped off when our time comes," he continued, not realizing how prescient his words would prove to be.

However, it wasn't only Mother Church that stirred enmity among Canterbury's townsfolk. Kent was the county seat, with the sheriff making his home here, and local tradesmen were a recalcitrant lot, mindful of their rights and others' slights. Brawls and quarreling had become so commonplace that a royal commission had been appointed to ferret out "malefactors and disturbers of the peace, citizens and other inhabitants of the city and suburbs, who have assembled in great numbers and stirred up strife, debates and contentions therein, sowing discord."

Margery laced her fingers through Thurold's and squeezed. "'Tis too fine a day to let that ugly old man spoil it. He's not worth a thought."

"Aye," Thurold agreed, with one last baleful look at the passing retinue.

Directly inside Canterbury's north gate was a blacksmith's shop, St. Dunstan's, named after the trade's patron saint. Margery generally walked past St. Dunstan's with nary a glance. Every village, town, castle, and abbey had at least one such establishment, and often several, some specializing in armor, others in household objects, some farmers' implements and still others a mixture of all. This shop was larger than many. Winter or summer the great furnace belched flames while apprentices scurried about or crafted various household instruments, knives and daggers—even fine jewelry—at a trio of long tables.

Today Thurold paused in front of the partition separating the shop from customers while Margery stood off to the side idly watching a lad near the forge squeezing a pair of leather bellows as a blacksmith expertly turned a glowing lump of metal with a huge pair of tongs. Then the blacksmith and a second smithy dragged the enormous lump out of the furnace and onto the floor where they broke off a sizeable chunk. Again using tongs they carefully moved the white-hot iron to a large anvil mounted on a stump.

Margery took sudden note of the second smithy. Unlike his partner, the man did not wear a felt cap to protect himself from wayward sparks, but rather tied his long black hair at the base of his neck with a leather thong. Even his bulky leather apron could not disguise broad shoulders, muscular arms, and legs long enough to set him a head taller than those around him.

"Ah, Fulco," Thurold called and the man, who'd just picked up a large hammer, looked up from the metal and flashed Thurold a grin. He was dark as a Moor, and his teeth appeared particularly white against his skin. His eyes flicked to Margery—eyes black as the charcoal stoking the forge. Then he and the other smith lifted their sledges and began pounding the metal, with Fulco's massive arms showing through the torn seams of his tunic as he worked.

Margery's stomach was doing so much flipping and flopping she might have ingested a live fish. She found it difficult to breathe.

'Tis the heat from the furnace.

She stared. The blacksmiths continued hammering the molten metal in alternating rhythm, "drawing" it out. She didn't know which she found more unsettling, the flexing and extending of those magnificent arms, or that snaking strand of hair that fell across a profile that looked as if it too had been forged from iron. This Fulco person seemed like some creature out of hell... or heaven.

"Where is that man from?" Margery managed to ask her step-brother.

"Who, Fulco the Smithy? 'ere, there and everywhere."

Seeing the look on her face, Thurold grinned. "Ye might close your mouth, Stick Legs. 'ave ye not seen a blacksmith afore?"

"Not like him," she wanted to say. She found it impossible to tear her eyes away. "I've not noticed him around."

"Fulco ne'er stays long in one place. His skills be in great demand so 'e's welcome at any castle. 'e originally hails from near Bury St. Edmunds."

Margery's eyebrows shot up. That was in the vicinity of their birth-place. "Jesus wept," she whispered. "If there'd been men like him about I might never have left Ravennesfield."

Thurold looked at her in surprise for his stepsister never so boldly commented on men. He couldn't remember her commenting on a man in that fashion, period. Not even *him*.

"I just meant he seems young to be so skilled," she hurriedly continued. She was sure her cheeks must be as red as if she were standing on top of the forge itself.

A pair of Augustinian monks who'd purchased hinges for a church door left the stall. The monks passed in front of them, breaking Margery's view.

"Fulco is one of us, you know," Thurold said. An odd remark for of course a blacksmith would be a commoner and not nobly born.

A farmer carrying a ploughshare stepped up to the partition.

Margery continued watching Fulco the Smithy work his iron. She knew that blacksmithing required infinite patience, pounding, returning to the fire, more pounding. Hour after hour, Fulco and his partner would alternately swing their hammers, slowly molding and shaping the mass until, if too soft from the smelter for weapons or chain mail, it would be turned into more prosaic implements from arrows and nails and undertakers' tools to torture devices.

"Dame Margery, good day give you our Lord."

John Calawe, mayor of Fordwich, smiled at her.

Spell shattered, she replied in kind and after exchanging pleasantries about the bounty of mouse-tails blooming so early in the year near the River Stour, she said to Thurold, "Let's be gone. We're due at the shop."

Margery risked a last glance at Fulco's great biceps, his dark face and black hair, his profile silhouetted by the flames of the forge, and something primal stirred within her. Even after she turned away, she felt the pull of him, as if his eyes might be on her when there was no falter of the ringing hammers, no indication that he'd even taken notice of her other than that initial glance. Silently vowing she would find a different route to Aurum, she stepped onto the street.

She would never again pass by St. Dunstan's.

She would never again allow herself to be disturbed by the presence of this Fulco the Smithy.

FOR THE NEXT month Margery walked past St. Dunstan's every day. At least every day that the blacksmithing shop was open, for with the Easter season there were more holy days and days of celebration. It became routine—in the morning on her way to Aurum and near dusk when she returned to her cottage. Throughout holy week and Easter Sunday, she even attended mass at Canterbury Cathedral rather than St. Mary the Virgin at Fordwich, hoping to spot Fulco among the massive crowds. When the shop was closed and she didn't see him she felt such an odd restlessness, even something of a panic, which she didn't understand. For when St. Dunstan's was open and she stopped, she didn't linger long enough to more than glimpse Fulco, or to attract attention to her presence. So she assured herself. Should anyone ask, she was simply satisfying her curiosity, for black and gold and silver smithing had much in common.

Or so she she'd explained to her maid, Cicily, who generally accompanied her on her sojourns.

"Research," she said, as if she must clarify the matter to her notoriously stolid maid. "Comparing techniques."

After all, blacksmiths worked "black" metals like iron while goldsmiths and silversmiths worked "white," but they were all metalworkers, weren't they? And other parts of their crafts were similar. A blacksmith's tools might be on a grander scale but to forge a suit of armor or chain mail required as much skill as creating chalices and broaches and reliquaries.

'Tis innocent. Harmless. At Aurum she had regular customers. Will, the innkeeper from the Chequer of the Hope, come round daily just to chat. Her behavior wasn't really that extraordinary.

So why, at the end of the Easter celebrations and with the renewal of regular routines, had she taken to walking the route alone? Her actions grew ever more inexplicable to herself, so how could she hope to explain them to others?

Besides, she rationalized, *I do not need to justify myself to anyone.*

However, even as she found herself hurrying impatiently until her first glimpse of Canterbury's north gate, she would pray, *Sweet Blessed Virgin, protect me from my wicked thoughts,* and force herself to slow as suited a proper matron. Sometimes she would order herself to walk past St. Dunstan's—very sedately of course--without even turning her head.

Only to have her body disobey.

She told herself that it didn't matter, that as engrossed as Fulco seemed to be in his work, he wouldn't notice whether she passed or stopped. Furthermore, he wouldn't care. Sometimes he glanced at her but more often he remained focused on whatever task was set before him. She wasn't used to being ignored, but there it was. She was no longer young and, though she could not well judge the blacksmith's age, he might be a decade her junior.

If he considers me at all, she told herself, *'tis as an old woman. Which doesn't matter. Even old women can look.*

Sometimes when Margery paused, Fulco would be bent over a table repairing or creating chain mail or hammering and shaping a broadsword on a smaller anvil. She'd once found him fitting armor for the lord of Chilham Castle, an enormous—and expensive—undertaking. A suit of armor could cost the equivalent of three years of a skilled laborer's wages.

But hadn't Thurold said that Fulco was the best of his kind? And perhaps such a time consuming process would keep him longer in Canterbury, for her stepbrother had also remarked that Fulco never tarried long. Was that the reason Margery continued her daily vigil? Knowing that the time would come when she would peer into St. Dunstan's and find him gone?

Most often Fulco and his partner would be at opposite ends of the big anvil, as they'd been that first day, working their iron. (Had she passed his partner on the lane she would have been unable to recognize him. No one in the shop beyond Fulco even registered in her consciousness). Fulco seemed to delight in this particular activity, in the endless rise and fall of his great hammer. Or at least she imagined that he did for his blows never faltered but rained down with rhythmic precision. Beyond that, she didn't give much thought to the smithy as an actual *person*. She wasn't curious about his past, his hopes and dreams, whether he was mean or kind, crafty or naïve, married or a widower. She looked upon him simply as a darkly beautiful object to be admired. And, oh, how she wished she could touch and stroke that object.

Before Fulco, Margery often spent the day at her cottage or at her grandmother's rather than Aurum. She might even travel to London for an accounting of business at the Shop of the Unicorn. After Fulco, her world had narrowed to the dusty road and her moments in front of St. Dunstan's. The rest faded to the times between.

What was it about him? Even a glance made her knees go weak with desire. Why? If she could put it into words, she might be able to make sense of it but she could not. It wasn't just his striking looks. There was something primitive, untamed about him. As if he'd arisen from the core of the earth in the manner of molten fire. Hell fire. For hell was located deep within the earth's bowels and she'd always imagined Satan as a huge, black, overpowering beast with fiery eyes that could lure the most saintly from the path of righteousness.

Which seemed an apt description of Fulco.

Mayhap you are a demon. For you've surely taken possession of me.

At night, Margery found it impossible to sleep. Her upstairs bedroom had one large window but when clouds covered the moon it was so dark she couldn't see the chest beside her bed or her hand when she raised it—and she imagined conjuring Fulco the Smithy out of that velvet blackness. If only she knew a spell that would bring him to her and send him away at her convenience. How long would it take to slake this particular thirst or would she simply burn hotter for him? She'd never been stirred by another man save Matthew Hart, and that had been such a tangled mess of emotions. Not so with Fulco the Smithy, whom she'd never even spoken to. She could boil it all down to one word: lust.

She didn't seek to know him any way but carnally, and in that way she imagined his rough hands on her, his massive arms crushing her, the feel of that iron body atop her as he claimed her for his own. The darkness was crowded with images of them in wanton positions doing wanton things that sometimes seemed so tantalizingly real her phantom lover might have resided in the room with her.

"I am going mad," she whispered.

At such times she would cross to the unshuttered window opening and gaze into the night, at the road passing beyond her cottage hedge, the masts of ships, darker than the dark itself, down by Fordwich's quay, and the bumpy blanket of treetops beyond new-ploughed fields. She would close her eyes and concentrate on the breeze blowing from the River Stour, willing it to cool her face, her fevered body. Sometimes she felt as if she were so hot she could be shaped like the iron in the blacksmith's forge, imagined Fulco running those great hands over her, molding her in whatever fashion pleased him.

Night after night with no relief.

So this is why priests call us insatiable.

After a particularly restless even, Margery visited her grandmother. If anyone understood passion it would be Maria Rendell. But when Maria asked whether something was troubling her, Margery found herself unable to speak of it. She kept thinking that she needed to be on the road, to make certain that Fulco had not picked up and fled since yesterday.

"I forgot I have an appointment at Aurum," she mumbled, rising from the bench. "I promise next time I will tell you everything." As if she could. As if there were words for something she herself didn't understand.

Margery forced herself to return to her garden, which already needed weeding, and vowed she would NOT surrender to this compulsion. For one day at least she would stay away.

And yet, by early afternoon her feet, as if of their own will, were hurrying her along the road to the north gate.

I will not, I must not, she thought, even as she did.

The day was unseasonably warm for the last day of April though, winter or summer, it was always hot inside St. Dunstan's.

Once at the shop, she noted that Fulco and his partner were at the anvil. And that Fulco had removed his tunic. Other than his leather apron, his torso was completely bare, his legs covered only with braies, revealing calves that were as defined as his arms.

Margery felt her jaw drop. Fulco's face and chest were covered with perspiration, causing his skin to glisten like dark silk. Once again strands of hair had snaked free from his thong and clung to his cheeks. His arms, fully displayed in all their glory, rose and fell. With each slamming of metal upon metal, sparks cascaded outward and upward.

As if by unspoken agreement, Fulco and his partner laid down their tools to take a rest. An apprentice approached with a jug of ale. After his partner drank, Fulco tipped the jug back, showing the muscular arc of his throat as he emptied its contents.

I must go, Margery thought, yet she remained rooted to the spot.

Fulco handed the jug back to the apprentice, wiped his brow with his forearm and then very slowly, carefully, raised his great arms, loosed the thong at the nape of his neck, caught the strands of loose hair back in the leather string and carefully re-tied it. Margery found herself mesmerized. Something about his actions was so sensual, strong and yet gentle. Not gentle... deliberate. Jesu, to imagine such fingers touching her...

And then Fulco turned to look directly at her, probing her with eyes black as the blackest night, and in their depths she saw a spark like those from his hammering, a spark that told her he desired her as she desired him. Their gazes locked. Her body felt as if it would burst into a flame so hot her bones, sinew, and flesh would immediately crumble to ash.

Finally, Fulco picked up his giant sledge, squared his massive shoulders and returned to his work. Margery somehow found herself back on the street.

I am no better than a bitch in heat. I AM a bitch in heat. Enough! I will return to London, she promised herself. *Right after May Day.*

May Day.

Tomorrow.

MAY WAS KNOWN as Mary's month so, in honor of Christ's mother, flower bouquets were regularly brought to holy places throughout the kingdom. But the first day of May was a different matter. Its origins dated back to pagan times and centered around fertility rites designed to guarantee bountiful harvests and fecund wombs. As usual the church put a religious patina over the ceremonies but a definite bacchanalian undercurrent ran throughout.

At dawn, Fordwich's lads had chopped down a towering birch, stripped its branches—all save for plumes at the top which symbolized new life—and carried it to the village green. There the giant pole was painted, planted, and decorated with garlands of woodbine, hawthorn, and other flowers freshly woven by maidens, also up with the dawn. Long colored ribbons were fastened near the top and streamed down to the ground. It was not lost on anyone that a maypole resembled nothing so much as a great phallus thrusting toward the sky.

While May Day catered primarily to the young, for it was they, after all, who would replenish the earth, Margery eagerly anticipated the festivities. Dressed in her most vibrant red kirtle—it was customary to wear one's brightest colors—she and Cicily walked from her cottage to the nearby green. A sizeable crowd had already gathered to crown the Queen and King of the May, who were making their way to their "thrones" before the maypole.

Margery recognized Annie, the beekeeper from Tancrey Island, as queen.

"But I've not seen the king," she commented, studying the lad, who was dressed all in green in remembrance of Jack in the Green, the woodland spirit who guarded England's forests.

Cicily refrained from reminding her mistress that she had most certainly seen the young man—near daily—over the past month. "He's an apprentice from St. Dunstan's. He mainly works the pair of bellows."

"Of course," Margery said vaguely, and her eyes swept the villagers, for the first of what would be many times, seeking Fulco. A part of her couldn't quite imagine him as existing apart from St. Dunstan's, and most likely he would celebrate at Canterbury. Still...

No matter. Tomorrow I will be London bound, and Fulco the Smithy will be banished from my memory as thoroughly as Mother Church banishes heretics.

At intervals throughout the day, two sets of maids, holding their colorful ribbons, wound their way, one group opposite the other, twining and untwining their streamers round the maypole. Then, to the accompaniment of a piper and later, musicians playing shawns and beating a tabor, the maids would repeat the ritual in a counter direction, skipping as they did so. After hours of drinking, their movements became more wanton, the gazes of the watching lads more desirous, their comments bolder.

Perhaps it was the profane nature of May Day, but to Margery it seemed that the sexual tension was thick enough to taste. The continuous heat coursing through her veins could not be solely attributed to the warmth of the sun. Just as odd, she repeatedly experienced a prickling along the back of her neck, as if someone was watching her. Silly, of course. Among so many fresh-faced beauties, who would notice a middle-aged woman?

With charming shyness, Queen Annie and King Hal held court over mummers, musicians, and performers as well as their subjects, Fordwich's townsfolk, who they could order about as they wished. Which they did sparingly for both blushed often and stammered the most timid of commands. When too overwhelmed, Annie had a tendency to cover her face and Hal to giggle nervously.

How very young you are, Margery thought, feeling a protective tenderness toward them. With their shining eyes, dewy skin and open, eager smiles, they seemed little more grown than Serill. *So, by contrast, why do I not feel so very, very old?*

Mayhap it was because she could dance, sing, drink, and flirt as much as she pleased. Mayhap it was because after today she would be shed of her obsession and her world returned to its rightful place. That would be no small thing, to be rid of her imaginary lover.

Margery threw herself into the festivities, even caroling with Fordwich's mayor and other local dignitaries. By late afternoon she knew she'd downed too many mazers of ale and was contemplating returning to her cottage for a nap. Somewhere along the way she'd picked up a garland of woodbine. Carefully, a bit over-elaborately, she wrapped her fingers between the delicate yellow, pink and orange petals so that she wouldn't crush them. She considered placing the wreath on her head, but even with her limbs—and her thoughts--loosened from alcohol she reminded herself that garlands were meant for the young and unmarried, whose hair was allowed to fall free.

Margery lifted the circlet to her nose and inhaled. Woodbine's scent was strongest around dusk, which was swift approaching. What did its fragrance remind her of? Summer and sunshine. Baby lambs and calves and foals trailing their mothers. Birdsong. Barefoot strolls beside hedgerows where the plant had a way of creeping among the hawthorn, blackthorn and hazel shrubbery until it spilled over in a riot of color reminiscent of swarms of butterflies.

She felt it, the ancient pagan pull. The harrowing and seeding of

Mother Earth. The harrowing and seeding of lovers. Already couples were stealing off to the privacy of the nearby woods.

Sunset bloomed, then faded, leaving a lingering stain on the horizon. Many of the elders had begun heading homeward. Margery drifted to the outskirts of the thinning crowd. The lightheadedness from the ale had begun to dissipate, though she swayed and hummed along with a group of carolers who were dancing and singing near the maypole.

How lovely they were in their first blooming—the broad- shouldered lads and the pink-cheeked maids with their unbound tresses shimmering softly in the dying light.

While we proper women have our hair hidden behind our wimples, gorgets, cauls and coifs. All trussed up like dinner partridges.

Priests thundered that only Jezebels allowed their hair down or their ears to be uncovered in public. Since the Blessed Mother had conceived through her ear, thereby retaining her virginity, removing one's headdress in public was brazenly advertising that the offender was a whore.

Aye. Even so, Margery Watson, this May Day's even, did something so contrary to propriety that, had any of those imaginary priests been watching, they would have gasped in outrage.

She undid her crespine and let down her hair.

Bending from the waist, Margery flipped her tresses in front of her, ran her hands through their thickness, raised up, shook them loose and tossed her head back until her curls cascaded free to her shoulders, her arms, down her back, all the way to her waist. After pushing her hair behind her ears so they would have been exposed for all the world to see, she placed the garland firmly atop her head.

And laughed.

Suddenly that sensation of being watched returned, stronger than ever. Margery froze, then slowly turned full circle.

No one.

To her left was a copse which ended at the banks of the River Stour. In the increasingly poor light, she couldn't distinguish much beyond the sketchiest of outlines. Near the trees the grass, thick with wildflowers, was particularly abundant. Stepping closer, she peered into the shadows.

Nothing.

Ah, well. She shrugged and bent down to pluck several flowers which she absently wove into her hair.

What a peculiar day this has been.

A sudden cheering from the vicinity of the maypole signaled that the bonfire had been lit. Tradition held that the fire would cleanse and purify the land in anticipation of summer's arrival, as well as increase fertility. But for Margery, the leaping flames could only mean one thing: Fulco the Smithy.

Will it ever be thus? she wondered, experiencing a sudden melancholy. *That every time I gaze into a hearth fire or even strike flint to steel I will be cursed to think of you?*

Church bells began ringing, calling out Vespers, reminding all to pause, give thanks for the day past and gird themselves against the dangers of the descending darkness.

Margery sighed. Time to return home. Tomorrow she would have to pack and her maid, who'd also drunk and danced in a most un-Cicily like fashion, would be nursing a throbbing head, and in a sullen mood...

From the copse she heard a nightingale's song. Then the whisper of something closer, what? Sensing a presence behind her, she started to turn. Almost immediately, someone grabbed her around the waist and pulled her tight against him. Margery gasped and reached down to claw away the stranger's hands. But, when she registered their size, the thickness of fingers and roughness of skin, she recognized her "assailant." Instantly her body responded; her every nerve ending ignited. Fulco the Smithy held her even more fiercely, his body as strong and unyielding as a rock, so that she could feel every inch of him.

Margery inhaled sharply and shifted position. Fulco eased his grip enough so that she could twist to face him. Without hesitation, she wrapped her arms around his neck and allowed his lips to find hers, to crush them with the strength of his desire. And hers. For she responded fully, as desperate as he to be sated.

Fulco pulled her into the densest part of the copse. As if by magic they'd both shed themselves of their clothing and he was atop her. His hair, freed of its leather restraint, curtained his face. Held captive by his gaze she felt as if she were falling, falling, as if this man could truly lead her to the inferno at the core of the earth. Where they would both be immolated in its flames.

And she would welcome it all. Anything. Everything.

She experienced such a hunger; an elemental craving to be possessed by him. And, oh, his body, as flawless as if it had been forged by the gods. There was little thought and no speech beyond moans and gasps as Fulco had his way with her and she with him. None of it seemed quite real and yet her senses were preternaturally heightened. She was aware of the grasses beneath her; the rippling of his shoulder muscles as her fingertips dug into them; their panting, which sounded like that of two spent animals. The prickling of his chest hair; his iron thighs against her own; the brush of his hair against her face and breasts as he moved downward to explore her body.

Margery's need was too great. She buried her fingers in his mane and pulled him back up so that her lips were once again against his, then reached down to guide him inside. He claimed her with a thrust of such violence that tears sprang to her eyes and she cried out. In pain. In exultation. In completion.

Too soon it was over.

But then, a lifetime would not be enough.

After their breathing slowed, they lay on their backs in the darkness, their arms and legs still touching.

She stared through the leafy canopy, feeling her heart gradually calm, the air cool her fevered body.

What had just happened? She couldn't fathom it. Her grandmother often spoke of the sun and the moon. Light and dark. But Maria's Phillip had been nothing like this. Fulco was the dragon in *Beowulf;* the lord of the underworld.

"Who are you?" She could feel the questions forming. "How have you done this to me?" Mayhap they should speak, reason through what was clearly unreasonable, attempt to make sense of a circumstance completely beyond her ken.

Margery shifted to face him, and rested on an elbow so that she could gaze upon him. Fulco's arms were behind his head and he was looking up through a lattice of branches to the heavens. Stars pricked the velvet darkness. She could smell the smoke from the bonfire, the sweetness from the crushed garland and flowers that had fallen from her hair. Most powerfully, she could smell *him*—the scent of new sweat and his passion, more faintly the acrid tang of coal fire and even more faintly something else, something almost sweet. Cinnamon? Whatever it was, the combination triggered a fresh rush of desire.

"Fulco," she whispered.

He shifted so that they were on a level and laid a finger to her lips, silencing her. He knew. He understood her doubts, her fears, her wonderings, her need, all of it without speaking.

Margery felt herself surrender. For it was no use. He would take her, she knew not where, only that she would willingly follow. She opened her mouth and slipped his calloused finger inside. His lips curved upward and his eyes drew her back into that place where words were unneeded.

Once again Fulco stretched himself atop her. All the while their eyes remained locked so that they could measure every caress, every pleasure, every new sensation, every wash of emotion as it was experienced by the other.

This time when they parted, Fulco pulled her to him, his front to her back, and started running his fingers over her, as if imprinting her curves on his fingertips. As if he were creating her as he created his pieces, only not with his tools, but with his touch. She placed her hand over his so that she might follow it as he traced her. She felt the softest whisper of his breath against her neck, and something broke inside. Was it all those years when she'd shuttered her heart against the pain of a dying relationship, pretending that it did not hurt, telling herself that she and her lover could survive if only she could reach the place where she felt nothing at all?

Margery had no idea how long she and Fulco remained in the copse. Only that the field around them grew still save for the occasional lament of the nightingale and the rustling from invisible forest creatures. In the distance, the bonfire had burned down to a soft glow.

Finally, Fulco pulled her to her feet. She'd only partially dressed and bundled the rest of her clothes in her arms since her walk would be a short one.

So, here it was, an ending that must be a disappointment. For what could be said after such an experience? Yet, how could they simply walk away, continue on with life as it was before? When Margery knew, at least for her, life could never be anything like before.

She gazed up at him. Though she could not possibly be feeling sadness, her vision blurred.

Fulco cradled his great hands on either side of her tangled mass of hair and whispered one word.

"Tomorrow."

CHAPTER 12

Fordwich

"*D*o you think 'tis possible to desire someone to the point of madness?"

Maria Rendell's eyebrows lifted. She studied her granddaughter, who, with her high color and shining eyes, did not appear mad but rather unusually healthy.

"Aye, I do." Maria's fingers curled over the arms of her throne-like chair which had been plumped with cushions and positioned to catch the cross currents from various tower windows. Colorful wall tapestries, most depicting scenes from Arthurian romances, stirred in the breeze.

"Is that how you felt about your lord Sussex, or your husband?" Margery pressed. "That you'd become mad from it all?"

Maria considered. She had endured a public flogging, invective hurled at her from pulpits across the kingdom, but it had been her moon who had driven her to distraction. For, beyond their lovemaking, she'd never been able to truly reach her husband. In thrall to a restless, discontented nature, he'd remained so frustratingly aloof. At least until after that night along the River Wear and the Scottish raid that had resulted in Richard's death and Phillip's disfigurement.

Feeling her way, Maria spoke carefully. "Passion is a grand thing—"

"Lust," Margery corrected. "Lust."

So, Maria wondered. *Who is this man?* She leaned over to scratch her faithful Canis between his ears. The great dog exhaled in pleasure, placed his grizzled muzzle on her knees, and gazed up at her with adoring eyes.

Margery was seated on a bench opposite her grandmother, hands clenched in her lap. "I understand that each of us has our rightful place in society, I do! Though the actions of people like me can hardly be judged important when compared to kings and queens and the like. Most of us go from birth to death with hardly anyone even taking notice. We're here and gone with no more consequence than sunlight glancing off a stream. And yet we constrain ourselves with so many rules—the church, our neighbors, our family..." She hesitated. "The ones we impose upon ourselves."

Maria nodded, though she had no idea where their conversation was leading. But she'd lived too long to directly ask questions she sensed could be more truthfully answered with tact.

"Duty and obligation. How I once chafed at those words."

Jackdaws drowsed in their cages, heads tucked beneath their wings. Maria removed Canis's muzzle from her knees and poured her and Margery wine from the small table between them. Leaning forward to hand her a goblet, Maria studied her granddaughter, whose gaze was fixed on a mass of wildflowers arrayed before the cold hearth.

"Sometimes we must do the right thing," Margery said, as if speaking to herself. "Even when we would prefer spinning lovely tales and living in another world."

"And what world is that?"

"A world without past or future. Simply me and... someone." This past month, Margery had come to realize that her peasant blood ran stronger than she'd ever imagined. At times she fancied Fulco the Smithy had been conjured from the heat and flames of his forge, and feared that all too soon he would simply disappear. *Poof!* Like smoke from an extinguished fire. Afterward, would she mourn among the ruins or simply look back in gratitude for her awakening?

Margery sipped her wine without tasting it. "I understand that a life together could never be as I've imagined. Not only would there be hardships and even empty bellies, at times, and discomforts such as I've not experienced for many years. But worse... how unendurable would it be if I cast aside my well-ordered life only to find that... someone... to be cruel and coarse? Or that he could not speak of anything beyond, 'Mend my clothes' and 'Fill my mazer.'"

"Daily living is the challenge, is it not?" While Maria was curious about the identity of Margery's suitor or lover or whoever he might be, she trod warily. "Mayhap priests are right when they assert that untrammeled desire must lead to tragedy." She continued, considering each word. "Though I've known passion aplenty, some of my sweetest memories are after my lord husband returned to me. When we would simply hold hands before falling asleep and in the morning awaken with fingers still entwined. Or when we shared a special look or laugh over some silliness or vexation. Or I might just study him when he was unaware and find myself filled with such gratitude for the gift of him I feared I might die from contentment."

This conversation was becoming too difficult. Maria did not want to be reminded of those Death had snatched from her. She swallowed hard, as if she might push down ancient emotions. "Love can run as deep as the sea, as slow as poured honey," she finished huskily.

"While a stream moves so unpredictably because its waters are shallow.Though I know 'tis impossible, that he... it... isn't even something I want, yet I find myself imagining such silly things. Like sitting beneath some spreading oak in some far away place, watching the sun set. Not even speaking. For I am finding communication can run truer without all the words."

"Sometimes," Maria agreed, though she'd learned from bitter experience that she, like the rest of mankind, too often filled her partners' silences with fevered imaginings. And that, so many things one professed to intuit with such certainty were later proven wrong.

"Words have such a way of wounding," Margery said, her thoughts harkening back to her last months with Matthew Hart. Wasn't it the safer course to stay silent? For, if one failed to utter the words, one could not be annihilated by them.

Margery reached out to caress Maria's cheek. *You are still so very young,* she thought, feeling such a desire to protect, to erase whatever it was that was causing her granddaughter turmoil.

"God has not created the partner who could fill all our needs. The only way we will not eat ourselves up with misery is if we determine that whatever our beloved is capable of giving us is enough."

Margery nodded. She knew that on one level, the same way she knew that her time with Fulco was drawing to a close. Perhaps that was the reason she found herself clinging so ferociously to the thought of him.

Silence stretched between them. Canis eased himself down beside his mistress and rested his head atop her slippers.

"Do not forget Serill," Maria said suddenly. "Out of everything, what I most regret is how my actions hurt my children. Thoughtless I was, and while I assured myself I meant no harm, that Thomas and Blanche were too young to be affected, 'twas not so. Even though we believe we are acting from the purest of intentions, the resultant damage can last a lifetime." Maria closed her eyes and leaned her head against the back of her chair. She was suddenly exhausted, and not because of age. Because of the ghosts that were being raised, ghosts she'd long thought safely buried at the crossroads of her past.

"So saith the old woman in the tower," she said, attempting levity. "Who pretends much and who actually knows very little."

Margery raised her great blue eyes, a mixture of Phillip's and her own, to study her. "At least you know more than I do. For increasingly I feel as if I am wandering alone within a forest dark."

AFTER CHURCH BELLS RANG VESPERS, Margery left her cottage for their meeting place. Generally, Fulco arrived first so that he could wash away the day's grime in the River Stour. Sometimes she would join him for a particularly exotic bout of lovemaking, but tonight she awaited him in the most secluded part of the copse, away from the river. She'd spread their blanket and set out a flagon of wine, as well as their usual bread and cheese. She sat very still, her senses alert for the whisper of his tread. She knew, though she had no idea how for Fulco had not spoken, that tonight would be their last night. What she did not know is how she felt about his leaving.

She heard him, slipping through the thinnest part of the copse, following the faint path they'd worn to the river.

She stood. "Fulco!"

He turned in surprise and then smiled in that way that immediately caused her body to flush with need.

He'd already shed his tunic and was barefoot, clad only in his braies. She approached him and slid her arms around his waist. He always seemed unusually warm to the touch, as if he carried the flames of the forge with him. "Do not," she said, referring to his bathing. "I want to taste you as you are."

Afterward, when they were nearing their usual time for goodbye, Fulco sat up and pulled her to him. She nestled against his massive chest and closed her eyes, savoring the moment.

He inched her away until he could see her face. "On the morrow I..."

This time it was Margery who placed her finger to his lips and shook her head.

"Please. You need not say it. I already know."

After they parted, Margery crept home and slipped into her bed. She did not cry. She did not hatch a scheme to somehow make him stay. Rather, she wondered what Fulco the Smithy had been trying to purge all those times they'd come together in the darkness.

"And most importantly," she whispered to the darkness, "What was I?"

～

THE FOLLOWING AFTERNOON Margery walked into Canterbury, as she'd not done since she'd started sleeping during the day and prowling the night. She paused at St. Dunstan's long enough to look for Fulco. Only to confirm what she already knew.

Returning home, she found a beggar boy waiting on the bench in front of her cottage.

"'e said 'e'd wait for ye, on the road near the old Roman fort, past Sturry."

The urchin did not have to clarify who "'e" was. Margery groped in her purse for a shilling and then set out for Sturry, a short distance away.

She spotted Fulco's wagon, which held a portable forge and the tools of his trade, alongside the road. The wagon and a muscular pair of harnessed bays faced north toward London, toward anywhere, really, for England was at his disposal.

Fulco was standing in the front of the wagon with his back to her, legs apart, feet firmly planted in a familiar stance. He must have heard her approach for he turned to watch. His hair, glossy as a raven's wing, hung free, and when she neared he tossed his head back and favored her with one of his rare smiles.

Life though pleasant is transitory... She reminded herself that she must not be sad, but grateful, as her grandmother had said.

Upon reaching the side of the forge wagon, she gazed up at him.

How long will it be before your face and form start to fade? Until you'll seem but a dream stitched from the darkness?

Fulco held out a scarred and calloused hand. "Come with me, my lady," he said. She was surprised—by his addressing her so respectfully, but even more so by his invitation. That she'd never expected.

"Leave? Us?" she asked stupidly.

He nodded.

"Oh!" She reached out and placed her hand within his own. While she'd indulged in such daydreams, she'd never imagined he might feel the same.

"I cannot," she whispered. "But oh, my heart, 'tis tempting."

"I know I've little to offer."

She shook her head. "I do not care about that." Which was largely true because, with her purse, they need never sleep beneath his wagon or scrabble for enough food or warm clothing. Her refusal had nothing to do with such mundanities. But, should she acquiesce, it would be as it always was in relationships. As it had been with the monster, Simon Crull. As it had been with the knight she'd loved. In the daily grind of weeks, months, and years their passion would be ground to dust and the magic of these past weeks obliterated.

"I would rather remember our time together as my secret treasure. That can never be tarnished but will ever remain perfect."

"The dream is all," he agreed, his expression almost fierce. At that moment, he reminded her of her stepbrother. Had she and Fulco communicated more with their mouths than their bodies, she might have uncovered a more complicated man.

Margery brought his hand to her lips and kissed the calloused palm.

Fulco slipped his hand from hers, raised his great arms, reached inside his tunic and retrieved a long metal chain and pendant.

He held the necklace out and coiled it in her palm. She examined the pendant, which was approximately the length of her index finger. It was the figure of a woman—a naked woman. Naturally rendered rather than in the usual stylized fashion. She remembered all the nights Fulco had run his hands along her body and now understood that 'twas more than an exercise in hedonistic pleasure. For there was no doubt of the figure's identity—with Margery's hair, its strands so lovingly delineated, tumbling free past exposed breasts, with her long legs and her womanly region as exquisitely wrought as if she were some pagan goddess.

It was indecent, no doubt of that. And the most beautiful thing she'd ever seen.

"I am so very... honored." She stared down at her miniature self, traced its metal curves as Fulco had so lovingly traced her curves of flesh and blood.

She raised her gaze once again to his. "I so wish..." If only they could disappear into an enchanted underworld where decades would pass like days and they would never grow old but would ever be together.

But Fulco was no faerie lord; he was simply a traveling blacksmith.

She returned his necklace. "Keep it. So you'll not forget me."

"There's little chance of that." Fulco drew away to his full height, slipped the necklace over his head and inside his tunic.

One last piercing look before he gathered his horses' reins and snapped them. The cart lurched forward, away from her.

Margery watched until the road took a curve and his wagon disappeared.

"You may forget me, Fulco the Smithy," she whispered. "But, by all that's holy, I'll not forget you."

CHAPTER 13

Cumbria and London, Summer 1379

$\mathcal{M}$atthew met his squire at the base of Lake Winandermere, at the end of a trail he'd often walked to fish. Jerome handed him the reins of his black destrier, Stormbringer.

"I've not ridden in five months," Matthew said, easing into the saddle. "For certes, I will be sore tomorrow."

"'Tis an easy ride," Jerome replied. Matthew was aware of his squire's gaze on him, no doubt attempting to gauge whether Matthew's accidie had passed.

I wish I knew.

Matthew felt as he had during his dead sovereign's campaign to be crowned king of France. What year had that been? 1360? The chevauchées had such a tendency to blur together, though Matthew had not forgotten the coughing sickness that had plagued him throughout. Just when he'd think himself cured, the coughing, shakes and spitting up of blood would return with increased vengeance. Similarly, while Matthew was currently hopeful he'd left his melancholia behind, only time would tell.

When they first glimpsed the massive slab that was Cumbria Castle, Jerome said, "Your sister is visiting. She eagerly anticipates your arrival."

Matthew groaned. "Is her husband with her?"

He shook his head. "She says Lord Ravenne be stout as a whale and she'd not put a horse through such misery."

Matthew smiled, relieved. "That sounds like Elizabeth."

"And your lord the duke will be at Knaresborough in a sennight."

Matthew nodded. That meant Serill. A reunion with his son would be a happy occasion.

Ah, thought Matthew. *Life will be good once again.*

At Cumbria Castle, Matthew struggled to slip back into familiar routine. He was particularly solicitous of his mother, Sosanna, who'd suffered enough without further pain from him. Though his interactions often seemed false, he reminded himself he was adjusting from his time alone.

I am fine. As Earl of Cumbria, I must be.

On the day before Matthew rode for Knaresborough, his sister pulled him aside for a walk along the castle curtain.

"How fare you?" Elizabeth asked in her blunt way. "You still seem preoccupied, I'd say."

"I am not sure." Matthew gazed at the far away Pennines, undulating like a dragon's tail. In the middle distance, fluffy bits of sheep dotted the rocky slopes while in the nearby meadows, grazing cattle were scattered like fallen leaves.

"I saw your leman."

Matthew eyed his sister, instantly wary.

Elizabeth clarified, "Margery Watson," as if he were too stupid to know or had too many mistresses to recall them all.

"I know who my leman is—was," Matthew said sharply, aware of a sudden tightening around his temples.

"She has opened a shop in Canterbury and stays there part of the year."

How should he respond? His gaze returned to the placidly grazing livestock, the rolling hills.

"She asked about you," Elizabeth persisted.

Should he inquire as to Margery's health, her activities, whether she looked happy or sad, whether she had taken a lover or was wed? Did he even care? What? His thoughts swirled inside his skull like an inchoate mass of demon-possessed clouds.

"I am looking forward to seeing our son," Matthew finally said before turning on his heel and practically fleeing down a nearby vice, leaving Elizabeth to gape after him.

SERILL HAD SPROUTED LIKE A SAPLING—A handsome sapling, Matthew thought, his heart swelling with pride. He was so overjoyed to see his son he felt like a lad in the blush of first love. While listening to Serill's tales of his daily duties, when riding or hawking together, even while crossing wooden swords in a gentle mock combat, Matthew found himself mentally devouring that sweet, earnest face, marking every angle and line so that later, when alone, he would be able to recall each detail. At times he longed to scoop Serill into his arms as if he were still a toddler. Mayhap it was because he and Ralphie, who seemed Serill's shadow, reminded Matthew so much of him and Harry, though the ages were reversed. He even enjoyed his sister's boys, Lancelot and Perceval. Or at least Lancelot, who had inherited a bit of his mother's dreamy nature. Perceval, more's the pity, seemed more a miniature of his father with his flaming hair and piggish manner.

The lot of women, Matthew thought, feeling sympathy for Elizabeth, whose dreams of romance, of a gentle suitor and perfect children had long ago been dashed on the rocks of reality.

Matthew met with his lord, John of Gaunt, and Henry Percy, Earl of Northumbria. *We lions of the north*, he thought, savoring the irony. *Among us three we could rule England, so charge our enemies. Though one of us has trouble distinguishing his arse from his elbow.*

When alone together in the duke's private chamber, Matthew diligently—though often unsuccessfully—tried to follow his lord's and Percy's political conversations.

John of Gaunt dissected a recent tax—another one!—fashioned to rise gradually so that the rich would pay far more than the poor.

"Mayhap that will soothe our critics," said the duke. "Though finances are always constrained. We cannot demand direct taxes unless the security of the kingdom is at stake."

Is that an invitation to perpetual war? Matthew wondered, though he did not ask aloud.

Henry Percy expressed contempt for all those who dared dissent. "'Twas a sorry day when the Commons were allowed to vote in the first place."

The duke, ever thoughtful—his enemies said calculating—reached for a slim manuscript from a nearby chest. "I've been reading something by John Gower."

When Matthew stared at him blankly, the duke clarified, "The poet. He's a friend of Geoffrey's."

Geoffrey Chaucer, a name that did not endear this Gower fellow in Matthew's eyes. Scribblings on a page seemed a poor substitute for worthwhile endeavors.

As if you have any idea what a worthwhile endeavor might be, his inner voice mocked.

"'Tis an allegory on the fall of man and the effect of sin upon the world." The duke held the book out so that Matthew could read the title, *Mirour de l'Omme*. The Mirror of Man.

"I have been pondering this part," John said, opening it to a book-marked page. He positioned himself so that the light from a long narrow window fell upon the manuscript.

> "'There are three things,'" he read,
> "'That bring merciless destruction
> When given the upper hand:
> A flood of water, a raging fire,
> And the lesser people;
> For the common multitude
> Can never be stopped,
> Neither by reason nor by discipline.'"

Henry Percy sneered. "As if poets, with their ink-stained fingers and endless ditherings, know a spittle's worth about human nature!"

Merciless destruction. Matthew thought suddenly of Margery Watson's stepbrother, who would certainly agree with John Gower's assessment.

"'Tis as if some sorcerer is magically emptying His Grace's coffers," said John of Gaunt. "There is never enough money. So now four pence a head is being suggested for everyone save children under fourteen and genuine beggars."

Which did not strike the duke as much of a hardship when a skilled woman could earn five pence and a simple labourer carting around stones three pence a day.

"'Tis the equivalent of two hens or a dozen eggs," Percy observed.

Matthew felt a buzzing inside his brain, as if it were being invaded by a swarm of bees. How many holdings did his lord lay claim to, scattered across how many continents? Matthew gazed about the duke's chamber, modest by John's standards. And yet one wall tapestry had probably cost more than many of his villeins made in a lifetime.

What peculiar musings. So unlike him. Where were they coming from?

"I will be visiting the rest of the family holdings in the midlands and south," Matthew said. "Mayhap I'll get a better feel for the common mood."

Too soon, he told himself. *I've returned too soon.*

In 1305, William Wallace, the Scottish hero and patriot, had been executed on the first day of St. Bartholomew's annual fair. Hanged, drawn and quartered, not sixty feet away from where Margery Watson stood seventy-five years later. Margery gave fleeting thought to the fate of Scotland's revolutionary, for John Ball had recently preached about his exploits at St. Paul's Cross, using Wallace's words against an earlier injustice to exhort the crowd. "I could not be a traitor to the king, for I was never his subject."

What a pass things have come to, Margery thought, *when an Englishman is quoting our ancient enemy to further foment dissent.*

At Lammas time, she'd traveled to London to reunite with Serill at the Savoy, John of Gaunt's city within a city. Though her son had mentioned visiting his father, Margery had not queried further. She did not care about the doings of Lord Matthew Hart. 'Twas true she occasionally daydreamed that her former lover had fallen heels over head for someone capable of taming his demons, whose personality fit so perfectly that this female phantasm had made him whole in a way impossible for Margery.

Fine. A pox on you both.

Sometimes, when she watched a mutual acquaintance stride purposefully toward her, she mentally braced herself for the revelation that Matthew was engaged to a great lady of the north, or already wed.

So be it. If Matthew Hart were still in her life she'd probably have drowned herself in the Thames. Worse, she'd never have met Fulco, or if she had she'd have been too faithful to have allowed herself to explore the more erotic side of her nature...

St. Bartholomew's Fair was most important for the wool trade, but all manner of stalls had been set up, some right atop the priory graveyard, including a portable booth displaying wares from the Shop of the Unicorn. Such activities had put Margery in close contact with Master Goldsmith Nicholas Norlong, who was a dear man, though she was surprised when he echoed some of Thurold's grievances.

"We be overrun with foreigners," he groused. "And the Flemings be the worst, for they grow wealthy at our expense. They've exported so much gold and silver there's not enough money here at home to pay a decent wage. And then they plot to flood the kingdom with useless luxuries."

Norlong would wipe his brow and continue with far more animation than Margery would have imagined. "There be some law-abiding folk who've turned to thievery, preferring the threat of the rope to the reality of empty bellies. Dame Margery, these be perilous times for us all."

Unlike Thurold, whose demeanor suggested he could actually right the kingdom with the mere force of his passion, Norlong reminded Margery of a clucking hen, running hither, thither and yon while chasing her chicks.

Her time with Nicholas grew increasingly awkward, particularly after he, sweating and stumbling over his words, proposed marriage. Nicholas Norlong was solid, even-tempered and with a head for business that, despite his laments, had the Shop of the Unicorn's coffers so overflowing they could hire the very best apprentices and journeymen in both London and Canterbury. Marriage made a certain economic sense. It would also provide companionship for those times when she felt lonely. They could grow old and stout together and if 'twas not love it would be friendship. He would read to her in front of the hearth fire and seek her opinion on business matters, and hold her hand of a morning, perhaps, when they descended the stairs to the Shop.

Would that be so dreadful?

I could, couldn't I?

No.

I am a rich woman. I need not marry anyone.

She imagined bedding the Master Goldsmith when she'd so recently enjoyed darker charms. The very memory of Fulco made her tingle and close her eyes until the fire passed. Being with Nicholas Norlong, round as a keg of ale, or with any man, for that matter, would be sacrilege. She would not erase such magic and overlay it with fumblings that would be near as repulsive as those she'd endured with her dead husband, Simon Crull.

Margery suddenly recalled Robin, her pet bird, dead, lo, these many years, smashed beneath the heel of one of her husband's thugs. Occasionally, she had allowed Robin out of his cage to feed and stroke him. Yet no matter how she'd cared for Robin, he had still been imprisoned.

Why would I willingly return myself to a similar cage? Say to Nicholas Norlong—or any man, "Here, open the door and put me on my pretty perch and lock me in and no matter how I might beat my wings against the bars, release me at your pleasure?"

She'd declined Nicholas Norlong's offer kindly, she hoped, but unequivocally.

"Might I ask again?"

Mentally comparing him with Fulco who had just taken her, and Matthew, who had so artfully seduced her, she wanted to say, "Merely asking permission proves your cause is lost."

Instead, she'd smiled and patted his hand. "You are a good man," she'd said. Which he was. And which, judging from his crestfallen expression, he correctly interpreted as "Never!"

On the third day of St. Bartholomew's Fair, when Margery and Norlong were starting to dismantle their stalls and pack up their wares along with other merchants, Margery looked beyond the tent pole and swore she spotted Matthew Hart among a group of other lords, standing, ironically, near a smithy's forge and displays of swords and chain mail. Matthew's back was to her but there was no mistaking the set of his shoulders, the color of his hair, the way he carried himself. After knowing him for a lifetime, he would not change so much in a year as to fool her.

Panic rose inside. She turned quickly away. Without waiting for Nicholas Norlong, she left the fair and hurried back to the Shop of the Unicorn.

Vowing that tomorrow she would retreat once more to the safety of Canterbury.

CHAPTER 14

Lake Winandermere
Fall 1379-Spring 1380

*J*n the fall of 1379, Matthew returned to Lake Winandermere. He repaired his hut, hauled in supplies and settled in for the winter. His foray into the world had been unsuccessful. He'd held himself together—at least he hoped he had—and had diligently visited each holding, gone over accounts with every steward and ridden at least a portion of every field and inspected every manor house and castle and outbuildings.

But inside he felt as if his soul were being chipped away by some evil sculptor until little remained save bits and pieces.

He had no choice but to once again withdraw.

I will resolve this accidie, he told himself. *I will not leave until I do. Or freeze to death in the process.*

The turning point finally came on the heels of an unusually mild winter, in the spring of 1380. When the moon was full and the night was warm, without so much as the breath of a breeze. Matthew recalled a time when he had ridden out under such a moon with Meg and just as suddenly found himself viewing Harry's dead face. His temples suddenly throbbed and as usual when such images surfaced, he expected that his mind would cause them to break and shatter.

But not this time. He was sitting with his knees drawn up, gazing outward over the black hole that was Lake Winandermere when he glimpsed a movement out of the corner of his eye. Turning his head he saw it, standing no more than ten feet away. An enormous hart, with antlers near the span of a man. The hart studied Matthew through calm, liquid eyes. Matthew returned its gaze. He fancied he could hear its breathing, inhale its scent. Moonlight cast shadows upon its antlers, dappled its gleaming coat. 'Twas not lost upon Matthew that he was face to face with the family namesake. Or that the antlers it sported were out of season. He parted his lips as if to speak—to question it?— for the stag must be a sign, an omen, a message in animal form. However, breaking the silence seemed a profane act. So they stayed as they were. Then, the hart bobbed its great head, as if in acknowledgement, turned and glided back into the shadows.

With the appearance of the hart it was as if a boulder had been rolled away from Matthew's heart, and memories—important memories—returned. First gingerly, then with more insistence. Peculiar, that what he had most feared, being crushed by the remembrance of his many sins, did not occur.

While Matthew's mind was filled with treacherous quagmires that he had long skirted, he now approached them and gazed within for longer periods, retrieving past events no matter how painful.

He conjured his life—who he had been—knight, son, brother—and where he had been—from Poitiers to the day King Edward had been laid to rest.

He returned to 1370 and Limoges, to the hundreds of women and children clustered on the sandy stretch of ground beyond the city. He saw again the pure September sky against which billowed the black clouds of the burning city, the reds, browns, whites, greens, and yellows which comprised the townspeople's clothing. He forced himself to look into the faces of those he'd killed. He heard again their screams and pleas, the wailing from those whose time had not come. He smelled the conflagration, his victims' terror. He recalled the grinning slash left by his knife, the scarlet stain which sprang from gaping throats, the stain which, after his victims crumpled and fell, soaked into the gravel like a fevered rain. He looked again across Limoges' field, saw the bodies tossed like sacks of grain, and beyond, his prince, propped upon his litter.

Who was to blame for Limoges? Edward? Me? Perhaps knight-hood itself?

"Tout est perdu fors l'honneur." Repeatedly, Matthew whispered the phrase. Sometimes it seemed to course through his head in rhythm with his blood. "All is lost save honor." Honor? What did that word even mean? He understood it in terms of his own kind—to keep his word, to treat his peers with respect, loyalty, and the largesse that was so much a part of Romances and dialogues and training and tradition—but how true was any of that in reality? Was it as much a chimera as courtly love, which was only a thin veneer covering the brutal reality of relationships dating back to Adam and Eve?

Honor. Regardless of how Matthew defined it, he had lost it long before Limoges.

When I lied to Harry about Cumbria. I went back on my solemn word that he would inherit. After that, 'twas just a matter of degrees, and all the rationalization in the world could not excuse it.

Nay, he'd failed to live up to its meaning even before his brother's engagement. So long ago he could not remember the first time. Was it honorable to heedlessly fornicate with the object of his desire of the moment, to leave a scattering of bastards about the kingdom, to lie to himself and others, to be arrogant and proud, to invade a country for reasons they might all dress up in pretty terms but which in reality had been conducted for far more mercenary motives?

Honor... knighthood. Knighthood and honor.

Could they be uttered in the same breath? Or did knighthood have naught to do with such lofty sounding concepts? Could knighthood be honorable when it broke one of the most basic of commandments, "Thou shalt not kill"?

However, killing was the way of the world. It was not only neces-sary but often laudable. To protect one's family, one's land, one's kingdom, one's villeins, fellow warriors. The world was a brutal place and he and his kind provided the wall between the rest of humankind and chaos.

But what if you create that chaos? A voice whispered.

He remembered Margery's jeremiads, which he'd dismissed as the mindless parrotings of her radical stepbrother. But now they nagged at him, as did snatches of sermons from various hedge-priests; as did conversations among tippled yeomen in smoky taverns; as did the criticisms from John Wycliffe and the mad preacher, John Ball.

Are we protectors or oppressors? If knighthood is false, I am false.

Despite Limoges, he had always perceived himself as a protector— of the poor, of England. If he was wrong, then what exactly was he? Where did he fit in God's plan? A knight could not be a merchant any more than a merchant could wield a sword.

But that was no longer true, was it? The lines between the classes were becoming increasingly blurred with merchants strapping on armor and knights indulging in commerce with ink-stained fingers, entering figures into manorial accounts as diligently as any scrivener. Yeomen were as important in battle as Matthew and his kind; some boasted even more so for they could slay from afar. If a knight could not be described in the time-tested definition of the word, or if he was perceived, not as guardian but as merciless brute, what did that mean? That Matthew's goodness, his rightness of place, had been naught but a febrile concoction of his imagination?

If 'tis so, does that not mean that my life has no meaning that I can even fathom? No purpose? What will I do then? I cannot exchange lives with those who possess a nobler, purer truth. I do not even know who they might be or the nature of any such truth.

Honor... Knighthood. Knighthood and honor.

How to define it? He *had* been fair to his vassals. He'd made certain his estates were well run. He had not been an ideal courtier, but love was largely chaffering, wasn't it? What man actually treated a woman according to the bleatings of troubadours? Courtly love was just a silly game cooked up by Eleanor of Aquitaine to keep her wandering husband under her heel. It had not worked two hundred years ago and he didn't know of any man past the age of twelve who took its precepts seriously.

Matthew thought of Desire and their affair, which had most certainly not been the stuff of romance, but of lust and a certain madness. But he'd confessed those sins and been absolved years ago.

And Margery? He had loved her to the best of his ability. He had always been generous with material comforts; he'd not beaten her or been unfaithful or cruel. He'd ever treated her with courtesy. Well, there had been times, but what man could not be occasionally ill-tempered when dealing with the vagaries of womankind? And, despite the difference in their stations, he would have wed her. If he could actually define love—a love that was honorable in its intentions—that he had for Margery Watson.

Matthew's confusion lay elsewhere.

He rummaged through shared conversations with his father and his prince and his duke, with John Chandos and members of the war council—and so very often, conversations with his brother. He conjured up Harry's face as a child—and as a corpse lying under the moon. Desire had described her husband as being kind and gentle. Aye, that Harry had been. And flawed, as all men were flawed, though with a heart that, unlike Matthew's, was incapable of malice.

'Twas undeniable that Harry had been weak, often more dilettante than dedicated, careless and immature, at least until well into his marriage. After Limoges? During Auvergne? At those times hadn't he acquitted himself as well as most?

"*I would not have minded being a priest,*" Harry had said. Matt winced at the remembrance, at the many ways he must have misjudged his brother, thinking Harry to be just like him or *wanting* to be like him. He recalled conversations from the March to Oblivion, conversations Matthew had dismissed as delirium.

"*Elizabeth and I went on pilgrimage to Glastonbury every year you were away. While she would hover about Arthur and Guinevere's tombs, I would climb the tor in the moonlight and I swear I could hear Arthur and all his knights whispering to me there...*

"*My favorite place was St. Michael's Mount. Cut off from Pensans and the entire world, so it seemed, and I would spend weeks there in the chapel atop the island, with the wind forever howling, and me sprawled upon paving stones icier than the grave, and I would have such visions..."*

When Matthew had thought to halt Harry's fantasies with sharp questioning, his brother had merely smiled that smile that was like a grimace upon his wasted face. *"'Twas not just gambling debts you had to pay upon your return from Bordeaux. I gave so many bequests... Pray to the saints they've not been wasted..."*

Harry the Pious. Not so much a condemnation from their father but an accurate appraisal?

Matthew had been so certain of himself and those around him when he now wondered whether he'd understood them at all. And now it was too late. He may have laid Harry's body to rest but not the memories, the questions, the regrets.

For weeks, Matthew puzzled over these and other related matters. As if sentences put to parchment, he withdrew them and examined them in the waning hours of the night, when he was fishing, or just sitting, staring across the waters.

Finally... Matthew made his peace. He decided that despite what he had personally done, the ideal of knighthood remained noble, remained honorable in the purest sense of the word—and that was all that mattered. Knighthood was as perfect as the grail itself. 'Twas in the quest for the grail that he, and others, failed.

There would always be naysayers, those who hated just to hate and criticized just to criticize, but those voices did not speak truth, at least about knighthood. And he had been a good knight. Not the stuff of Arthur and legend—and no such knights had whispered to him atop Glastonbury Tor or anywhere else—but Matthew had been as dedicated as most of his contemporaries. He'd done as he'd been told. He'd been brave; a worthy opponent in every campaign. He'd brought his brother, at least, out of Auvergne's mountains. He'd never abandoned Harry; he'd sacrificed himself so that his brother could survive another day, so that he might, God willing, indeed return to his wife and child. His father had loved him; his father had told him he would have done as Matt had at Limoges. Matthew had never betrayed his king or his duke and even with Prince Edward he'd served him to the end in spirit if not in body. Matthew had loved Edward of Woodstock as well as he could while honoring his own conscience.

And so it came down to this... after all those months, after all this introspection, Matthew could congratulate himself, finally. At least about one thing.

I have endured.

And that, he now believed, was enough.

CHAPTER 15

April, 1380, The Cherry Fair

*M*aria Rendell knew that this Cherry Fair would be her last. She had entered the world with the new century and she would exit this year. In her eighty years she'd witnessed four kings, insurrections, wars, floods, droughts, prosperities. The rise and fall of nations like the rise and fall of tides, like the rise and fall of her own particular lifetime. When she looked back, all of it had a rhythm, even though she'd been unable to discern such at the time. Now it seemed clear enough. But while the rhythm of kingdoms would continue its unraveling, hers had come to an end.

She knew the date of her death as certainly as she knew the rising and setting of the sun, the waxing and waning of the moon, the seasons one easing into the other. A part of her had always known, that this would be her year and the cherry orchard her death bed. As she'd known that her eyes were blue or that she had arms and legs—just another fact to be taken for granted. But how quickly the decades had passed! And over the past few years that knowing had gone from a prickling to a constant presence. Until now, if she'd been a mage rather than mortal woman, perhaps she'd have been able to turn to view Death, seated beside her. And say, "Welcome, old friend. 'Tis glad I am to finally meet you."

A lifetime trickling down to a handful of hours. She reminded herself that she must cherish every moment. To especially enjoy the cherry blossoms, which surely were the largest she'd ever seen, with the white so dazzling they might have been fashioned from angels' feathers. And, as if sharing a private message, a handful of trees— surely, those that had been behind her husband the night of their midnight meeting when he'd returned from the Scottish campaign— were arrayed in the deepest pink, the color of universal love.

Today, as always, she sat at the dais. Surrounded as she was by family, she found herself more than content. *I would like to know,* she thought, while gazing into the faces of her grandchildren and great- grandchildren, *how well you'll fare in life. I would like to see you grown.* Better not to focus on what she was leaving behind, but on her forthcoming reunion with all those she'd loved.

Maria knew what the priests said, that hell, or at the very least purgatory, most likely awaited her, as it did them all, so she would only meet with those who'd not been granted the grace to enter heaven.

I don't believe a word of it.

Clerics couldn't have it both ways, though they always tried. You can pray, purchase indulgences and faithfully execute your penances, wiping out your sins—and yet your first way station on crossing over would be purgatory? If you were lucky. So what purpose all the prayers, penances, payments of indulgences, month minds and endow- ments? The church could either effectively keep Satan from claiming you or it couldn't.

For Maria, the priests' personal reign of terror had ended some fifty years past, after her collapse before Thomas Becket's tomb. That and other related events had started her on a journey that ended here. With little concern for the state of her immortal soul and a firm belief that love was the one thing that remained eternal. And would encompass her upon her crossing—human love and the love of her Creator.

Maria's gaze swept the tables flanking both sides of the dais. She recognized many of the guests, their faces and forms gradually ravaged by time. As were hers. Recently, she'd been re-reading *Ecclesiastes* and ruminating on the preacher's words: 'One generation passeth away, and another generation cometh: but the earth abideth forever.'

Indeed it does. She inhaled deeply of the cherry blossoms. *In one form or another all this will endure long after mankind is not even a memory.*

"Are you feeling well, Maman?" Hugh Rendell bent over to kiss her cheek. All of her four children were in attendance and all had repeatedly asked her some form of the question.

She looked into Hugh's dear face—Hugh named in memory of her long-dead father—and nodded. "Do I look ill?"

Hugh smiled. "Never, Maman. You just seem... distant."

She patted his hand. "I feel fine. Better than I have in years."

Still she knew it was time. Verses from *Ecclesiastes* tugged at her thoughts like a child tugging her skirts, even as she greeted friends, gathered a great-grandchild into her lap and kissed his plump cheeks, or when she agreed that yes, this year's blossoms were indeed the most beautiful she'd ever seen.

"To every thing there is a season... A time to be born, a time to die... and a time to every purpose under the heaven."

Tomorrow evening she would have her bedding brought to the orchard where she would wait. Like a rendezvous with a lover or simply with a beloved. She sensed the dead drawing near—her parents, her twin, even grandparents she'd never met and the babe she'd lost. Aunts and uncles and friends, of course. But most of all she felt the presence of the men she'd loved. As if, should she turn her head, she might see Richard leaning against the trunk of a tree, framed by the cherry blossoms, shimmering the way his golden hair used to shimmer, smiling at her. Or her husband, his face exquisitely flawless, moving at the edge of the guests, slowly, deliberately making his way to come stand beside her.

He would bow and take her hand in his and then... There would be Richard, on the opposite side, and they three would walk away together, as they had so many years ago.

But they'd never walked together with her between them. There had never been that easiness in actuality for hadn't she ever been the serpent in the garden?

How young I was, how heedless, how selfish. And yet she'd long ago forgiven her former self, for along with all the flaws, she'd possessed the surety that love was enough, that if she was willing to sacrifice everything she would be rewarded with what she most craved. A transcendent love, a passion that rivalled anything in the Romances. Choosing to disregard the *denouements* of those tales, which seldom ended well.

Ah, the arrogance of youth. It was naïve, charming—and so necessary. *For if we ever acted as we do with age, kingdoms would not be built, loves would not be won and lost, children created, continents explored, necessities invented, wrongs righted. We would all be too lost in our moth-eaten maunderings to accomplish anything.*

"A time to love, and a time to hate... A time to plant, and a time to pluck up that which is planted... A time to kill, and a time to heal..."

I am not sorry, Maria thought, *for* anything.

That was the problem priests had with her, that she would never agree that loving two men was mortal sin. Besides, they three had paid the price for their actions, hadn't they? No need for penance when their choices, spun to their final conclusion, had provided consequence enough.

Maria could see them now, Richard and Phillip, their heads close together as they sketched out hasty wedding plans after her and Phillip's frantic flight to Rockingham Castle; Richard and Phillip, swords flashing, fighting almost to the death near the pharos beyond Dover Castle; Richard, England's mightiest earl, kneeling before Phillip, a mere baron, in the bailey at Fordwich Castle, seeking his vassal's forgiveness for having lain with his wife...

Canis shifted beneath her slippered feet, where she'd rested them upon his ribs. Her private footstool. Maria plucked a piece of chicken from her blawmanger and slipped it to her pet under the tablecloth. Jongleurs wandered among the guests, strumming their lutes, singing their songs; others juggled and performed the usual acrobatic tricks. Earlier she'd taken her great-grandchildren to watch a dancing bear. Hadn't there been such a bear nearby when she'd begged Phillip to marry her? For, when in the presence of this gallant knight who minstrels had lauded for his heroic efforts at the Battle of Bannockburn, how could she endure marriage to a man forty years her senior?

A man two decades younger than I am now.

Maria spotted her granddaughter in conversation with her father and beckoned Margery Watson to her side.

"Grandmere." Margery greeted her with a small curtsy. Maria raised her hand in a halting motion. "Do not ask about my health," she said imperiously.

She patted the bench next to her chair and motioned for Margery to sit. Once she was settled, Maria asked, "How fares your knight?"

Margery jerked back as if she'd been slapped. What a peculiar question! Her grandmother knew well enough that she and Matthew Hart had been parted nearly two years. Was her memory slipping? It could happen that quickly with the elderly. One moment they spoke in coherent sentences and the next they were jabbering like monkeys.

Margery reached for a goblet of cherry wine and raised it to her lips. She strove to be respectful but could not keep the edge from her voice. "You know I've not seen Lord Hart."

"You will." Maria gazed past the revelers into the distance where the cherry trees butted Fordwich Castle's curtain in a frothy wave. "I've been thinking about him. And others," she added vaguely.

Margery wanted to retort, "Well, I've not, not at all," but she feared her grandmother, like John Ball, could see things others could not.

"The sun and the moon," Maria said softly.

A chill rippled the length of Margery's body, as if administering a warning. She peered more closely at her grandmother. Maria didn't really appear any different. Her white hair was braided neatly behind her and her expression was calm. She wasn't drooling. She was dressed appropriately. She hadn't been wandering about with her slippers atop her head and clad in a floor rush. So what was happening?

Maria fixed her pale eyes upon her, eyes that had once been as blue as the summer sky.

And Margery knew.

~

ALL THE TABLES had been broken down, the white linen cloths bundled and carried to castle laundresses; trash collected; the paths created by hundreds of feet carefully raked to blend in with the untouched meadow grass; brown patches reseeded. Fordwich Castle was nearly empty of its guests, as was nearby Chilham Castle and surrounding inns, hostels and religious houses.

At dusk, Maria ordered her servants to take her mattresses and bedding into the orchard in a tradition that had begun following Phillip's death. Sometimes, when the weather warranted, she would sleep inside a tent, but tonight she knew that would be unnecessary.

Should I have told my children the secret? she wondered, as her maids led her to her destination. *That the orchard is a magical place, that during the fair it provides an opening between this world and the next, the way it is on Midsummer's and All Hallow's Eves?* (Maybe the magic was only there for her. Or maybe 'twas available year round to everyone. If one only decided to sleep there).

Canis bumped his muzzle against her hand. Did he sense her time was nigh? Animals possessed that power. But so did people. God often saw fit to warn His children so they might get their affairs and their souls in order. It was so with her. It had been so with the Black Prince, who had chosen to die on his favorite feast day, Trinity Sunday. As it had been with Richard and Phillip.

How to explain? Was it simply a subtle shift in perception, or in the nature of the body's humors? Maria had grown used to aging's aches and pains, but might not there be something different occurring in her body? Wasn't there an unusual tightening around her heart? And she couldn't remember previously experiencing double vision, at least when unaccompanied by a fever or other illness. Most markedly, she was struggling to stay in the present. She found herself wavering back and forth in time and had to remind herself, *My feet are here upon this carpet... I am in my room... at the dais... in the chapel... in the orchard.*

Three of Maria's four children still remained at Fordwich so she'd managed a private word with each before retreating to the orchard. She'd tried to say something special without arousing suspicion or alarm. Simply drop a comment into conversation so later they would remember and remark upon it.

"What a wonderful grandmother you've proven yourself to be, Blanche. As you were a mother."

"Hugh, you are the kindest man I've ever known."

Henrietta, who was, in Maria's mind, far too much like her name-sake, Maria's mother, to allow for the easiest of relationships: "Have I yet thanked you for the yearly pilgrimages you take on behalf of my soul?" Hoping it did not emerge as a criticism.

Thomas had already left, but Thomas out of all of them, would know...

Maria dismissed her maids after they helped her into her makeshift bed. She was immediately folded into the soft pile of mattresses, as if she were a child rather than full grown. Ever watchful, Canis stretched beside her. Periodically, he would raise his head to study her, or nuzzle her hand, as if seeking reassurance.

Overhead the stars flared like embers; the surrounding air seemed unnaturally still without even the hint of a breeze or stirring of nocturnal creatures.

Maria remembered another night when she'd been awakened from a fitful sleep by her husband's squire and ordered to meet Phillip here. Even while racing barefoot across the wet meadow grass, she'd fervently thanked God for she'd long feared Phillip dead.

It had been in the fall of the year. Or had it been closer to winter? Whenever, a storm had recently passed and as she ran among the fallen leaves and rotting cherries, thunder yet grumbled and lightning flashed in the distance.

It had been so very dark, like looking down a bottomless well. The rush light she carried had been a puny thing—though it had been bright enough to illumine Phillip's ravaged face when he'd drawn back the hood of his mantle. As if such a thing would matter!

And what a surprise, when it had been Phillip, her wandering husband, so chary with his declarations of love, rather than Richard, who had ultimately proven himself faithful. How Richard had professed his adoration, how he'd showered her with tokens of his affection, how passionate he'd been, risking all to have her at his side. She'd believed that her lover, out of everyone, would prove her constant.

How wrong I was.

It had not been death or another woman or even his brother the king's deposition and murder that had proven the earl false. It had been their Savior, Jesus Christ. When Richard had been dragged from her he'd been the most ardent of lovers, only to return a holy man.

Because you forsook me for God, was that supposed to make your betrayal more acceptable? To erase all the pretty words, the lovemaking, our time together with a shrug of your shoulders an "You see, I had a vision! You do understand, don't you?"

Maria was surprised that, after all these years, Richard's perfidy still rankled. 'Twas not a saint she'd needed, but a man of flesh and blood.

Which God gave me, didn't He, with Phillip's return?

Maria felt as if a hand were squeezing her heart. She managed to inhale and monitored her breathing, careful not to worsen a pain that remained more a nuisance than actual discomfort.

I've never forgiven you for forsaking me, she thought, and was taken aback at the revelation. All these years she'd told herself otherwise, for how could she be jealous of God? But there it was. And yet, Richard's desertion—now she would call it that—had released her to freely love her husband. Otherwise, she might have been forever torn between them, never to have experienced those golden years with Phillip.

I do forgive you, my love.

The stars, the night around her seemed to flicker. To dance. She saw Richard and Phillip, faint, pulsing in and out, as if playing hide and seek from her. Followed by her beaming twin and her parents... and others she'd treasured, who had gone before.

"Oh," she whispered or thought she did. For they seemed to be surrounding her, all looking so young and lovely. And so very happy— even her mother, who'd never smiled so sweetly in real life.

The orchard appeared to glow, as if illumined by a sea or charcoal braziers or candles. Around her a silence, as if even nature was holding its breath in anticipation.

Canis's ears pricked forward and he emitted a low whine.

Maria noticed her hands upon the counterpane. They were gnarled, the fingers and joints thickened, the little finger on her right hand crooked from an old injury. Ah, age. First, leveler; then destroyer. Her body had served her well but it had outlived its usefulness.

I'm done with this shell, she thought. *I am ready to be rid of this cage.*

'A time to weep, and a time to laugh; a time to mourn, and a time to dance;'

Maria closed her eyes. She was becoming disoriented. She had to think where she was.

I have not danced in a very long time.

Her limbs had grown heavy. She should see if she could lift them but it was too much trouble. With great effort she managed to open her eyes.

Where am I? Oh, aye, in my chamber.

No, that wasn't right. In the apartment on London bridge, awaiting Richard's arrival. Wasn't he angry at his brother the king?

But Edward II is dead. All our Edwards are dead...

Isn't it night? But 'tis so bright. And how can mere humans look so radiant, as if they are not flesh and blood but angels?

Maria watched them approach, watched as one separated from the others to approach. She remembered that walk, but it wasn't quite the same; she couldn't quite place the difference.

Then he was at her side.

How odd. So very far away, she heard a dog howling. But it was so faint, like the hum of an insect...

Maria gazed up at him. His face and form were so wondrously brilliant her eyes should be dazzled, but the light was somehow soothing.

He reached out his hand, as if asking her to accompany him in a roundel.

"My lord," she whispered. "I am so happy to see you." She paused to listen, rejoicing in that voice she'd so missed all these many years. "Aye, it has been such a very, very long time."

CHAPTER 16

Fordwich, July 1380

Margery Watson leaned out her bedroom window and waved to Oliver of Tutbury as he paused on the cottage step to gaze up at her.

"*Bon soir, ma belle*," Oliver called before turning to leave. "Sleep well and dream of me."

Margery knew the young knight was disappointed to receive nothing more than a kiss and perfunctory parting embrace. Sometimes she wondered whether all her inner heat had burned out with the departure of Fulco, for she'd not been stirred by any man, not even on this particular summer's night so ripe with sweet promise. Certainly not with Oliver Tutbury. Such a pretty boy he was, hardly a man at all. Since their meeting at this year's Cherry Fair, he'd embarked on something of a courtship, for marriage to a wealthy widow—with noble blood, no less—was an acceptable match for a second son. So far Margery had allowed him to sit at her feet and woo her with the usual love songs. In a moment of weakness, she'd even removed his cap and buried her fingers in his dark hair, though it had been another black-haired man she'd been imagining.

Remaining at the window, Margery breathed in the lush air, the fragrance from the flowers below. Only the chirruping of insects and trill of a nightingale stirred the silence. A full moon, warm as amber, inched its way across the liquid blackness of a sky devoid of stars. Canterbury's lights glowed on the horizon; the narrow roadway spun in a dark ribbon past her cottage. Margery could see, in all its glory, the copse where she and Fulco had lain together. She shivered in remembrance, as she had shivered when he'd touched her. Madness. But what sweet madness! They'd been playing with fire in every sense, and she did not regret it, not a minute. Oliver of Tutbury, any man—save one and she didn't want to think about *him*—was so anemic in comparison. Why even bother?

Since Cicily had departed for London to care for an ailing grandchild, the cottage was quiet. Margery stepped away from the window to a small chest beside her bed. Absently, she loosed the pins from her hair, shook it free and picked up her comb, ignoring the missive next to it.

She thought of her grandmother, resting beside her husband within the Church of St. Mary the Virgin, and wished she could seek Maria's wise counsel.

"I do miss you, Grandmere," Margery whispered, though she chastised herself for her selfishness. For when Maria had been discovered with her faithful Canis stretched out stiff beside her, her maids had enthusiastically described their lady's expression as "blissful." Soon after, the usual talk of sainthood and miracles had circulated. But when Margery imagined her grandmother, she was strolling in some rather foggy version of paradise, arm in arm with her sun and her moon.

Happy and not to be bothered.

Replacing her comb on the chest, Margery picked up the nearby letter. A retainer wearing the Hart livery had delivered it yestermorn. The message had been direct: Matthew Hart had returned from Cumbria and wished to see her.

A pox on you, my fine lord, she'd thought after reading it once, then twice, and yet a third time. She'd picked her way through its contents, studying it as intently as she would her star chart. As if its message would reveal a deeper truth with as much accuracy as the heavens revealed one's fate.

She ran a finger over the seal. If only that simple act could provide some clue beyond its writer's terseness, when all it did was cause her heart to flutter like a captured bird's.

What were you doing in Cumbria, withdrawing from your duties to your liege lord and your kingdom? Brooding, drinking, wenching, throwing yourself into the role of overlord, whatever that means in that uncivilized place?

She remembered what Matthew's sister had said about her brother being "alone." Had he become a hermit? Or a ferryman, for Matthew often talked about that great lake, Windy something. She imagined him ferrying travelers across a vast expanse of choppy waters, though that did not seem an occupation that would interest the man she knew. Or thought she knew.

Regardless, whatever Matthew Hart had been doing, he'd had no problem wiping her out of his thoughts as easily as chalk from a writing slate. Not a word in two years. It was true they'd officially ended their relationship, but she was still the mother of his son, still his long-time leman. He might have shown better manners.

And now here he was, as if he had a right. How dare he think he could just pop his head out like a mole from its burrow and expect her to clap her hands in joy.

When what I'd like to do is chop your head off with a garden hoe.

Margery picked up a small wooden robin beside the letter and the comb. Following his return from his first campaign, on the heels of Edward the Black Prince's glorious victory at Poitiers, Matthew had given her the bird. She'd tucked it away so long ago she'd had to hunt to find it. Yet hunt she had and here it was.

The robin's once bright breast, with the chipping away of paint, had been reduced to a scarlet prick. She ran her thumb over its smooth surface, which felt as warm as if it were indeed alive. She'd once considered the trinket her talisman but what had it protected her from? Not heartache and tears, surely.

Tomorrow I'll bury it in my garden or throw it in the Stour.

Closing her eyes, Margery pictured Matthew as he'd been when he'd presented his gift. So young, so virile, so over-brimming with confidence.

How impossibly innocent we were...

Margery's thoughts drifted back, from the first time she'd glimpsed him in the fens, ordering her to "Come out," to their first kiss; their sweet days and nights together when each was enough for the other; their shared creation of Serill; Matthew's physical strength, the feeling of safety she'd always experienced in his presence. That Matthew Hart fitted himself perfectly into every part of her soul.

But the other Matthew? She'd not forgotten his blindness to the faults of his kind or his black moods, which had sucked her down along with him. Matthew Hart meant Limoges and war and violence and death. Sometimes a lifetime of experiences meant that you must drive a stake in a relationship the way you would the heart of a heretic before burying him at a crossroads. So that he could never roam again to terrorize and torment and destroy...

Enough.

Thinking to close the shutters, Margery returned to the window. While leaning out to grasp the latch, she spotted a man on horseback headed in her direction along the otherwise deserted road.

Odd, at this hour. Perhaps it was Bobby Carter returning from the George and Dragon. But he would be afoot. Oliver? He seemed too indolent a suitor to decide to press his case so quickly after she'd rebuffed him. Perhaps a lone priest or someone headed to Fordwich Castle? But few traveled alone after dark.

Oh, well.

Margery closed the shutter and sank down upon her bed. In the flickering candle flame, the hart's seal glistened like a splotch of blood against the parchment.

She rested her head in her hands.

How dare you think to upend my life again?

After a few restless minutes, Margery departed her bedroom and descended the stairs, her bare feet slapping softly on the wooden boards, her unbound hair brushing against the back of her chemise. Sometimes when she couldn't sleep, when she felt an impatience with what increasingly seemed like an impossibly well-ordered life, she would sit on her rough wooden bench among her flowers until the moment passed.

After exiting the cottage, she opened the gate leading to the backside and eased onto the crude bench. She inhaled deeply of the perfumed air, imagined it settling upon her like a lover. Lovey, her cantankerous gander, her chickens, her bees in their skep, were all settled in for the night. The area was blessedly still.

Why did you have to write? Why could you not have let things be?

The clopping of horse's hooves grew louder. Soon the stranger would pass on his way... where? It did not matter. She could not see him nor he her. She was safe and protected, here in the dark.

The clopping ceased. She heard the creak of leather as the rider dismounted in front of her cottage door.

It must be Oliver Tutbury.

Annoyed, she rose and moved toward the front of the cottage. The candle's glow leaking from between the bedroom shutters cast a few narrow bars upon the grass, but it was easy enough to remain hidden. She would be able to see the interloper without being seen. She'd not answer the door, and in a future meeting, if Tutbury mentioned his return, she would chastise him for his disrespect. "I was asleep," she'd say. "I did not hear you."

Margery peeked around the corner, expecting to see the young knight.

"By the rood!" she breathed. "What is he doing here?"

For she'd recognize Matthew Hart anywhere, no matter how uncertain the light. He'd said nothing in his letter of paying a call in the dead of night.

She found herself shaking, though she was sure it was not with excitement.

Oh! This would not do. She cast about for a place to hide. If she stayed in the shadows he would eventually go away.

Matthew approached the door, which she noticed with sinking heart, had been left open.

"Meg?" he called, stepping into the doorway.

There was no getting around it. She'd just have to face the unpleasantness.

She addressed him from the shadows. "Go away! I do not wish to see you."

He spun around in surprise, then stepped in her direction, pausing after opening the side gate until his eyes adjusted. Margery was grateful that darkness would hide her expression, which she was certain registered nothing save disdain. She could see him well enough in the moonlight, however, and with that one swift appraising glance she noted that he was not the same troubled man who had fled London, more's the pity.

Matthew approached her. Margery stayed in shadow.

"Do not," she said. He stopped, though too close for her liking. Raising her chin, she stepped back. "You are not welcome here."

"I realize the hour is late, but you knew I would not forever stay away. I have been impatient—"

"It does not matter the hour, whether 'tis midnight or noon. The point is you are *never* welcome in my cottage or in my life, so off with you."

Matthew seemed more amused than upset. "I've long anticipated our reunion; I'd hoped for something more pleasant."

She snorted. "What reunion? 'Tis not as if you'd gone off to battle and are coming home to your lover. Which I am no longer."

"Might we discuss this inside? I would not have everyone from here to Canterbury eavesdropping on our business."

"If you think to pretend that these past two years did not occur, that you can just barge back into my life you are truly mistaken."

He reached out as if to draw her toward the front door. "Meg—"

Margery doubled her fist and hit him in his jaw with all her strength. Caught off guard, Matthew reeled back.

Margery scurried past him, thinking to slam the door and bar it against him.

He caught her arm and spun her to face him.

"You have a strong hand, Meg," he said, rubbing his jaw. "You'd make a passable fighter."

"Be gone or I'll do it again."

"I guess I do not have to question whether you are angry with me..."

"I took a lover," she said breathlessly. "And I'm not sorry."

How childish she sounded, like a child tattling on a playmate. But there it was. No man would want his property despoiled by another. *Be shocked and horrified and be gone.*

Matthew raised an eyebrow. He did not speak for a long time, as if measuring his response. "You need not confess," he said finally.

"I'm not confessing," she said. "I'm... bragging." She suppressed the urge to giggle. This was all too preposterous.

Matthew stepped past her, into the cottage and looked around. "Where is he, your lover? Will I have to fight him for you? I will, you know."

"Do not mock me," she said. "And I did not give you permission to enter my home."

"I apologize for my bad manners."

Matthew's gaze held hers before travelling slowly up and down her body. She was aware of the thinness of her chemise but would allow herself no show of discomfort.

"You are overbold, sirrah."

What did she read in his expression? Desire, or something else? A simple knowing? *"Ah, yes, now I remember. This is what you look like. This is what I've come to claim."*

When he did not respond, she appraised him in kind—or at least she hoped she did—as impersonally as if she might be pondering different styles of fabric. *Which one should I choose? Which is the most practical? Which is the most finely worked? Which will feel most comfortable next to my body?*

"I have to admit you are looking well," she said reluctantly. "The haunted look has left your eyes."

She would give him that much. He appeared rested and fit. But there was something else, something indefinable in his demeanor that bespoke a deeper change. She felt it once again, that indefinable energy that had drawn her to him a lifetime ago.

"I left some ghosts in Cumbria."

"Well, you should have left yourself there, as well," she said tartly. She would not allow herself to soften toward him, even in the slightest.

Matthew slid his arms around her waist and pulled her to him. His lips met hers and he kissed her deeply, possessively. As if he had a right! Despite herself, Margery felt herself yielding and knew what she must do...

She raised a clenched fist but before she could hit him again, Matthew caught her wrist.

"Really, Meg, is that any way to welcome me home?"

FOR THE NEXT three days Margery went to her goldsmithing shop and followed her usual routine, keeping an eye on the new apprentices and waiting on customers. Pilgrims comprised a large part of Aurum's business, purchasing paternosters and other religious-themed objects. A favorite was a pilgrim's badge, constructed in gold or silver, depicting the head of Thomas Becket, complete with miter, and framed by four swords representing the four knights who'd murdered him. The badges were popular among the wealthier who shunned the base metal trinkets sold in stalls surrounding cathedral precincts. Ordinarily Margery felt a quiet pride when displaying the finely worked badges, for she'd personally designed the mold.

But not now.

Each time someone approached or she emerged from the shop's interior she expected to see Matthew Hart standing there. Upon their parting, soon after that stolen kiss, he'd promised he'd be back.

But when?

So eager he'd seemed that Margery had felt a certain smugness. Now she would be in command; now she would be dismissive. Now she would make him apologize for all the times he'd hurt her and still she'd not relent.

I will tell him, "I am done with you," and he will be so devastated...
Where was he?

Will, the tavern keeper from the Chequer of the Hope, visited as usual. A pleasant enough fellow, who, like many others enjoyed grousing about the state of the kingdom. Usually, Margery didn't mind. He sounded like Thurold, who was off with John Ball somewhere, and the laments were so familiar she could recite them herself near word for word. But today Will's voice grated.

"John of Gaunt is king in all but name... the good and virtuous have been humbled allowing vice to stalk the land... Our young king must have a care to his counselors, who have not his best wishes at heart... greedy church... oppressive taxes..."

But then Ernald, a quietly reliable apprentice who kept to his tasks and never mentioned politics, looked up from his delicate tap-tapping of a pendant on a small anvil and said, "There will be a reckoning."

He spoke so fiercely and unexpectedly that Margery was snapped out of her lassitude. She'd become inured to such threats for that's all they were. And, since her acceptance into the Rendell household, she'd reconciled the different blood flowing through her, hadn't she? That ancient conflict surrounding her birth was no longer an issue.

But Ernald's use of a "reckoning" somehow gave his words an apocalyptic quality, as if mouthed by an Old Testament prophet rather than a skinny twenty-something with a scraggly beard and stained teeth.

Margery felt as if a cloud had descended above High Street, casting the narrow lane in darkness, as if the bustling crowds possessed a sinister air, as if her hard-fought acceptance of her identity, her heredity, might be an illusion. She'd become comfortable in her position as a shopkeeper, as well as the recognized by-blow of a great lord. Furthermore, her tryst with Fulco had somehow married those two sides of her heredity.

Or so she'd assumed, looking back on it, now that she was no longer certain.

With Matthew's return, old doubts, insecurities and conflicts were once more pressing to the fore.

How can this be? I resolved all that.

But mayhap she hadn't. Mayhap she'd merely packed everything away the way she did out-of-season clothing.

And now the season was changing...

But Matthew had not returned, which caused further puzzlement. Had he been toying with her once again, thinking that after he stirred her emotions, he could disappear for another two years? She felt like kicking something in frustration and had to refrain from snapping at her fellows during the day or her maid, who had returned from London, at night.

When she tossed upon her bed, Cicily, who slept on a pallet tucked in the alcove, would call, "Be ye sick? Have ye a fever? Are ye in need of a sleeping potion?"

If only Margery could cease the infernal racing of her mind. She wished she'd taken Fulco the Smithy's hand when he'd offered and swung up beside him on his forge wagon. They would have travelled to parts unknown where Matthew Hart would never find her. She would prefer a lifetime of sleeping under a wagon to this torment.

It was all too confusing to contemplate.

Yet contemplate it she did.

As a widow I am allowed a blessed measure of freedom. But what does "freedom" even mean? What do I really seek? Not to be a man's property? To be shed of emotional entanglements? To be able to walk through life without loving too much or hurting too deeply or being too disappointed when my husband or paramour degenerates into my captor, or becomes cruel or indifferent or unfaithful?

On this third night following their meeting, Margery crossed once again to the window, which she'd left unshuttered. No rider darkened the road.

I do not even know how to define love, she thought. She examined the concept as if it were a multi-faceted jewel or mayhap a curious creature that had crawled out from the muck to be poked and prodded and explored. She re-examined her and Matthew's years together, particularly those last miserable days. Everything following Limoges had been one long descent into darkness. And after the death of their king Edward, the final plunge into a waking nightmare.

I cannot go back there. When their relationship had been crushed amidst the weight of Matthew's melancholia. Their lives had been intricately woven together for so very long, but if viewed objectively, the warped and twisted threads far outnumbered the perfect.

Cicily stirred on her pallet and shifted, causing the straw to rustle.

"Oh, Grandmere," Margery whispered. She'd taken to addressing her grandmother rather than a bevy of the usual saints. "What should I do?"

~

THE NEXT EVEN, when she returned from Aurum, Matthew's stallion was tied in front of her cottage.

Margery hesitated. So now here it was. "Give me strength," she prayed to all and sundry.

Matthew opened the garden gate, careful to make certain that Margery's gander, Lovey, did not slip free, and met her at the front door. Lovey protested with a great squawk and spreading of his wings before strutting back to a far corner of the backside.

"I was beginning to think I dreamed you," Margery said, hoping that her frown belied the frantic pattering of her heart.

"I wanted to give you time to think. And for my jaw to heal."

Margery opened the cottage door and reluctantly gestured for him to enter. In passing, Matthew's arm brushed hers. Cicily had been arranging bread, cheese, and wine on a table near the hearth, but when they entered, she greeted him with a curtsy before discreetly withdrawing.

"Might I serve you something?" Margery maneuvered away from Matthew toward the table. "Wine?"

"Aye."

She poured from a jug into a goblet, pleased that her hands remained steady. When she extended the goblet their fingers brushed; instinctively she drew back.

Matthew gazed deeply into her eyes. She was first to look away.

He laughed. "Am I going to have to woo you, pluck you a tune on my lute? Will you reduce me to that?"

"I've heard you sing. And your musical abilities are even worse." From outside, Lovey squawked in protest of something. "Rather like my gander."

"I would be insulted if you did not speak true." He drank deeply. "So let us dispense with the music and get to the heart of it."

The window shutters were open and the kitchen-living area was pleasantly cool. Cicily had arranged flower bouquets on the table and various chests while Margery had woven hawthorn boughs above the door, creating a pleasant mingling of fragrances.

"Two years is a very long time," Margery said. She gazed into that face that had once been so dear and remained so very familiar. And which no longer belonged to her.

"We've been parted longer."

"That we have," she agreed.

More than six years when she'd been married to Simon Crull and Matthew had been in Bordeaux with his mistress. Many months during campaigns. But their last parting had been different. They'd been married in all but name and both had agreed their relationship must end. It wasn't that their love had died exactly. There had been no looks or words that conveyed the message, "I do not love you enough," "I do not love you at all," and "I am so sorry I no longer care."

She worried the hem of her sleeve, not meeting his gaze. The room, which was large enough under other circumstances, seemed uncomfortably close. "Mayhap a love that simply crumbles away is less sad than a love whose heart remains beating but because of events and tragedies and challenges has been irretrievably damaged."

"Is that how you view us? For I do not." Matthew took a step forward as if to embrace her, but he merely crossed to the dining table to place his empty goblet beside the evening repast. Then he returned to her side. Margery retreated to the window overlooking the road, darkening with evening's shadow. Carts rumbled past, loaded with barrels, probably the last leavings from Fordwich's port. A stray cat, tail twitching, crossed behind the carts to disappear beneath a hedgerow.

How to say what was in her heart, if she even knew what resided there. "Sometimes the very things that draw people together are the things that ultimately drive us apart. Everything that we shared... the differences in our stations. So much always seemed to come between us."

Matthew came up behind her. If she leaned back, she would graze his chest. She fancied she could feel the heat radiating from his body. *Do not touch me. Do not.*

"We can conjure a thousand reasons to remain separate and think ourselves into a headache," Matthew said. "I'd rather make it very simple."

"You never were one for complications."

"I've had two years to ponder my troubles.'Twas painful but I faced down my demons and I am no longer tormented."

She turned to face him, her gaze lingering on his face. "I can see that."

His every movement, word, gesture, the very look of him told her so. What changes had marked his absence she could not say, but the signs were unmistakable.

"And now I am here to claim what is mine. You are mine. You always have been. As I am yours. We can fight it all we please or we can accept it and step forward together."

"How cocksure you are, my lord." A flicker of anger arose and she felt her cheeks flush. "I think I'd rather not be claimed by anyone."

He smiled. "You've long known I am not nimble with words. I did not mean to offend. I am simply stating fact, though mayhap inelegantly."

Voices drifted from the open window—Clarice conversing with Bobby Carter, snatches from a hymn, *'In dulci jubilo, Nun singet und seid froh...'* No doubt from pilgrims seeking shelter beyond Canterbury, which would be emptied of rooms. Soon church bells would ring Vespers, soon Fordwich, Sturry and the countryside would draw into itself like a dog bedding down for the night.

"You know well enough how laid low I was," Matthew continued. "But now that I've sorted through my past, I no longer fear the future; I embrace it."

Margery's eyes filled with sudden tears. She felt an ache in her chest that made breathing difficult. "I canna do this," she whispered. "I can see that you've changed. But so have I. So has... England." Dropping all pretense, she whispered, "This is an ancient war, my love." The term of endearment slipped out unbidden. "'Twas not only Limoges that drove us apart. Do you not remember, our last months together? All we did was fight and wound each other. I'll not go back to that."

"Nor I. We need not. We will not."

He brushed away a tear from her cheek. She shook her head as if to warn him against trespassing further. "'Tis more than that."

How to explain? All her life she'd straddled two worlds, trying to reconcile one against the other. She'd been like a weathervane, bobbing this way and that, depending on whether she was with Matthew and his kind or Thurold and John Ball. Only recently had she thought herself freed of that ancient conflict. But had she really reached a resolution or had it been easy to think so when she didn't have an all too human reminder standing before her?

"When you were gone I found it so easy to fit into my various roles, slippery as an eel, darting in and out. But with you here, I am afraid that, despite our best intentions, we'll become stuck in those old patterns and grievances, and end up as miserable as before."

He stroked her cheek with the knuckles of a hand. This time she did not pull away. Rather she suppressed the urge to reach out to rest her palm against the side of his face as she'd done countless times, to smooth the lock of hair that forever tumbled over his forehead.

"Life can be simple, Meg." His voice was low-pitched, persuasive. How dark his eyes in the shadowed room, how dear his countenance. "Just toss all the dead weight overboard and say, 'This is what I choose. This is what I will fight for.'."

"We cannot resurrect the dead."

"Our relationship is not dead. 'Twas just a bit dormant." He stood so close now she had to crane her neck to be able to see his expression. "Let us go to Cumbria. I will retire forever from court—"

"Hah! There is always a war to call you out—"

"Foreign wars no longer hold any appeal."

But there could be wars much closer to home. What if all those decades of John Ball and Thurold and others stirring their cauldron of grievances would finally cause it to bubble over? What had Ernald the apprentice said, a reckoning?

She suppressed a shiver of foreboding. "You will always trod a far grander stage where events, rather than your wishes, will dictate your actions. Who knows what you might be called to do and you will respond as you always have. 'Tis your duty and your obligation. It cannot be otherwise. But that puts you at odds with any relationship we might think to build together. I am tired of being hostage to events."

Matthew waved a dismissive hand. "But that is the nature of life. Things ever happen that we cannot control. And once we make peace with that, much of the frustration ends."

It was on the tip of her tongue to say, "What a philosopher you've become," but why mock him when he spoke true? It was just disconcerting to hear her man of action speak in such an introspective fashion. A stranger had indeed returned to her.

Matthew's arms settled upon her waist. When he pulled her close this time, she allowed it. He kissed the crown of her head. "For so long I fled all thought of the past, of all the sins I'd committed, the mistakes I made. But when I finally ceased running..." He told her about his withdrawal to the shores of Lake Winandermere, about his struggles, about the appearance of the great stag, and about his resolution.

"I have committed terrible acts," Matthew said. "But I did as my prince commanded, as our priests command before we go to war and they absolve us of all sins, past, present and future. I have always done what I was charged to do. If I am wrong then our society is wrong and that cannot be. I am a knight with a set of duties and obligations. We each have them. If I am a man I cannot be a hawk. We are what we are. You are. I am. Your brother is. John Ball is. Even Lawrence Ravenne is. I have accepted who I am, and what I have done. I am not a philosopher; I do not know why there is evil in the world or whether committing evil deeds has made me evil. When I hear such matters debated I can never get to the rightness of them. But I have come to my own conclusions and I can live with them and I have forgiven myself. 'Tis enough for me."

Margery leaned back in his arms to better gauge the meaning of his words. She felt off-kilter, as if she'd just stepped from a well-worn path onto uncharted territory. For this man she did not know, these words, these observations would not have emerged from the Matthew Hart of two years past. She wanted to lecture him, shake a finger at him and say, "How can you be at peace when your soul is so stained?" Not so much to seek an answer but to poke him as she would a caged animal in order to provoke a reaction. For if she criticized him, she knew exactly how he would respond. That pattern of behavior was familiar, and as destructive as it had been, they could both have played their respective parts without thinking. She condemnatory; he defensive. Or vice versa.

But if she believed Matthew had changed—and she did—why would she seek to wound him? That was not love or even the kindness she would extend to a casual acquaintance. And was it not the height of arrogance to lecture Matthew Hart on his sins, when her soul was just as stained? Weren't they all God's broken creatures seeking mercy?

The sounds drifting from the windows—villeins chatting as they returned from the fields, a child's laughter, the distant bleating of sheep, the even song of various birds, the squeaking of a laggard cart and jangle of harnesses—all faded until it was just they two. "'Tis all happening too fast," she said. "I need time to think."

"I am forty-three years old. At times I can only dimly remember that other Matthew Hart. Sometimes I cannot fathom his actions or some of his choices. But I do not hate him. I have compassion for him, as I do for all of us. Do I deserve what I most crave, which is a quiet life with you? I do not know. Only you can answer that. But 'tis why I am here. To ask you to return to me, to us. Marry me, Meg. I would give Serill a name. I would spend my days with you. I do love you. I always have. "

Wasn't it just like life, to be so certain of the future and then to have it all upended in a moment? Marriage? Removed from all that was familiar? Being swept away into the wilds of some unholy land? Thinking to build a new love on the fault line of an old? Throwing herself into a cage? Or embracing a second chance for happiness?

"What say you, Meg?" When she did not respond, he said, "I will wait as long as it takes for an answer."

Margery still did not speak, but in her heart she already knew.

CHAPTER 17

Spring 1381, Kent

When describing the English character, the court chronicler, Jean Froissart, wrote that Englishmen—women being too unimportant for inclusion—were of a "haughty disposition, hot-tempered and quickly moved to anger, difficult to pacify and bring to sweet reason. They take delight in battles and slaughter. They are extremely covetous of the possessions of others, and are incapable by nature of joining in friendship or alliance with a foreign nation. There are not more untrustworthy people under the sun than the middle classes in England. However, the gentlefolk are upright and loyal by nature while the ordinary people are cruel, perfidious and disloyal... they will not allow them (the upper classes) to have anything —even an egg or a chicken—without paying for it."

And later, when Froissart chronicled the Great Rising, he said that it arose in the "mean season." Actually, the final burnishing of the Peasant's Revolt occurred around Lent—that stretch of weeks between Shrovetide and Whitsunday of 1381. This was when mendicant friars traditionally preached their public sermons in English at every preaching cross, and regular clergy in churches across the land—all with one message, that Christ died for the sins of all men, not just a privileged few. The Easter season was second only to Christmas in merrymaking and holidays for the common folk that Froissart had dismissed as "cruel, perfidious and disloyal." It was during these resultant gatherings that the message was spread and de facto leaders emerged. These men were generally involved in some form of local governance, were tradesmen and largely literate. Thus they could read from secret missives and provide a uniform message which helped account for the seeming spontaneity of the revolution, but was actually the result of a more sophisticated network. Sparks of discontent there had been a plenty. Now the sparks would catch hold with results that would reverberate long past the mean season of 1381.

'Twas not traditional to be married during Lent, and Margery and Matthew had long made plans for a mid-summer wedding in Cumbria. In the nine months they'd been re-united they had returned to London and resided at Hart's Place, but now Margery happily anticipated retiring to Cumbria Castle. From Matthew's descriptions, her previous imagining of his earldom had metamorphosed to a place of unspoiled beauty, away from the pollution of London and endless crowds, and divorced from political and court intrigue. Perhaps as important, living in Cumbria would shield her from the disapproval, even scandal, that would inevitably accompany the Earl of Cumbria's marriage to a woman so far beneath him in station.

For Margery, the months passed in a pleasant blur. She found herself falling in love all over again, found herself behaving sometimes like a moonstruck youth. Matthew was the man she'd long loved, but he was also different. There was a calmness at his core, a peace that drew her, everyone, it seemed, in a way that his more youthful cocksureness had not. He could be just as formidable a knight, as commanding a lord, but his temper seldom flared, he seemed more accepting of challenges large and small, and he was certainly more concerned with her welfare, her happiness than the Matthew of old.

Her faerie knight, but more than her faerie knight. An old love blended with a new and Margery increasingly counted herself blessed.

It was not until late April of 1381 that they were ready to travel north for the wedding. In order to be unencumbered by baggage carts and pack horses, they had sent most of their household possessions ahead to Cumbria. They planned on a leisurely journey, with a stop at Kenilworth where Serill was lodged, and then on to Bury St. Edmunds to visit Matthew's sister. Or more precisely have her visit them. Elizabeth Ravenne would then accompany them to Cumbria Castle, though her husband would not. Matthew had finally confronted Lawrence Ravenne with the murder of Margery's mother, an act that Ravenne had first denied. Had Alice Watson's death been so unimportant that he could not remember slicing her near in two and leaving her crumpled in the shadows of a village lane while her children looked on?

Finally, after Matthew continued pressing him, Ravenne shrugged a half-acknowledgement, before saying, "She would have died of plague, regardless. And I could not have her contaminate me."

Had Ravenne not been married to his kin, Matthew would have challenged him to a wager of battle right then.

What a trial his poor sister had endured these past three decades. *If God is good*, Matthew thought, *you will be welcomed straight to heaven.*

Or, mayhap, Lawrence Ravenne would die soon for since the time Matthew had last seen him he'd lost a tremendous amount of weight and perpetually complained of stomach pains and other related inconveniences. However it happened, Matthew hoped that the devil might soon claim his brother-in-law so that his sister might be granted the freedom to tend to family demesnes as she saw fit and to write her poetry and stories, if she still had a mind to do so. Peace. Elizabeth deserved that much.

On Ascension Day, the paschal candle was extinguished in England's churches one last time to remind believers of the darkness of the world without Christ and church bells were rung. While all the ingredients of the rebellion continued moving apace.

Of course few, certainly not those like Margery and Matthew, had any inkling of the impending storm. Instead, focused on her wedding and her journey north, Margery had only one more task to complete.

And that, she feared, would be a most uncomfortable one.

∽

THUROLD WAS IN MAIDSTONE, where John Ball had recently been imprisoned for preaching seditious sermons, and Margery sent word that she must see him. Rather than endure an awkward meeting with Matthew, she and Cicily rented a pair of palfreys and set out at dawn. As the sun rose, they joined pilgrims heading for Boxley Abbey to gawk at a talking Christ upon the cross; merchants laden with pack animals; and workers driving their sheep and cattle to market. Margery noticed a different mood among the travelers—more politics and less piety—and often heard the phrase, "'When Adam delved and Eve span, who was then the gentleman?'"After that, there would be a sudden silence and then a change of subject. Or was that her imagination? Though she didn't imagine the frequent mention of John Ball or how descriptions of him had changed over time—from fool to nuisance, now to prophet and to some, heretic. When Margery had always known him simply as a good man who ever dreamed big dreams, worthy dreams that would never come to pass.

The day was sweet, smelling of flowers and meadows and fresh-turned earth. Bare-legged boys dotted the fields, using slings with deadly accuracy to prevent scavenging birds from flying away with newly-sown seeds. Herds of cows, hides already summer sleek, grazed in pastures dotted with yellow and orange and purple wildflowers. An occasional maypole still standing in a village green, coupled with drooping garlands tossed atop hedges and fence posts, attested to recent May Day revels.

Margery thought of her smithy. Where might Fulco be? It had been two years since she'd lain in his arms. That time did indeed seem like a dream, though occasionally, when she saw a man with long black hair tied in a thong, she felt her heart lurch and was so relieved when it wasn't him. She was happy with her lord. Which did not mean that she would not keep her tryst close to her heart and privately cherish it and Fulco the Smithy forever.

After reaching Maidstone, they found Thurold and ate bread and cheese in an inn along the River Medway. Then, as sunset stained the sky, Cicily retreated to their lodging and Margery and her stepbrother strolled beside the water. An occasional fishing boat yet slipped along its sluggish surface while others, tied to docks, bumped gently against each other or sprawled like giant beetles upon the bank.

She dreaded telling Thurold about her pending marriage, though she suspected he already knew. He'd given no indication but increasingly, he seemed to have eyes and ears everywhere.

As they walked, they discussed inconsequential things. Inn and shop signs creaked in an intermittent breeze which also brought smells of excrement and decay from the river and endlessly churning waterwheels. Was it her imagination or was Maidstone quieter than normal? Few townsfolk clustered outside doorways or in public areas and something felt... different. Was it an air of expectancy, as if Maidstone and its inhabitants were waiting? But for what? It reminded Margery of the atmosphere before a storm but when she scanned the twilight she saw only the first stars, like candle flames, pricking a cloudless sky.

"I've stumped along so many streets, seen so many villages," Thurold said. "Though most often na like this. In France and Italy 'twas na much more than slaughter and destruction. And, all too often it seemed, we only ended up harming those like us. Ye might part the rich from their coin but somehow 'tis always the poor what suffers."

Rather than defending the natural order of things, which actually meant defending her lover, Margery stayed silent. She'd heard Thurold's lamentation so many times but tonight it was delivered more in contemplation than anger. Was it because of the hedge-priest's arrest? Or because Thurold knew about her and Matthew?

As they walked, she surreptitiously studied her stepbrother. He was still dagger-thin, his face wrinkled as a walnut and burned a permanent brown from suns in countries she could not imagine. When had his hair gone grey? His gait stiffened? He'd begun awkwardly holding his right arm? She had a sudden image of him, graceful as a cat, racing across the fens, luring Lord Lawrence Ravenne away from her during the time of the Great Pestilence. She remembered the night that her stepfather Alf had been killed, when he and John Ball had rescued her from a life of drudgery in a dying village.

"We be a long way from Ravennesfield, aye?" Thurold asked, as if reading her thoughts.

"That we are."

At that moment, Maidstone's bells rang. After they faded, he said, "How many times 'ave I heard bells in how many foreign cities? Did they ever ward off demons? Or did the townsfolk consider us to be the demons?"

Margery didn't know what to say, so she merely nodded in the dark.

"All those nights on all those campaigns I would study the stars, stars like tonight, knowing that our fates be written there—our births, our deaths, the rise and fall of kingdoms. I wanted so bad to be able to unravel their meaning. But I'd no priest or astrologer to show me that particular alphabet."

"Mayhap 'tis best not to know." She opened her mouth to tell him about Matthew but he went on, "Our time be at hand. When Simon Sudbury imprisoned John Ball this time, I knew, we all knew something was different."

Earlier, Margery had seen the Archbishop of Canterbury's palace on the east bank of the Medway, a hulking reminder of the church's power. Was John Ball locked away in its dungeon? Could he smell the river? Did the walls drip, did water seep in with the rise and fall of its flow, was the air fetid with its odor? Was John being starved? Tortured? He'd already been excommunicated and yet he had not ceased his exhortations. The one thing she did not wonder was whether John Ball was afraid.

"'Tis an odd thing, what causes folks to say, 'Enough,'" Thurold said. "We've reached that crossroad."

Margery remembered the criminals she and Cicily had earlier seen swaying like grotesque wind chimes from various gallows along various crossroads they'd passed. Chilled, she pulled her cloak closer.

"...this last poll tax be the worst. And then we be called criminal because so few can comply, for most 'ave not even one thickpenny of their own. 'Tis so clear now that finally, finally, they, the invincible ones, 'ave miscalculated. We must always 've felt that they be wiser than us, as well as richer, but 'tis na so."

"Thurold—"

"This time when they hold out their hands we will bite off their fingers."

Margery shivered. A black dog, which had been padding along beside them, veered off into an alley. Didn't Satan come in the form of such a dog, or a bear, or a raven or a goat or as a multitude of other animals? Evil was omnipresent, as was death. And love and happiness. It all depended on where one chose to look.

"I am going to wed Lord Hart," she blurted and braced for the inevitable outpouring of rage. Instead her confession was greeted with a sigh. They walked on, their steps barely heard among the other night noises, while Margery awaited a reaction that did not come.

"I admire you and John Ball and his like, I do. But things are simpler for women. I have spent too many years worrying and wondering and doubting and all I want now is to live the rest of my life with M'lord Hart in Cumbria, to enjoy whatever portion is left to me. The other..." she waved an arm into the darkness, "I just canna grasp all of that."

"I've waited forever for this moment," Thurold said, "and now I feel... nothing."

"Because you do not believe that anything will ever change? Think how long we've lived and what we've expected and hoped and longed for. How much ever came to pass? How is it even possible to alter the natural order? The lords could not choose their heritage any more than could we. 'Twas an act of God—"

"And how wonderful that God allowed them to be born in fine warm manors," Thurold said, his temper flaring, "and with nurses to feed and clothe and fuss after 'em so they can grow up to take our food, our clothes—"

Margery rested a hand upon his arm until she felt the tension drain away.

"Someday we will be free," he finished softly, "for ye cannot kill an idea. 'Tis all I can believe, that when we speak this time they will finally hear. But if that canna be, mayhap it will be for Serill's heirs or even mine, wherever they might be."

Margery wondered, for the first time, about Thurold's life beyond John Ball and their cause. Had he ever fallen in love? Begat children? Did he regret forsaking the ordinary for the occupation of a mercenary, the cause of a revolutionary? And what sort of a sister had she been not to have questioned?

"I wish I knew the future." His voice was wistful. "I wish I could read the signs."

In the periphery of her vision she saw what appeared to be the tail of a comet disappearing to the northeast, roughly in the direction of Canterbury. She prayed Thurold had not noticed such an omen, that his attention was elsewhere, upon the ruts and refuse beneath their feet, the sighing stands of reeds and rushes and cattails, the whispering river.

"I've never heard you so melancholy."

"Mayhap the fury's been worn from me."

"So does that mean you will not hate me for marrying Lord Hart?"

Thurold snorted. "We no longer be children, are we? I do na like it but ye've long known that. And we all must follow our paths."

"What is written on the stars?"

"Aye." Thurold turned and placed his hands on her shoulders. In the lantern's glow from a tavern window his expression was troubled. "I know things," he said, his manner urgent. "And I ask ye to heed me. Take Serill and go north with your knight, far away from London. Go soon."

Margery swallowed hard. She didn't ask her stepbrother to explain the meaning behind his cryptic words.

She was afraid she already knew.

CHAPTER 18

May, 1381 Maidstone and East Anglia

hirty years past, ominous portents had presaged the time of the Death—earthquakes, pestilential vapors, rivers turning to blood, animals giving birth to malformed young. If you could read the signs you knew that a horror of unimaginable magnitude was about to descend upon the earth, and later, when clergy proclaimed that the Pestilence was divine judgment for man's wickedness, no one disagreed with their interpretation. It was ever thus. When catastrophes were imminent, so were the warnings. Winter in summer, relentless winds howling like banshees, ceaseless rains—or no rain at all. Leaves turning in the wrong season; buds refusing to bloom; trees bearing withered or blackened fruits; stunted or malformed crops.

In 1381, when England was on the precipice of an event about which chroniclers would long ponder, were there omens? Birds flying backwards, the sun standing still or traveling from west to east, new or peculiarly bright stars appearing on the horizon, corpses leaving their graves to haunt once-familiar byways?

Wise men, such as the monk and chronicler, Thomas Walsingham, later claimed the Peasants' Revolt to be the work of God, who was once again punishing His children—this time Londoners—for their sinfulness. But at the time, most Englishmen and women went about their routines with no idea of the gathering violence, with not even a glimmering that in a matter of days their lives would be forever changed. Some could not shake off an uneasy feeling; others were troubled by inchoate nightmares; still others would raise their gaze to sweep the horizon or, like an animal sniffing out prey or predator, seek a certain scent upon the wind. The atmosphere was thick with something unusual, wasn't it, something ominous, foreboding? Or was it only in hindsight that people looked back and said, "Aye, we should have known. The signs were there all along."

One man, for certes, understood. John Ball. On April 28, 1381, when Archbishop Sudbury had ordered the hedge-priest's arrest for "sowing errors and divisions" and attacking the church hierarchy, Ball had calmly asserted, "I have twenty thousand who will rescue me." He'd not added that the time of his arrest, in the period between Easter Day and Ascension Day, could not have been more auspicious had John chosen it himself.

Stupid, stupid apostate, he'd thought, smiling benignly at the Archbishop, while silently sending a weary prayer of thanks to his Creator ending in, *Finally!* All the seasonal holy days and festivities, which brought with them long periods of idleness and large gatherings, provided the perfect environment in which John Ball's followers could spread word of his imprisonment and instructions for the forthcoming insurrection.

Even now, as John waited in his cell, he knew his army was massing. The message was simple: the lords had finally gone too far, just as he'd known they would. Push and push, take and take, until nothing remained and the villeins must turn upon their tormentors like cornered badgers. After more than two decades of sleeping under hedges, of being persecuted for his message—nay, not his message, but Christ's—after years of hardship, the seeds John had sown, watered, and nurtured, had finally matured. The Bible said, 'Sow the wind, reap the whirlwind.' Soon the harvest would be gathered, and for the oppressors, what a bitter harvest it would be. Throughout the countryside, to all the places John had preached, his followers had already sent their coded messages, telling Englishmen the revolution was at hand.

> "John Ball
> Greets you all,
> And doth you to understand
> He hath rung your bell.
> Now with right and might,
> Will and skill,
> God speed every dell!"

Archbishop Sudbury's Maidstone palace stood between the square-pillared church of St. Mary's and the squat prison where John and other offenders against clerical law were incarcerated. The Archbishop's palace was a graceful building made of native ragstone, boasting two Norman towers and a cluster of steeply pitched roofs. The cost of its upkeep would keep a hundred children in wheat and brown bread for years.

'Tis you, Sudbury, who should be excommunicated.

John stared out the high narrow window of his cell, which looked directly out onto Maidstone's main road, the widest in all of England. Upon that highway the first of his peasants, God's children, would arrive to free him. Then they would free England. Soon all goods would be held in common. Soon there would be no more villein and gentlefolk; soon all would be one and the same. When Adam delved and Eve span, there had been no gentlemen.

Nor will there be again, John thought, as he watched and waited.

ON MAY 30, 1381, a poll-tax commissioner, Thomas Bampton, summoned the men of three Thames-side villages to Brentwood to inquire among them who had evaded their rightful tax. When Bampton demanded that the villagers pay their due, they refused and chased him and his men out of Essex.

King Richard's advisers sent Sir Robert Belknap, Chief Justice of the King's Bench, to restore order. From among the local people, Belknap swore in jurors who were willing to make statements against the offenders. After accusing Belknap of being a traitor to the king, the commons forced him to turn over his list of the treacherous jurors' names. Then they ran the jurors down, cut off their heads, and cast down their houses.

On Whitsunday, a great number of common folk—some said fifty thousand—assembled in Essex. The rebels marched to the manors and townships of their enemies and razed their houses or set them afire. They caught three of Thomas Bampton's clerks, cut off their heads and stuck them upon poles as an example to others. They then proceeded to slay all the Black Robes, jurors, large landlords, and servants of the king and John of Gaunt that they could find.

The revolt spread beyond Essex. Gathering in bands, peasants besieged all the roads leading to Canterbury. They compelled all pilgrims to swear to be faithful to both King Richard and the "commons," as they called themselves.

The village of Dartford, on the River Darenth, was the first stop on the Pilgrim's Way toward Canterbury. Here a tiler called Wat, incensed by a poll-tax collector's insistence that his daughter disrobe to prove she was beneath the legal age of taxation, seized a hammer and bashed in the collector's head. He then joined the rebels. Along with a man named Jack-Straw, Wat Tyler took charge. He ordered all available official documents seized and had them burned in Dartford's streets.

All that night the commons continued their pillaging, as well as their march toward Maidstone, a distance of more than twenty miles.

To free their leader.

John Ball saw them early the next morning, swarming across the highway, spilling into the fields, brandishing their homemade weapons. He heard them shouting his name.

"Thank you, Father!" John breathed. After decades God had answered his prayers. After centuries of oppression, God would free England. John had been right when he'd repeated throughout the years, in the same manner as when he would pray upon his paternoster beads, that 'twas impossible to kill an idea. That belief, the belief in a cause so right it could not be obliterated no matter how hard the trying, had sustained him through the darkest of times...

Terrified of the mob, prison guards immediately opened the gates. John emerged to deafening cheers, where he was met by the rebel leaders, Wat Tyler and Jack Straw—and one other.

"I knew I would find you here," John said to Thurold Watson.

"John Ball hath rungen the bell," Thurold replied with a grin, "and its clamor will be 'eard throughout the kingdom."

AFTER MARGERY and Matthew travelled to Kenilworth where Serill was a page, they three travelled to Bury St. Edmunds. So far the journey had been pleasant enough with only the occasional rumor causing Margery a twinge of unease. Nothing concrete and snatches of gossip were easy to dismiss. Besides, their troupe was well armed. Sometimes she thought upon her recent trip to Maidstone and Thurold, and the May Day garlands all tossed and trampled among the hedges. Odd how those particular images, for no discernible reason, would temporarily darken her mood.

Margery hadn't been this far north since she'd first journeyed to London more than two decades past and she tried to orient herself in a landscape that was the same. And not. There had been so many abandoned buildings and farms and fields in the aftermath of the Death. That at least was different.

She had forgotten how flat this area of England. Matthew's men remained dressed in chain mail and were well-armed, but the atmosphere was relaxed. Margery did not mind that she was the lone woman for Cicily had refused to leave London for "such wildness," but Matthew had assured her that at Cumbria she would have a hundred maids if she so wished. With Matthew and Serill flanking her the days seemed like an extended holiday. The occasional afternoon storm kept down the dust of the roads and the hours were pleasantly passed talking, singing or enjoying the scenery. Occasionally, Jerome,

Matthew's squire, would remove the lute lashed to his saddle and pluck a melody.

Being with Serill was such a delight. He seemed so happy to be with them, and acted his best grown-up self in the presence of the other knights. Easy to see all the things he'd learned in the Duke of Lancaster's household, though Margery liked it best when he forgot about being a page and returned to being a boy.

Sometimes, to pass the time, Serill would ask them riddles. Many were as old as creation though she and Matthew pretended they'd not heard them.

"Why do dogs so often go to church?"

"I have no idea," said Matthew, winking at Margery, for that one had been ancient when he was a boy.

"Because when they see the altars covered, they think the masters go there to dine."

They all laughed.

"My turn," said Margery. "How many straws go to a goose's nest?"

"I know the answer to that," said Matthew, for that was also well worn.

"I'm at a loss," said Serill, though he might have been playing along.

"None," Margery said and then she and Matthew and a couple of other knights completed the answer. "They can't go anywhere. They don't have feet."

That last night before they would reach St. Edmunds Abbey, where they would stay until Matthew returned with his sister, they bedded down at a comfortable inn in Stowmarket.

Before drifting off to sleep, Serill wrapped his arms around her, as he'd done as a small boy, then laid back and with a half-smile, asked, "Why do men make an oven in the town?"

"Because you can't make a town in an oven."

As Margery kissed her son on the forehead and smoothed his hair, her heart was full.

CHAPTER 19

Bury St. Edmunds Abbey, June 1381

"I will be back tomorrow with my sister," Matthew said, from atop his destrier. His men were already mounted. Edmundsbury Castle was a half day's ride from Bury St. Edmund's Abbey but knowing Elizabeth, she would have carts and furnishings suitable for a dozen wedding celebrations. Best to count on a delayed return.

Margery blew her lover a kiss before she and Serill returned to the abbey.

Margery's host was Prior John of Cambridge, a thin-lipped priest with the mind of a lawyer and a ruthless singlemindedness when it came to gathering money. Prior John was in charge of Bury St. Edmunds Abbey and since Matthew had provided the abbey with a generous donation, the prior was at his obsequious best around him. However, after Matthew's leaving Prior John had virtually ignored Margery, leaving her and Serill to stay in their small quarters or explore the well-attended abbey grounds.

Quiet.

Peaceful.

And with no idea that Matthew had unwittingly deposited them in the maw of the beast. For, not only was Bury St. Edmunds Abbey one of the most powerful in England, it was among the most hated, with charters that gave it a stranglehold over both the town of Bury St. Edmunds and the surrounding countryside. It held the city gates, possessed the wardships of all orphans in the district, collected fees from the estates, and lent money. Its archives were stuffed with bills against the city's influential citizens, who whispered "the abbot's papers have a sharper edge than the headsman's ax."

As Margery and Serill finished a spartan repast tucked away in a tiny part of the abbey palace, a former chaplain named John Wrawe and a band of rebels entered Bury St. Edmunds' south gate. As Margery and Serill left the palace to stroll in the Abbot's Garden, situated behind and to the south of Prior John's grand residence, the rebels marched toward the abbey. As Margery leaned over to caress the red petals of a damask rose, she heard the first shouts. Like a stag upon scenting the hunter, she stiffened and cocked her head.

"Hush!" She ordered Serill, who had been humming one of the ballads Matthew had recently taught him.

"I know things," Thurold had said. *"Take Serill and your knight... go soon."*

Margery felt the hair prickle on the back of her neck.

"What is it, Maman?"

Margery put a warning finger to his lips. Of course nothing would happen, not in this peaceful abbey with its comforting jumble of buildings and beautifully tended gardens, but she heard a rumble like that of men on horseback. Her eyes caught the cross atop the central tower of the abbey church. Was not Saint Edmund the guardian of the abbey as well as the town itself?

She tensed, trying to place the sound, which sounded a bit like the growl of thunder, though the deepening sky contained not a hint of cloud. Had Matthew and his men returned? But it was much too soon. And why would they be making such a noise? Had there been another call-up of troops? Mayhap a criminal being chased by a sheriff and his posse? But wouldn't such matters have been discussed during their meals with Prior John? The peasant unrest? But Prior John had dismissed that particular subject with a wave.

Grabbing Serill's hand, Margery hurried to the garden entrance. Tromping feet. Angry voices. Louder. Serill was watching her, his eyes wide and frightened so she tried to compose her expression. But she knew, aye, she knew.

"This is the moment." Thurold had said. *"'Tis an odd thing, what causes folks to say, 'Enough.' We've reached that crosssroad."*

Margery could see a portion of the Great Gate, which gave access to the Great Court and the abbot's palace. The gate had been built for defensive purposes in 1327, following a previous riot. A portcullis hovered overhead, like the fangs of a wolf, but no guard had moved to lower it. What did that mean? If something dangerous was occurring they would close the gate, wouldn't they?

Torches leapt against the stone walls of the gate, echoing the flames of the setting sun. The first rebels appeared, carrying pitchforks, staves, and bows slung over their shoulders.

"Do not stop," Margery whispered, heart hammering against her ribs. "Go on."

Surely they would not attack Bury St. Edmunds Abbey. Thurold and his like might claim to hate corrupt friars and bishops, but such was just talk. Particularly when a priest was their primary spokesman.

Peasants spilled through the gate, spreading out across the Great Court. Some headed toward the cowshed, brewery and other supply buildings to the left, but most made their way straight toward the abbot's palace, brandishing their weapons and chanting, "Prior John!"

"Mother Mary!" Margery breathed. She glimpsed the prior bolting out of the palace's back door, toward the meadow and the River Lark which bordered the back of the abbey.

Margery pulled Serill into the shadows of the garden hedges.

"Maman, what is it? What is happening? Who are those men? Are they with Father?"

Seeking a hiding place, Margery's eyes swept the area—the tiny garden chapel, the Reredorter and outbuildings, and the abbey church which stood huge and solid against the darkening sky.

"Something... troubling is happening but we'll be safe," she whispered to Serill. "We'll hide in the church."

"I do not like this, Maman. I wish Father were here. He would kill them all and rescue us—"

"We must care for ourselves until his return." Mind racing, Margery pulled Serill toward the abbey church. She and Serill both had daggers, but they would prove useless against a horde. They must hide and hope for the best until she could devise a better plan. Perhaps Matthew and his men had seen the mob and were even now returning...

When Margery and Serill reached the Monk's Cemetery, they heard angry voices close by. Something crashed. Margery crouched behind a small monument, pulling her son down beside her. The palace was ablaze with the rebels' torches as they went from room to room searching, she presumed, for Prior John. Some had smashed windows and tossed out silver plate, reliquaries, and furniture. Like rats deserting a granary, priests, monks and servants poured out into the courtyard, their shouts adding to the din.

Margery scooted past the cemetery, along to the south entrance of the church, entering through St. Botolph's Chapel. The chapel was so dark Margery had to rely on the memory of an earlier visit to guide her. The shrine of St. Edmund, located behind the high altar near the shrines of Saints Jurmin and Botolph, was the focal point of the apse.

Should we have fled the abbey like Prior John? She wondered, while groping her way toward the opening which led to the shrine. But she was unfamiliar with the area. No, they must hide and wait until Matthew's return.

"We will be safe here. No one will violate sanctuary," Margery said with more conviction than she felt. She led Serill toward the high altar in front of St. Edmund's shrine. The cathedral was one of the largest in the country; surely they could find a hiding place in its vastness.

A scream pierced the silence. Margery imagined she heard the thud of running feet across the cemetery lawn.

"Listen to me." She lifted Serill's chin, trying to better see into his eyes. If those outside were like Thurold and John Ball, they were nursing a lifetime of grievances. Who could predict their level of violence? And they would not give her a chance to explain—what? That she knew John Ball, that she sympathized with their cause, that she was one of their own? But who and what was she really, in her sumptuous clothes and with her prosperous business, with noble blood coursing through her veins, and with both a son and a lover in service to the most hated man in England?

"Should something happen, should you and I somehow become separated, if those men should find us, whatever you do, do not mention your father or most of all, the duke. Pretend you know naught of any lord."

Serill's clothing didn't contain the Lancaster badge, that was something, though the rebels would only be momentarily fooled.

"You must be like Thurold. Repeat what you've heard him say about our lords. Do you understand?"

"Will they kill us if they think Father and my lord Duke are our friends?" Serill asked in a small, frightened voice.

"Just do not speak of them." Sinking against the altar, Margery gathered her trembling son against her, stared into the darkness and prayed.

Crash!

The chapel door was thrown back on its hinges. Serill jumped; his arms tightened around her.

Voices, several in the chapel area. Margery's heart pounded so loudly she could not hear.

I must stay calm for Serill's sake.

She looked around to see if he might somehow escape, whether she might be able to distract the rebels long enough for him to safely slip away. But where would he flee? He was so young, only eleven. How could he survive without her?

They wouldn't hurt a woman, would they? But the heads? The screaming...

It was dark in the chapel. Perhaps they wouldn't see her.

Margery heard footsteps approaching. More voices. Then what sounded like one man nearing the altar. She removed her dagger, placed Serill behind her, and looked around. No place to hide.

Trapped.

A figure came in view. Shadowed, but he was huge and bulky, an impossibly formidable opponent.

Doomed.

Then she was face to face with the man. Margery blinked. Surely in the dimness her eyes were playing tricks on her.

Fulco the Smithy?

What had Thurold said? *"He's one of us... He travels from castle to castle... He's from Bury St. Edmunds."* Had Fulco been an instigator, moving around in order to stoke the fires of the insurrection? Might he be one of its leaders?

Margery stared at Fulco. He returned her gaze, looking every bit as surprised as she felt.

"Please don't hurt my son," she wanted to say, but somehow she could not utter the words. They'd never needed words before... and now?

Fulco looked younger than she remembered. Coarser, as if he were naught but a common villein.

Dear God, what did I do? What have I done?

Then, a shifting of the light revealed a glimmering of a chain around his neck, just peeking from his tunic. And Margery knew. She saw not a rude peasant but her midnight lover, her gift from the pagan gods who'd thawed a heart that had been packed in ice.

"Ah, Fulco," she whispered.

The months fell away. They might have been back by the River Stour with him above her, staring into those beautiful black eyes as they made love.

Without looking down at her son, Margery said, "We are fine, Serill. Do not be afraid."

She stepped away from him and approached Fulco.

Motionless, he watched her. She stopped when they were as close as they'd once been, close enough to feel each other's breaths, close enough she imagined they might hear the beating of their respective hearts.

Reaching inside Fulco's tunic, Margery withdrew the necklace with her metal image and clasped the pendant in her fist.

She gazed up at him. Fulco bent down until their foreheads touched, and there they remained. As if they were two travelers, returning home to each other after a long and weary journey.

"My love," she wanted to say. He wasn't that exactly. Matthew Hart was. But whatever Fulco the Smithy meant to her, no man, not even her beloved, she knew, would ever fill that secret corner.

Fulco wrapped his hand over hers and they stayed motionless, foreheads together, sharing their breathing, as if something magical within its mingling would forever bind them together.

"Maman?" Serill's frightened whisper returned her to the present. As did a sound from beyond, coming closer.

"Hide in the crypt." Fulco said. "I will return when I can and find you a way out."

They stepped away from each other.

Fulco turned and strode away, back toward the rebels. "There's no one here," he shouted, "Let us move on."

Matthew reached the north gate of Bury St. Edmunds early on the morning of June 9, 1381. He, Lawrence Ravenne, and an armed troupe of 30 knights had left Edmundsbury Castle at dawn, immediately upon receiving word of the rioting.

As his destrier galloped through cobblestoned streets toward the abbey, Matthew surveyed the damage. Some houses had been pulled down and the area was strewn with wreckage, but he saw no rebels—a good sign.

When they reached the Abbey's Great Gate, however, he saw that the portcullis was half raised, and beyond, a bonfire blazed in the Great Court where peasants were feeding manorial rolls into the flames.

The palace had obviously been sacked. Upon entering the Great Court, Matthew's gaze swept the rubble, fearing to see the bodies of Meg and Serill. From the area to the south, where the small church of

St. James huddled near the much larger abbey, fifty more rebels congregated. They carried three heads on pikes, one, Matthew noted, still dripping blood. Dreading the worst, he forced himself to study them but saw only the severed head of Prior John and two others.

Lawrence Ravenne drew rein beside Matthew. "Bastards! 'Tis Sir John Cavendish, our chief justice, and John de Lakenheath, the monk who exacted manorial dues and fines."

"They'll exact nothing again from any man," Matthew muttered.

Ravenne withdrew his sword. "The whoresons will pay dearly for their perfidy."

"Nay!" Matthew grabbed his wrist. "Wait until I've found Meg and my son. Then I'll run them through myself."

They crossed from the Great Court through the narrow Cellarer's Gate to the Palace Yard which abutted St. James' Church. Making no move to either attack or flee, the rebels watched their approach.

Dread, Matt experienced, dread unlike anything he'd thought imaginable, worse than those dark nights at Winandermere. Was this his payment for Limoges, for all his sins? To lose Margery and his son?

Motioning the other knights to stay in the Palace Yard, he passed beyond St. James to the Great Cemetery surrounding the abbey church, where the peasants were gathered.

He addressed the apparent head of the rebels, describing both Margery and Serill and finishing with "They were residing at the palace. Where are they?"

John Wrawe, the leader, stepped forward with a menacing swagger.

"I left them both at the palace," Matthew continued, well aware that Wrawe might mean to challenge him. "You must have seen them." He deliberately removed his sword from its scabbard and rested it across the pommel of his saddle. "If they have been harmed in any way, I will personally see that none of you leaves this abbey alive."

The other peasants began muttering among themselves. Some were eager to confront the knights, no matter how well armed. They themselves carried pikes, flails, bill hooks, and plow handles, which could easily bludgeon a man to death. And Matthew Hart was far enough from the others that he might provide an easy target.

"Do you think to threaten us?" someone shouted from the rear.

"'Tis no threat." He surveyed the ruined abbey and the decapitated body of the monk, de Lakenheath, sprawled near St. Botolph's chapel, then raised his gaze as if he might spot Margery atop the roofs, leaning from a shattered window, rising heavenward among the burning embers.

Uneased by the knight's expression, John Wrawe manner became more placating. "I swear by all that's holy we have not seen them."

"You would not mind then that we search the abbey."

Without awaiting a response, Matt returned to Ravenne and the others. "Half of you keep an eye to the rebels. I've no desire to end up with my head on a pike. If they make a false move, kill them all, starting with their leader."

"Why wait?" Ravenne countered. "Why not dispatch them now?"

"Not until we find Margery," Matt said sharply. "They might be lying. If they are holding her and Serill hostage, they could murder them both and we would not even know."

"They would not dare."

"They have already dared plenty. Now, take some men and search the church and the southern part of the grounds. I will search the palace and the rest of the abbey. Do not leave so much as a stone unturned. I do not intend to leave Bury St. Edmunds until my family is with me."

During a haphazard search of the nave, Lawrence Ravenne and his men found two terrified monks huddled on the steps of St. Edmund's shrine. Matthew uncovered several others in hiding about the abbey grounds. Upon checking the stables, he noted that Margery and Serill's mounts were missing, but so were many others.

While returning to the troupe, he tried to formulate a plan. It was obvious that England was in the middle of some sort of insurrection, though to what extent 'twas impossible to say. After so many years of idle talk, some malcontents had acted. How many? Was this the extent or were they part of a larger mob? What had been the catalyst? The poll tax? A poor harvest? Some sort of local dispute with the abbey? If so, the violence might be confined to Bury St. Edmunds. But if that were not so, if all of England was experiencing similar revolt, his first duty was to protect King Richard. Which meant he must head south to London.

But what about Meg and Serill? Since their bodies had not been found, he assured himself they were safe. Perhaps they'd fled on horseback. But a lone woman and a boy on dangerous roads? And where would they go? Would Margery think to travel to Cumbria? But she would be unfamiliar with this part of England and his holdings were weeks away. Would she return to London or to Canterbury? Matthew cursed himself for leaving her, for ignoring what now appeared to be warnings of pending danger.

"We have dawdled long enough," said Ravenne, interrupting his musing. "We must attend to business here and then ride for London and the king."

Matthew nodded. London was three days away unless they rode like madmen and the weather cooperated and they were not met with bands of rebels. His first duty was to their monarch, but still...

He eyed John Wrawe and the rebels, some of whom were drifting away, seemingly done with confrontation. Wrawe did not appear inclined to fight. But they had murdered members of the clergy... And at this moment he did not care. At this moment all he could think of was his family.

"Leave me a handful of men. I will continue my search while you head for London."

A huge black-haired peasant, hair tied back in a thong, impudently grabbed his destrier's bridle near the bit with a massive hand. Matthew gazed down, temper flaring, thinking to challenge him.

The man stepped closer and spoke in a low voice. "Your lady and son escaped on horseback."

Fulco the Smithy did not explain that he'd retrieved their mounts and guided them free of the abbey. "They be London bound."

Matthew gazed into the man's black eyes. "I thank you," he said. Fulco released his grip on the horse's bridle.

Matthew raised a mailed fist and with a sweeping gesture said, "We all ride for London."

CHAPTER 20

London

On the Feast of Corpus Christi, John Ball celebrated mass upon a makeshift altar at Blackheath, a bleak stretch of land seven miles outside London covered by scrub trees, yellow gorse, and bracken. Blackheath was usually no more than a resting place for trade caravans and a playground for venturesome boys but today thousands of peasants knelt upon the broad chalky strip of commons to pray that God would champion their cause.

After John Ball completed mass he stepped before the altar, which was decorated by a cross and candles and bordered by two rude banners. The peasants stood, their garments making a rustling sound like fallen leaves dancing upon the wind. Behind John the morning sun bathed the bearded faces of his followers in a golden light.

God's light, he thought. As God the Father and His Son would be their leader this day. *I am but His vessel. Our cause cannot fail because the Almighty has chosen the time, and 'tis He who will lead us to victory.*

Throughout the countryside the rebellion had spread, just as John Ball had known it must. In East Anglia, from Bury St. Edmunds outward to eastern Suffolk where rebels had plundered the houses of tax collectors, justices of the peace, escheators, and other officials. Norfolk and Norwich had been attacked, and in Yarmouth the jail had been opened to release the four prisoners held there.

In the rest of England, the revolt had been more sporadic. Cornwall, Devon, and Dorset had suffered no outright rebellion, but homicides, highway robbery, burglary, and violent gatherings increased. From the midlands, John of Gaunt's Duchess had fled north to the towering fortress of Pontefract—only to be refused admission by the frightened custodian. In Surrey, Middlesex, and Hertfordshire, which surrounded London, villagers had burned manorial rolls and manors, and killed all the Black Robes.

And now all had gathered at Blackheath, before John Ball, the man who would lead them to a new society. King Richard was in the Tower of London, surrounded by his advisors, and he had agreed to travel to Greenwich this morning to meet with them. The rebels were certain His Grace could be persuaded to embrace their vision of a new world.

Not our vision, John thought, his eyes sweeping the crowd and beyond, to the low roofs of London's western suburbs. *Our Blessed Savior's vision, my vision. I must sustain their minds, just as their bundles of bread crusts and meager rations have sustained their bodies. I must inspire them so they will approach their lords, not as serfs creeping to the feet of their masters, but as men created equally in the image of God.*

John began his speech with the familiar rhyme, "When Adam delved and Eve span, who was then the gentleman?"

A cheer swelled from the ranks, but it was quickly suppressed. For a long moment, there was only the flapping of the homemade banners interspersed throughout the crowd. Then John Ball launched into his sermon, a sermon all had previously heard in one fashion or another. While he slipped into the familiar pattern of countless past speeches, it contained an added edge and urgency for he was not portraying some nebulous future, clothed in mist like the autumn hills, but an obtainable reality.

"Things will never be well in England so long as there are

villeins and gentlemen. They have leisure and fine houses; we have pain and labor, the rain and the wind in the fields. How long we have suffered, back into the darkness of time, and if we do not change it now, our children's children will suffer as have we, as have our ancestors. We have lived as animals, but we are God's creatures, the same as any lord. Servitude was introduced by evil men, against God's will. If it had pleased Him to create serfs, he would have appointed in the beginning those who should have been serf and those who should be lord. The only servants that should be allowed are servants of God."

The rebels listened intently. Now, this moment, everything would be different. They'd suffered enough. Events, their plight, had brought them to this day and they must seize it. If they did not dare, or if they dared and failed would the moment be forever lost? One thing for certain: should they fail, they and most likely their families would all be killed. So they must either act or return quietly to their cottages and farms and occupations and hope that the lords would not exact vengeance for the damage already wrought. But when had the upper classes ever forgiven them anything? They had no choice now but to continue along this path.

John Ball concluded, "We must hasten to act after the manner of the good husbandman, tilling his field and uprooting the tares that destroy the grain. We must rid ourselves of the tares of society—all those who have oppressed us."

The crowd chanted, "For King Richard and the true commons!"

Let them believe as they would, John thought. *Let them believe that when 'tis over, they will look to the king as their leader.*

John knew better. No man above—no man below. And that included Richard of Bordeaux.

IN HINDSIGHT, the outcome of the Peasant's Revolt seems inevitable, but not during that fateful summer. Tens of thousands of rebels descending on London, most of Richard's trusted advisers out of the country, many soldiers away at war, while the boy king and his remaining council holed up in the Tower of London?

One of those who rightly feared for his life was Simon Sudbury, Archbishop of Canterbury, who had been responsible for John Ball's imprisonment and was one of the most hated men in London, if not all of England, for the part he'd played in the introduction of the poll tax. After His Grace and his councilors returned from morning mass in St. John's Chapel, Sudbury confronted King Richard on his demented plan to meet with the rebels.

"They could kidnap you or worse." His homely face was a mask of worry; his thick fingers endlessly twisted his ecclesiastical ring. "Anything could happen."

A proud man Sudbury had been, and corrupt, many said. More interested in earthly power than tending his spiritual flock. Aware of the rebels' animosity and perhaps sensing his impending fate, Sudbury had earlier relinquished England's Great Seal and begged to be retired from public office. But when he had laid the seals of his office on the table, not a lord volunteered to assume the responsibilities—or the dangers—that accompanied those seals.

"I must meet with them." Richard's voice cracked and changed octaves. "The commons will not harm me, their true king. I am told they wish to convey their grievances against my councilors and ministers and members of my family. They hold that those around me have mismanaged the land, and I mean to discuss the matter with them. I may not agree with them, but 'tis time to acknowledge them."

Richard's decision greatly vexed his councilors. Though none could agree on a course of action, it was inconceivable that England's sovereign should risk death by meeting with a bunch of rabid dogs.

Matthew watched Richard and Henry of Bolingbroke, both aged fourteen, born within three months of each other. Bolingbroke, John of Gaunt's eldest son, his hair a darker shade than his cousin's and with a stocky warrior's build, was quite a contrast to young Richard, who still retained more of his mother's beauty than his father's bold mien. Young and inexperienced as Henry was, he said little but he was alert and he had a calmness about him that lent him an air of authority beyond his young years. Watching the pair, Richard in command, Henry ever respectful as befitted his subservient position, not even the most adept soothsayer—and certainly not Matthew Hart—could have predicted that two of England's kings, one present and one future, were housed together in the Tower. And that, in less than two decades, one would overturn the other to take the crown for himself. Or that Richard II, who had retreated here for his protection, would someday be imprisoned in this great pile of stone and pain.

For it seemed, that, not only did England's players seldom change, neither did human desires.

Robert Knolles, the famed mercenary, stepped up beside Matthew and followed his gaze. "Let us hope the mob does not learn that John of Gaunt's first born is in the Tower. They'll be screaming for the poor lad's head along with Sudbury's."

Matthew grunted. He was glad Knolles was part of those advising the king. The old mercenary had a mansion in the city which was massive enough to house a garrison of one hundred twenty experienced soldiers. Should the worst occur, that was a comfort. Matthew did not doubt that Robert Knolles could keep at bay a legion of demons with a handful of men.

As far as the rest in the Tower, all the royal uncles were absent. Some of the remaining council had already proven themselves frustratingly indecisive or endlessly bickered among themselves, though several like himself and Knolles were seasoned soldiers harkening back to Poitiers.

I myself am torn, Matthew thought, hovering in the background of those currently imploring the king. He had said very little since his and Lawrence Ravenne's arrival at the Tower two days past. The other barons had apportioned his share of advice, though none really knew what to do. If John of Gaunt had been in London, matters would certainly have been better. As it stood, six hundred men-at-arms and archers against ten to fifty thousand rebels made for discouragingly poor odds. In addition, his mind kept drifting away from the present danger to fears about Margery and Serill. What might have happened to them? His primary duty was to protect his king and kingdom, but when everyone stood around dithering or quarreling, he could barely contain his pacing, his need to be... where?

"I do not intend to see London destroyed by vermin," declared the city's fiery mayor, William Walworth. "I am certain I could raise six thousand men who would easily send the rebels back where they belong."

Matthew tried to shake himself free of the ennui that intermittently plagued him. Over and over, he mentally returned to Bury St. Edmunds Abbey and the trip to London, calling up the buildings and the country-side and the questions he'd asked of various people they'd met through-out, to see what he might have missed. Some clue as to Margery and Serill's whereabouts. Trying to think as they would have thought. Trying not to dwell on the direst possibilities. No denying that the country was in rebellion, but there were still quiet spots. The black-haired man had said they were London bound. But was he telling the truth? And what if Margery and Serill had been captured? They were hearing the most alarming tales, including rapes...

Matthew forced himself back to the matter at hand, which was the ability to raise an effective force against the enemy. Addressing William Walworth, he said, "I do not believe you could raise six dozen men, lord mayor. Do not forget that on our ride from Bury we saw countless rebels, many with their bows slung upon their backs. I need not remind any of you how devastating a long bow can be. We are not up against untrained rabble. I'll wager many of them fought in the French campaigns."

"Aye, and mercenaries can never be trusted," chimed in Lawrence Ravenne. "Look what they did to the Queen Mother when she was returning from Canterbury."

"They did not do anything to the Queen Mother," Matthew snapped, clenching his fists. "They helped her chariot out of the mud." Two days of being confined with a gaggle of contradictory and quarrel-some men—of whom his brother-in-law was the worst—had severely tried his patience.

"They kissed her and rubbed their faces against her!" Ravenne exclaimed. "They near frightened her to death. How dare they take such liberties! They should be strung up for the very thought."

"They are still Englishmen," Matthew countered. "Some of them probably even saved your arse at Poitiers. I think Englishmen should not fight Englishmen unless it cannot be avoided."

"I can understand why you are soft on peasants, when you've spent half your life consorting with one," Ravenne responded. "But you sang a different tune at Bury, when you could not find your whore. You were ready to run through the lot of them."

At his epithet, Matt felt a hatred so fierce that his vision blurred. Ravenne might be his sister's husband and the father of her heirs, but he was a worthless sot who had murdered Margery's mother and created such chaos with his careless brutality...

But I am also a murderer of innocents. Most of us here have blood on our hands. Matthew turned away, lips tight. *We must remain united or we will all perish.*

The hatred drained away, leaving a weariness that he'd not felt since Winandermere. And he couldn't, wouldn't return to that place.

As if ridding himself of a pesky gnat, Matthew shook his head. He would focus on one thing only. He, they all, must protect Edward of Woodstock's son, England's rightful king, and the kingdom over which he ruled.

THE FOLLOWING MORNING, King Richard and his advisors set out from Traitors' Gate, which opened directly onto the Thames. Richard, Matthew, Lord Salisbury, Ravenne and several others rode in the first barge followed by a large armed guard in four more boats.

The morning was warm and fine, the Thames a reflection of the cloudless sky. It was hard for Matthew to believe that danger awaited them, but Bury St. Edmunds had also seemed safe. The royal barge skimmed toward the royal manor of Rotherhithe with the gaily dressed king standing in its prow.

The sloping banks of the Thames were black with men, wave after wave of rebels. Though some cheered King Richard, more hurled oaths and threats.

"Damme!" Forgetting his earlier animosity, Lawrence Ravenne sidled next to Matthew, as if seeking protection. "We have dug our own graves," he muttered, his face the color of whey. He clutched at his stomach, which had been torturing him for days.

"'Tis like the French at Poitiers," Matthew said. "Remember how they counted more than raindrops and yet we bested them? If need be, we will do so again." Though privately he wondered whether he had survived every battle only to be torn apart by a half-armed mob of his own countrymen.

"They were French, not English..." The rest of Ravenne's reply was lost in the rebels' taunts.

King Richard's boats stopped twenty yards from the shore. From the rail of the royal barge, His Grace addressed the crowd.

"Sirs, I have come to listen. What have you to say to me?"

A thousand rebels screamed an indistinguishable garble of demands.

No matter how Richard tried, his voice was lost in the din.

"We canna hear ye," shouted those on the banks. "Come ashore so we might talk."

Richard turned uncertainty toward Matthew and the others.

Matthew shook his head. "'Twould be folly, Your Grace. They could hold you hostage."

Lord Salisbury yelled that an audience was impossible.

"Aye!" Lawrence Ravenne raised his voice to address the closest rebels. "You are in no fit state nor are you suitably dressed to talk with your king."

Matt shot his brother-in-law a look of disbelief. "We are in the midst of a rebellion. Think you they care how they're dressed?"

"They should. If they cannot treat their sovereign with respect, why should we waste our time with them?"

"Because they outnumber us ten thousand to one."

How had Elizabeth endured this donkey all these years? How had such a creature been allowed to live when so many fine men were moldering in their graves? Matthew saw the faces of his father, his brother, his prince, his king, so many, and shivered, like a hound shedding water.

When the rebels realized King Richard would not step ashore, they wrote out a petition demanding the heads of John of Gaunt, Simon Sudbury, the treasurer Robert Hales, and several other highly placed officials, and had it rowed out to him.

Following a hurried conference, Richard's councilors decided the situation was too dangerous for him to remain, and turned the boats around.

"Treason!" the rebels cried. Some brandished their weapons; others removed their longbows from their shoulders.

The barons circled protectively around Richard.

"They will not hurt me," His Grace said. "Have they not repeatedly sworn they are loyal to me?"

"But the rest of us were not included in that oath," Ravenne demurred, his eyes apprehensively scanning the shore.

On either side of Richard's barge the oars dipped and cut through the water, while the peasants vented their rage until it sounded as if the Apocalypse had arrived.

'Tis all over, Matthew thought. *They will cut us down and we'll die like dogs, not warriors.*

The royal barge sped back toward the Tower, past the peasants packed as numerous upon the shore as grains of sand. Not one man fitted arrow to bowstring. Not one man used his weapon against England's king.

CHAPTER 21

London

$\mathcal{L}$ ate in the afternoon of June 14th, Margery and Serill caught their first glimpse of London—the needle-spire of St. Paul's Cathedral, thrusting above the treetops. St. Paul's was a comforting sight, for Margery had imagined a city razed to the ground. Throughout their four day journey they had sometimes met with fellow travelers who carried news, while hiding from bands of rebels swarming the area. Most bound for London, she presumed.

"Soon we'll be home, sweetheart," Margery said to Serill.

Thanks to Fulco the Smithy, she and Serill had had horses to ride and safe passage out of Bury St. Edmunds Abbey along with instructions as to the safest route back to London. Fulco had argued against their return but Canterbury was overrun and to head north for Cumbria —traveling a good three weeks in totally unfamiliar terrain—would be courting death. An unescorted woman and a boy, even if they were fortunate enough to attach themselves to a travelling merchant or a train? She'd asked Fulco about Kenilworth, which was one of John of Gaunt's residences, but he'd shook his head. "'Twill be a favored target," he said. "The roads there be too dangerous."

While London might be a primary destination of the rebels, it was a vast city and only a very small part—perhaps the Tower and Westminster and the grand palaces—would be targeted. Not the entire city. She hoped.

"I will risk London," she'd said to Fulco, not adding that she had a better chance of finding Matthew there. And of course he would return to London to protect his king. Fearful for her father, she'd further queried Fulco for details about Canterbury, in case Thomas Rendell was ensconced at Fordwich Castle. She learned that Canterbury Cathedral, its town hall and Canterbury Castle had all been assaulted. Peasants had publicly burned all the rolls and writs and crippled the related machinery of royal and civic government. Her formerly taciturn lover had provided a surprising amount of detail, once again reminding her how little she'd known her midnight man.

"Do not fear for your father," he'd said, as if reading her mind. "He be a knight after all." This last was said without inflection so whether he was being sarcastic, sympathetic or merely stating a fact she could not say.

Even in the midst of danger, even as they reached London's outskirts, Margery found herself remembering her and Fulco's final moments. Serill had been struggling into his saddle and surely she and Fulco had been blocked by her mount so he could not possibly have seen them in one final passionate embrace, could he? But how could they not have behaved thus, when they all might be dead at any moment and he'd saved their lives and he meant so very much to her?

Please keep them safe, she silently prayed over and over, referring to Matthew and Fulco. Then she added John Ball and Thurold and her father—and King Richard of course...

"Do you think Father is already to London?" Serill asked, while their mounts plodded wearily along the last stretch of highway.

"Aye, and let us hope that once there, we will be able to quickly find him." She had gambled that the rebellion would have ended by the time they reached the city, but she'd been wrong. Thurold and John Ball had been proven right, after all. The fissures had run deeper than she could ever have imagined.

The heat of the afternoon settled upon them. They neared Bishops-gate. No heads on pikes above the entrance, a good sign. In fact, though there were many rebels pouring into the city, others had donned a festive air, as if they were countrymen bound for sightseeing. While there were few women among the press, no one bothered a lone matron and a child, most likely assuming they were attached to others on horseback. But not all were jolly. Some bore the familiar expressions she'd so often seen on her stepbrother and John Ball—set jaws, deter-mined visages with eyes cold and hard or blazing with a fanatical passion.

"Ah," Margery gasped, heart sinking.

"What is it, Maman?"

Above the tree tops and beyond the River Thames, Southwark was on fire. The merry afternoon, the jocular travelers created a macabre contrast to what must be unfolding—for pockets of flame were also flaring in London's suburbs. Hart's Place was in the suburbs. John of Gaunt's Savoy Palace was in the suburbs. If Matthew had retreated to either place he might be dead now.

They had not escaped anything traveling to London. But, Margery told herself, the Shop of the Unicorn was far away from those places and this was a rebellion against lords, not tradesmen.

And so she and Serill entered London.

"I AM GOING to Hart's Place," Margery said after she and Serill were safely inside the Shop of the Unicorn.

"You cannot," said Nicholas Norlong, wringing his hands. "They are attacking Lombards there and putting all the buildings to the torch. Surely, Lord Hart is in the Tower with His Grace the King."

"I must at least try to find him." Margery had changed her clothes into a rough servant's gown. "And I'll start with his townhouse."

"Ye canna go wandering around dangerous streets..."

"I need to know," she said stubbornly.

"Dame Margery, some of London's apprentices have turned on their masters, hacking them to pieces. While our Shop enjoys a good reputation, what if we meet someone who holds a grievance or decides to settle an old score? Or who is simply caught up in a frenzy of bloodletting?"

"I will go alone if I have to," Margery countered, reaching for the bar to unlock the shop's door.

Followed by Nicholas Norlong and an apprentice named Peter Brown as her reluctant escort, she began her search. Parts of London appeared deserted, others normal, yet others manifestly dangerous. Margery collared passersby, who repeated what might have been rumors—that Fleet Prison had been breached and all prisoners released; that churches, hospitals and mansions were being destroyed in specific areas of town, areas where Margery had often visited, shopped in, or strolled through. Beside her, Norlong and Peter Brown, whose name suited his dark hair, eyes, and skin, cursed, muttered together, or cast apprehensive glances as they scurried along the streets.

I would have been better off alone, she thought. *They are shopkeepers, not protectors. You might be able to create a dagger but you certainly will not be able to wield one.*

They strode across Holborn, toward their destination. Judging from the wreckage they passed, Margery held out little hope for Hart's Place. Nicholas Norlong was right. This part of London had been decimated. The burning ruins of a dozen mansions, all belonging to other prominent people—lawyers, courtiers, and clergy—lit their way. Flaring up, dying down. Margery imagined the bonfires of hell would be identical.

"Dame Margery, this is madness," cried Nicholas. "No one remains here, of that 'tis obvious and who knows what may greet us around the next corner?"

"Whoever was here is long gone," Margery countered. She and Serill had braved far worse on their journey. "The area appears more deserted than anything, but I must see for myself."

Peter Brown glanced nervously behind, as if death and destruction would appear from the ruins.

The acrid smell of smoke caught in Margery's lungs, growing even stronger as they rounded the final turn to their destination. She held her breath. God grant Hart's Place had been spared. God grant that, if Matthew and his retainers were there, they had barricaded themselves inside, where they would be protected from the chaos.

"Oh," she breathed, her hands unconsciously clasping over her heart.

Hart's Place was rubble, no different from all the rest they'd passed. Tongues of flame licked sporadically at a few foundation timbers, a portion of stone wall still stood, but more Margery could not see. The back, where the garden was located, was out of her sight line.

Nicholas took her arm. "Dame Margery..."

She shook off his grasp and circled the ruin, hurrying to the garden. Of a summer, she and Matthew had often lounged here in order to escape the heat where they would read a Romance, eat a light lunch, sip wine and converse, and occasionally make love in some of the more secluded areas. Now it was as deserted as the rest of the property, and possessed of an unnatural stillness, as if all life had departed with the wreckage. Only patches of ground had been spared the rebels' tromping feet. She couldn't even hear the Thames, now visible beyond the burned or trampled hedges and broken trellises. In the mud flat leading to the river she spotted what appeared to be a garden statue, knocked from its perch, but upon closer inspection saw that it was a body sprawled face-down on the ground.

Margery closed her eyes. *'Tis Matthew.* Dread filled her. Norlong and Brown were standing near a half-destroyed fish pond, as if staring at it might return it to wholeness. And allow them to pretend that they had not noticed Margery or the body.

Gingerly, she approached the corpse. It could not, would not be Matthew. Bending over the figure, she grabbed its shoulder, pulled until it flopped over upon its back and the face was visible. Not her lover at all, but a stranger.

"Dame Margery, I must insist we return to the Shop."

Margery started at Nicholas's voice. He'd shaken his timidity long enough to creep up closer behind her, but she knew his insistence on leaving had little to do with a desire to protect her.

Stubbornly, she shook her head. "The Savoy is close to here. Lord Hart might be there..."

"Surely he will be in the Tower. Let us make inquiries through other means. I do not want to end up like this poor devil."

Peter Brown added, "One of the rebels earlier said the king and his men've left London all together; that not a one remains to face them."

"Return if you must," she said sharply, "but I am bound for the Savoy." She gathered her skirts and strode away from the wreckage. Suddenly she thought of her stepbrother. If he were anywhere, he would be at the destruction of John of Gaunt's palace. And if she could find Thurold, there she would also find answers.

THE AREA around the Savoy was thick with rebels. All day, following their aborted meeting with the king, they had vented their frustration with an orgy of violence and retribution. But no one disturbed Margery or her companions. What the trio did not know was that Wat Tyler, John Ball, Jack Straw, and the other leaders had issued strict orders that neither thievery nor killing would be tolerated. One man caught stealing a silver goblet had been drowned in the Thames. And John of Gaunt's mistress, Katherine Swynford, along with their children, had recently been allowed to leave the Savoy without incident.

The trio passed through the palace gates, Margery's gaze sweeping the area for bodies, for her stepbrother. She was more heartsick than afraid. Regardless of John of Gaunt's sins, regardless of the legitimacy of the commons' grievances, what was the purpose in destroying such beauty?

They reached the outer buildings of the Savoy, then the palace itself, and with each step, she felt more off-kilter, as if made dizzy by fever. Impossible to believe that such a faerie castle, filled with treasures so flawlessly beautiful they could have been created by angels, that so much cunningly crafted stone and wood and tile and metal could be as easily obliterated as a child's construction of blocks. Rebels had fallen upon prayer rugs imported from the east, rare weapons and relics from the great hall, tapestries and silver sconces, and tossed them all in bonfires. They broke up priceless ornaments and threw them in the Thames, and smashed jewelry with their hammers. They hacked stacks of gold and silver plate into tiny pieces and stuck remnants under their belts as souvenirs. They ransacked the duke's state chambers, including his wardrobe. They used their torches to burn the napery, sheets and coverlets, beds and head boards. In the Privy Suite, they ripped the red velvet curtains off the duke's bed and slashed it into ribbons. From the Avalon Chamber they smashed a marble mantel that had taken two years to carve. They pitched dainty bancas made from rare oriental woods out windows once covered by stained glass.

Will John Ball be here? Margery wondered, looking for the flowing robes and massive form that would tower over the others.

"Thurold Watson? John Ball?" she queried those she passed. Inevitably, she was met with a shrug of the shoulders or shaking of the head.

Flames from the palace's great hall and the surrounding buildings cast the entire area in garish silhouette. Disregarding the danger from the spreading fire, rebels darted inside to witness first hand its destruction. The blaze strained upward to the intricately carved ceiling beams, toward the pale crenellated towers that had been the Savoy's trademark.

"Thurold will be here somewhere," she said to Nicholas. "Keep an eye out."

Norlong's face was the color of the ashes even now being carried away from the roaring, leaping flames. Peter Brown had pulled his hood over his face as if that might hide him from scrutiny.

Finally, she spotted her stepbrother, standing with several other yeomen who had tied one of the duke's cloaks—of a beautiful Lancastrian blue decorated with pearls—around a tree trunk and were using it for target practice.

"Thurold!" She yelled and waved, but in the din he could not hear. She ran up to him just as he was fitting an arrow into his bow string and jerked his arm, spoiling his aim.

Cursing, he turned on her, his expression flitting from rage to surprise.

"Who is left inside the Savoy? Who have you killed?"

"What are you doing here? I thought you, at least, were tucked away in the north. 'Tis na safe to be about—"

"What do you mean "at least"? Have you seen Lord Hart? My father?" Before Thurold could reply, the palace was rocked by an ear-shattering explosion. Barrels of gunpowder had been mistakenly cast on the great hall's bonfire, causing the entire building to erupt. Some peasants, who had been enjoying the duke's wine cellar or were clustered around the bonfire, were caught inside.

Margery covered her ears to blot out the screams of the dying. Thurold pulled her down next to him, where they crouched until they were certain no debris would hurt them.

"Is Lord Hart inside? What have you done?" she yelled into Thurold's ear. His eyes glittered, his expression was so strange that she was momentarily afraid of him.

"Why do you, even now that our victory is assured, think of him? You chose the wrong side, sister. We are going to win. We are going to crush them all under our heel."

They both stood. Around them packs of rebels running, yelling, scurrying about, bent on more destruction.

"This is wrong," Margery cried. "What good does it do to create paradise if nobody remains to enjoy it?"

Thurold's anger drained away; he reached out to pull her hood over her face as if to protect her. "I should na frighten you. Hart is not here. All of them be in the Tower with the king. I saw your...'im earlier, on the royal barge at Greenwich. And I've 'ad no word of your father which means he's a'right. Now begone from 'ere. Return to the Shop. Stay shut away until 'tis over."

And how long will that be, she wondered but she did not ask aloud. Instead, taking Thurold's word that Matthew was safe, she did as he bade, and, beckoning to her companions, allowed them to escort her home.

∽

NOW THAT EVEN HAD DESCENDED, Matthew stood on the battlements of London's Tower, facing into the city, where a multitude of fires flared against the night. He had heard of the burning of the Savoy, as well as the Temple, which was the headquarters for England's lawyers, and contained the city archives. He had not heard, but was certain, that Hart's Place was another casualty. With Hart's Place, he had lost memories of his father, his brother, his childhood—and Meg. But that seemed the very least of his troubles...

Below the Tower, on Tower Hill, many rebels had bedded down, effectively blocking any escape. Some had positioned guards outside the tower walls while others had encamped round St. Catherine's Wharf upon the Thames. The light from their fires created a soft glow against the star scattered heavens. Like the watchfires lit on Midsummer's Eve to keep away faeries and evil spirits.

Only this evil is flesh and blood, Matthew thought. *This evil is English.*

It was still hard for him to comprehend that the commons would revolt. Baronial wars were an accepted way of life, though not so much during Edward IIII's reign. But for peasants to turn on their lords was against God's natural order. They might have a handful of legitimate grievances, but he would never forgive them the destruction of the duke's property—or his own. And if Margery and Serill were dead, he would murder every last one of their leaders, that he vowed. Still, the faces he'd seen along the banks were the faces of fierce and courageous fighters from French campaigns. Matthew sighed. He felt exhausted by the tension of the day and worries about his family. Yet he knew he would not sleep.

Absently, he listened to the king's sentries, keeping vigil at their posts, arguing with the rebels. Disembodied threats jangled in the darkness.

"We will not leave until we obtain from King Richard all we want!"

"Tomorrow we will storm the Tower and kill you all."

Another shouted for the head of Simon Sudbury, a third for the treasurer, "Hobbe the Robber." Then the voices evaporated, like clouds torn apart by the wind.

Candlelight from the turret in which Richard and his councilors were closeted spilled onto the battlement. Inside Matthew knew his peers were still arguing a course of action. Richard remained temperate, refusing to call on loyal citizens or the Tower garrison to put down the rising. Instead, seeking common ground, he expressed his desire for another meeting. Which many of his advisors, fearing for their necks, counseled against.

Sir Robert Knolles, the freebooter, called from the Tower door. "His Grace has come to a conclusion. He wants to meet the rebels on the morrow at Mile End. He seeks your opinion."

Matthew sighed. His gaze wandered across the city, as if to probe its secrets. In a few hours the drunken shouts would die down along with London's fires and the city would settle in as it always did. Thoughts of his family and their welfare were always in the background, even as the kingdom crumbled around him. He imagined Margery, could actually see it, both her and Serill lying dead somewhere along the route to London, rebels having slit their throats and tossed their bodies in a heap somewhere.

"Are you coming?"

"Aye." He thought suddenly of that long ago time, the night before his knighthood ceremony, when he and Robert Knolles' nephew had wagered with loaded dice. When Harry had been alive and no one could have imagined that England would ever come to this...

Knolles prodded him. "His Grace awaits."

Matthew passed a hand across his eyes, as if to rub away the past, turned and moved along the battlement toward his king.

CHAPTER 22

London

At seven o'clock on the morning of June 14, 1381, Richard II rode out from his stronghold, bound for Mile End. The peasants who were gathered around the Tower exit parted enough to allow the king and his royal party past, then closed ranks behind them.

The day was already uncomfortably warm, with an unpleasant sultry edge. No wind stirred the dull green dress of the commons, or the royal pennons carried by Richard's outriders. The white harts clung close to the spears upon which they were fastened, like fearful children hiding their faces. Beneath his pourpoint, sweat trickled down Matthew's back and arms—as much because of tension as the heat. They were riding into a snake pit, that much he knew. His every nerve was taut, his attention heightened as it always was before conflict.

Plain-garbed men either watched sullenly or shouted insults, calling for the heads of Richard's ministers, though there were some shouts of "Long live the king!" Many pressed close, grabbing at stirrups and bridle reins. Matthew's destrier, Stormbringer, snorted and nervously tossed his head, shying away from the rebels. It required much forbearance for Matthew to keep his sword sheathed, to keep from smiting the hands grabbing at him, to ignore the taunts.

Taunts from fellow Englishmen.

So difficult to accept that his countrymen were now arrayed against them. But now was not the time for musings about England's sorry state of affairs. Now, he, they all must be on the alert for if any of the mob lost his temper and acted impulsively, goading the others to violence, Matthew and his fellow knights would be hard pressed to protect their sovereign.

Ahead, he could just glimpse the white feather in King Richard's hat as he followed Aubrey de Vere bearing the sword of state. Though Richard must surely also be aware of the danger, he continued to act with remarkable composure.

Prince Edward would be proud, as I am. My lord's offspring is proving to be a king worthy of my life.

Which was good. Because Matthew would not wager that any of them would live to view another sunset.

Beside him, Lawrence Ravenne swore. "Look at the whoresons," he said between clenched teeth. "How dare they lay their filthy hands upon their king?"

A grunt was Matthew's only response.

They passed through Aldgate, onto Hog Lane, to where the road ran directly to Mile End, an attractive village a mile beyond the city. Mile End possessed a handful of taverns and was a favorite for vacationers, who enjoyed strolling its open stretches and partaking of the fresh air. Today Richard and his men were greeted by twenty thousand villeins and freemen.

Matthew's eyes scanned the endless sea of faces. He thought suddenly of Thurold Watson, who would surely be here. Might he know Margery and Serill's whereabouts? Or what about that Lollard priest? If he spotted John Ball, he would at least shout out a query.

King Richard calmly approached the rebels. Wearing his blue and silver coat and jeweled gloves, and with his exquisitely fashioned boots thrust in shining silver stirrups, His Grace appeared more a creature of fantasy than flesh and blood. So bedazzled were the commons that no one answered him when he first addressed them.

"My friends, I am your king and lord. What do you wish from me?"

Finally, one rebel, Wat Tyler, the ex-soldier from Kent, dared to come forward, to act as spokesperson. "We want you to set us free forever, us and our descendants and our lands," said Tyler and a handful of other chosen or self-designated leaders around him. "And to grant that we should never again be called serfs or held in bondage."

Richard graciously agreed to these points and all the others they presented, as if they were of no consequence. Did he really mean to grant such boons? Surely not; surely he was simply stalling until reinforcements would arrive from elsewhere in the kingdom. But even a compliant king could not agree to the last.

"All ministers of the crown who are obnoxious to the commons must be punished."

If Richard were shocked by this demand—for he well knew that the commons found many of his own friends and relatives obnoxious—he merely demurred with a mild shake of the head. "There shall be due punishments for those who can be proven traitors by due process of law. I cannot promise more."

He then had the commons form two lines. "I confirm to you that you shall be free," he said, and granted a full pardon for all the wrongs done by the people of Kent, Essex, Sussex, Bedford, Cambridge, Stafford, and Lincoln—providing they returned quietly to their homes.

Beside Matthew, Lawrence Ravenne mumbled, "Aye. Promise them lakes filled with wine and a sky flung with diamonds, so long as they depart."

Matthew nodded. If Richard actually meant to honor such ridiculous demands, their entire society would disintegrate like sand castles at high tide. Besides the rebels had been so violent, 'twould take generations to heal the wounds.

King Richard then ordered thirty secretaries to begin drawing up the letters containing his promises; representatives of each county were given royal banners as proof of his protection. Flushed with their victory, some of the commons began to disperse.

"'Tis over then?" Ravenne asked, relief evident on his face.

Matthew could not quite believe it, particularly when the rebels realized that the king could actually grant few if any of their demands. They could *hope*, but their hope would prove ill-placed. Centuries of grievances would not be soothed with one conciliatory meeting.

Matthew's doubts were well founded, for when King Richard and his bodyguard returned to London they found that rebel gangs still roamed the city. Most shocking of all, the Tower drawbridge had not been raised, leaving His Grace's residence vulnerable. Because the rebels had arrived bearing one of the young king's royal standards and also his letters patent with a ribbon hanging from it to which was attached England's Great Seal, the guards had allowed them entrance.

Inside, four hundred men, led by an Essex man named John Starling, had ransacked King Richard's rooms and even intruded into the Queen Mother's quarters. There Joan of Kent, still abed, promptly fainted, only to be ignored as the rebels probed with their weapons beneath her bed frame. The king's cousin and John of Gaunt's son, Henry of Bolingbroke, was saved by a member of the royal guard named John Ferrour, who hid Henry in a cupboard and who would much later be pardoned "in a wonderful and kind manner." By protecting young Henry of Bolingbroke, Ferrour had this very day unknowingly altered the course of English history.

Simon Sudbury and the treasurer, Robert Hales, however, would find none to save them.

Sudbury was saying mass in tiny St. John's Chapel on the second floor of the White Tower. Several others were there, including the hated Hales. Sudbury had previously heard all their confessions and was chanting the Seven Penitential Psalms when the chapel door flew open. Just as he intoned, "All the saints pray for us," the rebels, led by John Starling, burst in.

"Where is the traitor?" Starling cried.

Knowing his time was at hand, that the peasants had every intention of violating sanctuary, Simon Sudbury regained his courage enough to step forward.

"Behold the Archbishop whom ye seek." John Starling and several other rebels pinioned his arms behind him. "No traitor, no plunderer of the Commons he," continued Sudbury to no avail.

Robert Hales and three others were also tied. Then the Archbishop of Canterbury was led up to the battlements and shown to the cheering crowds now filling the courtyard, and even those beyond the walls who, in last night's darkness, had been crying for his head.

Time to kill a churchman, nay, two churchmen, for Robert Hales, Grand Prior of the Knights Hospitallers, was also dragged to Tower Hill. A substitute block and axe had to be found for these spontaneous executions. John Starling volunteered to wield the ax.

An executioner was a professional whose skill, often passed down through the family, lay in performing his duty as swiftly and painlessly as possible. There was an art to decapitating a man, as there was to his hanging, drawing and quartering. Unfortunately, John Starling had not the expertise or the desire to expeditiously dispatch Simon Sudbury.

Sudbury's arms were unbound and he was given a few minutes to pray.

The archbishop cried, "Take heed, my beloved children in the Lord, what thing ye now do. For what offense is it that ye doom to death your pastor, your prelate?"

His guileless act only infuriated Starling and the rest who replied that Sudbury should know all too well his many sins.

"Oh, take heed lest for the act of this day all England be laid under the curse of the interdict."

As in the bad old days of John Softsword and his quarrel with Pope Innocent? If the peasants were aware of such ancient history, today they scoffed.

John Starling ordered Simon Sudbury to lay his head upon the improvised block.

Starling swung. The first blow inflicted a deep wound to the archbishop's neck.

Sudbury cried, "Ah! Ah! This is the hand of God!" Instinctively he raised a hand to the wound. The second swing amputated several fingers.

Eight blows it took to sever Sudbury's head; Hales and the others not so many. All their heads were then carried to London Bridge where they were set upon stakes.

Later John Starling would stalk about London with the bloody ax suspended around his neck, boasting that it had been his hand that had killed the Archbishop of Canterbury. Even after the Essex peasant was eventually brought to the gallows, he continued exulting in his deed.

In Chepe, the decapitations continued, this time with an eye to prominent citizens such as Richard Lyons, who, during the Good Parliament, had tried to bribe Prince Edward and the old king with barrels of gold. Lawyers were targeted. Apprentices fled from shops and warehouses, armed and crying, "Clubs! Up, Clubs!" to beat their masters. In the Vintry, commoners massacred forty Flemings and left their headless corpses heaped in a pile. One hundred fifty more were dragged from their homes or from the churches where they'd sought sanctuary, and killed on the spot.

After word reached King Richard of the White Tower's breach, he and his men retreated to the Wardrobe, which had once been used for transacting important business, as well as storing valuables, and where the Queen Mother was now ensconced. Still seemingly unruffled, His Grace comforted his mother before putting his clerks and secretaries to work copying out the changes he had earlier promised the rebels.

With night's fall, terror reigned. The more rational had already begun abandoning London for their homes, leaving only the most savage.

Understanding in his heart that their cause was lost, even John Ball had retreated, if only temporarily. Right now the commons appeared to have the upper hand but John knew better. Freedom, equality, had been in their grasp, he believed it, but the rebels would pay dearly for their lack of restraint. When it came to brutality, they would be no match for their lords, regardless of the disparity in numbers.

John Ball need not be a prophet to know what was about to unfold.

ON THE NIGHT before the final fateful confrontation, Thurold Watson visited the Shop of the Unicorn. He was in high spirits, confident of victory, boasting of the commons' superior numbers, the lords' refusal to fight and the king's seemingly malleable acceptance of even the most outrageous demands. Listening, Margery found her temper unraveling and bit back sharp words. No good could come of this, regardless of the outcome. Was Thurold meaning to taunt her when he knew of her fears for Matthew? Or was he simply euphoric—and insensitive—because the realization of his dream seemed within his grasp?

More like a nightmare, she thought, watching her stepbrother pace from the counter in the front area to the furnace, anvils and smithing tools, and back again. Since the revolt, the Shop's doors had been barred and its windows barricaded. Currently, Serill and the servants, quiet as whispers, were huddled in the living quarters. No doubt some feared that members of the rabble might pull them from their hiding places into the streets. As they'd pulled dozens of Flemings from the Church of St. Martin in the Vintry for committing the unpardonable crime of mispronouncing "bread and cheese" as "broke and case"—and beheaded them on the spot.

"I am beginning to question whether your friends are proving worse than those they seek to overthrow," Margery said, after Thurold fell silent. Only a single candle, its flame dancing when he passed, lessened the gloom in the long, narrow room.

"What mean ye?"

She shrugged, telling herself they mustn't quarrel, but unbidden the words spilled out. "You've killed hundreds of foreigners, not to mention the Lombards whose mansions you've also sacked. And you seem to take great delight in slaughtering the city's lawyers, tax collectors and jurymen on the slightest pretext."

Thurold waved his hand imperiously, as if such deaths were of little importance. Margery's mouth tightened. Hadn't that always been one of the commoners' lamentations against their lords—their arrogance and indifference to the lives of others?

"If this is how you behave when you rule," she persisted, "what makes your tyranny preferable to John of Gaunt's?"

"Someone must allus lose. This time 'tis they, and they must pay the price. After all the evil ones be killed, ye'll see the rightness of our acts."

"John Ball did not see the rightness! He withdrew in disgust."

"Priests be na like soldiers. They've no stomach for bloodshed." Thurold paused to face Margery.

He thought of Wat Tyler, one of those who'd come forward to act as leader after John Ball had retreated. John might be a priest but he had more courage than a hundred soldiers, and Thurold was ashamed of his cavalier description of his friend. Men like Tyler were more interested in saving themselves from the axe than furthering any larger cause. But admitting to such doubts might somehow cause God to look unfavorably upon the uprising and they'd come so far...

Margery and Thurold glared at each other. In his plain garb Thurold appeared indistinguishable from thousands of other rampagers she'd seen this past fortnight. But he'd been true to his vision from the day he'd met John Ball, or perhaps from the very beginning, as a wee one tucked in his cradle. Furthermore, though the rightness of a cause did not mean that it would prevail, Margery *did* believe Thurold was right. And admired him for his passion, as she loved and admired him for so many things.

"I wish..."she began, but she had had no idea how to continue for she could not formulate what it was she sought.

Thurold balled his fists, then expelled his breath in an involuntary sigh. "I know King Richard's promises might be empty as air. I just so need to believe."

That Margery could understand. She touched his arm in a conciliatory gesture.

In a soft, barely heard voice, he continued, "I dreamed last night of Alice. I swear, 'twas so real."

She was surprised by this unexpected twist to their conversation. She couldn't remember the last time she had dreamed of her mother.

"And Giddy, too."

Margery's eyebrows lifted. She hadn't contemplated her half-sister in years and when she tried to conjure Giddy, she kept shape-shifting into Serill. Had the three-year-old's eyes been dark like Thurold's or blue like Alice's? And what about the color of her hair? Had it been the same shade as the broom Alice had used to sweep the earthen floor? As golden as summer wheat? As brown as the banks along the stream behind their cottage? Or red? Somehow that seemed right. Ugly, Margery had thought it, the color of sunrise before the day arrives. Orange, pink. The same color as Lawrence Ravenne's?

Sweet Jesu, no, do not let me even think such a thing...

"...'Twas na like a regular dream. 'Twas more like... they were standing right above me, where I'd bedded down."

A chill raised bumps along Margery's arm. Apparitions often appeared as harbingers of someone's passing. Death had a way of announcing itself in advance if you just learned how to read the signs. A bell might toll without agency of human hand, or an owl might hoot, or one might hear three knocks upon the floor of their room, or an enormous black hound might appear out of nowhere.

Aloud, she asked, "What are you trying to say?" She wanted to cover her ears with her hands.

"While I believe the bad old days be forever gone, the violence is na over. If Alice and Giddy's appearance means my time is nigh..." Thurold shrugged. "We all know how cheap is life. And I do na fear death."

She crossed herself. "You must not speak like that."

"I would rather die swift than rotting away in bed, too weak to rise and lying in me own filth. Death surrounds us, Stick Legs. Especially a soldier like me. 'Tis a tiny thing, really. 'ardly worth bothering about."

Margery thought suddenly of her dead husband, Simon Crull—another she had conveniently wiped from her memory. What was the saying, "He who most resembles the dead is the most reluctant to die?" That had been Crull, hadn't it? She had a sudden memory of her husband in the moments before he'd died, after she'd poisoned him. Her standing over the goldsmith, him gazing up at her, his expression alternating between pain, surprise and hatred; his hand clawing in her direction, as if, even at the last moment, Simon Crull might somehow bully her into saving him. Reveling in every moment, she had watched until he'd drawn his last breath.

Ah, something she dared never confess.

But why think of Crull now?

She misliked this quick tallying of the ancient dead, this intrusion of her mother and sister into the present. Were Alice and Giddy trying to warn Thurold to prepare for death? To offer comfort and support of some sort? Or had recent events simply caused her and Thurold's heads to swim with fevered fancies?

"I want you safe," Margery said, slipping her arms around his waist and nestling against him. "I want Serill safe. I want... all those I love to be safe. For at least a while longer. I will pray for that."

"'Twill be as God wills it," Thurold said.

She drew back so that they could gaze into each other's eyes. She was almost of a height with him, when once he'd seemed so tall. Slivers of memory: strolling down a rutted road, her hand stretched up to grasp his, him teaching her to count in English, "One, two, three," over and over; carving her a spinning top and showing her how to make it stand and twirl; making a game of gathering eggs; playing fetch with their dog—oh, what had been his name? A lifetime together, much of it lost in childhood forgetfulness, but which bound them together all the same.

After a final embrace, Thurold crossed to unbar the door. Margery called his name. He turned to look at her. She had to ask it, the worry that had been there since their parting.

"Have you seen Fulco the Smithy?"

Thurold frowned. Of course he would not know about them for she'd never told anyone and she assumed Fulco hadn't either. He would think it a very curious question.

"I thought I saw him a while ago," she said, rushing on. "Is he safe, do you know? Is he one of the leaders?"

Thurold's frown deepened. He stared at her a long time, as if weighing the meaning behind her words. "I've not seen him," he said finally. "But if any man can take care of himself, 'tis Fulco the Smithy."

And then Thurold was gone.

ON THIS LAST day of meetings, when John Ball's worst fears would be surpassed, King Richard issued a proclamation that all commoners still in London should meet him in East Smithfield near the hour of Vespers. Then, believing that violence was inevitable, the young regent and his knights received absolution at Westminster Abbey. Though reports put the number of rebels at half their previous count, two hundred knights were still a poor match for five thousand. King Richard and his men rode out to meet their fates, and all of them, save His Grace perhaps, wondered whether they would survive to day's end.

CHAPTER 23

Smithfield

East Smithfield was the open space just beyond Aldgate where
weekly horse markets were held, familiar to all. Since Smithfield was surrounded on all sides by buildings, it was strategically safer
than yesterday's meeting at Mile End. To position themselves at best
advantage, Richard's knights gathered on the east side of the wide plain
in front of St. Bartholomew's Hospital. The rebels, loosely drawn up in
battles, stood to the west. Brightly colored pennons, including the royal
banners King Richard had presented at Mile End, dotted the ranks.
Though some rebels cheered His Grace, more watched warily or
openly taunted the royal party. Others, who had dined in taverns or
enjoyed the wine in the houses of murdered Lombards, were drunk and
quarrelsome.

A sudden silence settled over the field. Matthew's shoulder muscles
tensed; with each breath he seemed to inhale danger as if it were a
living thing. He was certain that the last few days, the give and take
and concessions were simply a preamble to this moment. Not only
their lives but England's future hung in the balance. They could not,
would not fail their king. Hopefully, the day would pass without blood-

shed, but he was seasoned enough to interpret the expressions, the body language, the *feel* of the moment to reckon otherwise.

Late afternoon sunlight lightened and shadowed the faces of the rebels. A cooling breeze rustled dozens of banners. The jangling of an occasional bridle bit as a horse tossed its head sounded unnaturally loud in the strained atmosphere.

King Richard was the first to act, beckoning London's mayor, William Walworth, to his side.

"Ask them to send me their leader," he ordered softly.

That would be Wat Tyler. Flushed with the success of these past days, as well as tipsy from the hippocras he'd enjoyed, Tyler received Walworth's message contemptuously.

Before riding to meet King Richard, he turned to his men. "I will talk with HIM, of course, but if I give this sign"—he demonstrated with his arm—"advance and kill them all. Except Richard himself."

Had Tyler foreseen what fate soon held for him, he most certainly would not have earlier boasted to all within earshot that he would "shave the beards"—behead—all who opposed him. Nor that soon the only laws in England would be those he himself imposed.

Dressed in dirty green and astride a small hackney, Wat Tyler crossed the plain to halt before the sumptuously attired king and to set the final act in motion. One other accompanied Tyler—his banner bearer, Thurold Watson.

MARGERY CREPT along Cow's Lane, toward Smithfield. Abutting the open area were the stone walls of St. Bartholomew's Hospital, and beyond, St. Bartholomew's Priory, which was her destination. She'd decided to brave London's streets alone because she felt in her very bones that today would be the beginning or the end of something momentous. And that she must bear witness—for herself, her son, Thurold and John Ball. And for Matthew.

Margery reached the Hospital just as King Richard's party rode past, ten abreast. When she spotted her lover among the others, looking well and whole, Margery slumped against a nearby wall in relief, and sent upward a prayer of thanks. She dared not call out to Matthew or distract him in any way, but rather gazed after until he and the others had disappeared from her line of sight. She then cut across the open field, reaching the priory. Now she had a clear view of the young king, as well as Wat Tyler and Thurold riding forth to meet him.

"By God's bones," she swore upon recognizing her stepbrother. Thurold had not expressed much faith in the tiler, yet here he was, carrying the commons' banner.

An ill omen, for certes, she thought, feeling a strong sense of foreboding. *Too exposed... Alice and Giddy... The dream... A foolish fancy...*

Margery's attention drifted from Thurold to the press of knights. She finally spotted Matthew, this time closer to the edge of the royal party.

Let this end peacefully. Let us leave London and retreat to Cumbria, far away from politics and intrigue and hopeless causes.

Wat Tyler reined in his mount next to King Richard. Dagger in hand, he dismounted, half bending his knee to his sovereign. Then, to the horror of the watching noblemen, he seized King Richard's hand and shook it.

"Brother, be of good cheer and joyful," Tyler said. "Within a fortnight you shall enjoy the praise of all true commons. And we shall be good companions."

Richard appeared unaffected by Tyler's boldness. Not even when he gestured toward the assemblage, saying, "All of these men are under my command. They have sworn an oath to do exactly as it pleases me."

"I see naught wrong with that," His Grace replied agreeably. "But why have the commons not returned to their homes? All that you have asked has been conceded."

Wat Tyler issued a coarse oath. "None will go anywhere until we obtain *all* for which we came." He launched into a rambling catalogue of grievances that made little sense to the king and none to Matthew, who was within hearing distance. Annoyed as he was by Tyler's familiarity, Matthew's attention had been caught by the banner bearer, whom he immediately recognized. Their eyes met, held. Matthew's lips parted. He wanted to call out, "Have you news of your sister? Know you where she might be?" but he must put aside his personal needs and concerns. After the crowd dispersed he would corner Watson, but now he must focus on his king's wellbeing. Still Matthew stared, as if he might read in the yeoman's face some clue as to his beloved's whereabouts.

An indecipherable expression flitted across Thurold's visage before his gaze travelled to Lawrence Ravenne, seated next to Matthew upon a skittish roan destrier.

When had Thurold Watson last seen his former lord? Matthew wondered. Surely, it had been decades ago. Ravenne generally paid scutages to avoid military service so their paths would not have crossed during more recent campaigns. Where else might Watson have seen Lawrence Ravenne? Hard to gauge his reaction, if reaction there was, for Thurold's eyes were in shadow. And Ravenne had greatly changed, particularly with the recent weight loss, which had caused his face to wrinkle and features to blur in the surrounding flesh. But enough to be unrecognizable? Margery had said her stepbrother had vowed vengeance for the death of Alice Watson, but that had been so very long ago. If Thurold *did* recognize Ravenne, would he consider this his opportunity to settle ancient scores?

Matthew's grip unconsciously tightened on the pommel of his sword before he mentally dragged his attention back to the interplay between King Richard and Wat Tyler, now wrapping up a long soliloquy in which he'd raised every issue from Lollardy to the abolition of the forest laws.

Richard replied, "Such changes as you suggest would require much thought and earnest discussion. I will grant all I have the right to concede, save the regalities of my crown."

An uncomfortable silence passed between the two. The western sky was beginning to darken with the first hint of sunset, the air to cool. Shadows leapt from the first battle of peasants to reach King Richard and the pair positioned halfway between. Stray rays of sun caught coifs, the occasional spear tip, caressed the rich brocade of the king's tabard, his jeweled gloves.

Matthew shivered and leaned forward, every nerve taut. He sensed that the next few moments would determine everything...

"A drink of ale!" Wat Tyler bawled. "I am thirsty!"

From the ranks, a yeoman bearing a flagon scurried forward. After rinsing his mouth, Tyler spat on the ground at the king's feet, gulped down the rest of the ale, wiped his mouth with the back of his hand, and stared truculently at Richard's men, who angrily returned his gaze.

In full view of the king, Wat Tyler vaulted into the saddle.

"He dares too much," Ravenne muttered. Mayor William Walworth's face flushed red. Robert Knolles muttered, "Bloody hell." The other knights had also endured enough of Tyler's outrageous behavior. Better to risk death than such indignity to their king. Matthew knew the moment had come; Wat Tyler was about to pay full measure for his disrespect, for being the convenient focus of the nobility's hatred, as well as a living, breathing symbol of the commons' treason.

"I recognize the man who calls himself Wat Tyler," Ravenne shouted. "He is a notorious highwayman and robber."

Tyler, who had already begun heading back toward his men, jerked round his hackney. As did Thurold.

"Come forth and identify yourself, liar!"

Ravenne stayed where he was. "I only speak the truth. And 'tis so —you should be hanging from the gallows. You are the greatest thief in all of Kent, nay, in all of England."

"Shut up," Matthew said. "Remember our first duty is the king's safety."

But it was too late. The unraveling had begun.

Wat Tyler flushed; his gaze swept the crowd, seeking the man who had dared humiliate him.

"I know who insulted ye." Thurold Watson pointed toward Ravenne. "The devil 'imself."

"Then 'tis the devil we'll kill."

Matthew unsheathed his sword as Tyler and Watson urged their horses across the separating distance. Passing King Richard, they approached the royal party.

"Fools!" Matthew breathed. So be it. Both men had sealed their fates.

William Walworth planted his horse in the rebels' path. "You are under arrest!"

Wat Tyler swung his dagger at Walworth, slicing through the mayor's tabard—only to have the blade slide harmlessly off the armor beneath. Walworth hacked his sword downward, wounding Tyler in the head and neck. One of the king's squires, John Standwick, dashed forward and ran Tyler twice through.

Meanwhile, Thurold Watson had planted his banner in the ground, and dagger in hand, maneuvered his mount through the struggling men to ride straight toward Lawrence Ravenne. Ravenne remained open, vulnerable. Thurold raised his dagger toward Ravenne's face, toward his unguarded eyes. He felt the yielding flesh as his weapon found its mark; heard Ravenne scream. When he crumpled forward, Thurold plunged the blade between the large links of Ravenne's gorget. Blood spurted outward as the blade severed a carotid artery. Thurold felt a fierce surge of triumph at the sight of Ravenne's blood, its warmth upon his face and fingers.

Thurold did not see, until it was too late, the flash of sword off to his left. He tried to jerk back, but Matthew's blade caught him along his right shoulder and slashed down to his breast bone. He felt a moment of surprise, of searing pain, before crumbling from his horse.

"Kill! Kill!" The rebels screamed. They readied their pikes and fitted notches to bowstrings. Some held up their index and middle fingers with the back of their hand facing outward in the time-honored gesture of English yeomen taunting their enemies.

Maneuvering free of the three bodies, Matthew joined his fellow knights, who had positioned themselves to meet the onslaught. But before they could act, King Richard spurred his stallion toward the oncoming mob, raised his arm and signaled them to halt.

"Sirs, would you shoot your king? Do you seek a leader? I will be your captain, as well as your king. You shall have from me all that you seek. Only follow me to the fields without!"

Lurching to a stop, the rebels hesitated, then, surprisingly, lowered their weapons. First a few, then *en masse*. Without looking back, Richard walked his horse toward Clerkenwell, north of Spitalfields.

As if hypnotized, the commons followed him. They forgot the mortally wounded Wat Tyler, still alive and calling feebly for help. They forgot Thurold Watson, crumpled on the ground while his frightened mount raced away across the green. They forgot the treachery of the lords, many of whom, led by Mayor Walworth, were already racing back toward London with the intent of commandeering enough volunteers to permanently crush the rebellion.

Matthew and half a hundred trailed Richard and the peasants. Ravenne dead. Now Elizabeth would be a widow; their eight boys fatherless. Because of his position Ravenne's death had to be avenged, but beyond that? He was sorry he'd had to kill Thurold Watson, even thought it had been his duty.

How will I tell Meg? He wished he hadn't been the one. *But how could it have been otherwise?*

He'd had no choice. And if he hadn't struck the peasant down, someone else would have. Thurold Watson could not kill a lord, no matter how well deserved. And at least Thurold's death had been swift, even honorable in its own fashion.

Matthew continued close to King Richard, watching, waiting for a suspicious movement. Would the rebels, realizing that they were in danger of losing all, take the king hostage? Or worse? And when Mayor William Walworth returned, as he soon would, well, then, Smithfield's green would run red with blood.

London's sky was a montage of color, the light starting to grow uncertain. Something made Matthew dare a glance back at Wat Tyler, Thurold and his dead brother-in-law. Plainly, he could see several figures around the trio, including a woman, seated and cradling the head of one.

Matthew squinted to sharpen his vision. "Meg!" he breathed. Safe.

231

Here. She must have witnessed everything. What would she think? What would she say? Would she understand? Curse him forever?

He hesitated. He could not desert the king. He twisted back around, assessing the situation. Richard was well guarded; the danger at least momentarily lessened. Reining his mount, Matthew galloped across Smithfield, calling Margery's name.

Margery raised her face to his, cheeks shiny with tears.

"Meg."

As outnumbered as Matthew was, he dared not risk dismounting. After addressing her, he had no idea how to continue. "You are alive," he said finally. "I had so feared..."

Margery continued staring at him. Save for the moans and gabble of Wat Tyler and the nervous shifting of bystanders, there was only silence. Matthew saw that Margery's gown was dark with Thurold's blood. He averted his gaze. *So much blood I've seen, so much until it means so little.*

"I am sorry, Meg," was all he could think of to say. It seemed that he had spent most of their shared life either apologizing for his actions or trying to explain them.

"I wish you had not..." her voice trailed away.

"You know that I had no choice, though I too wish otherwise." There was no explanation, no words. He'd done what must be done and he suspected Thurold Watson, being a soldier, would have agreed. But such an insight would not comfort Margery and he'd not even attempt it.

Gazing up at the man she loved, Margery felt such a confusing mix of emotions. She'd had a perfect view of everything and at the moment she'd seen Matthew move upon Thurold, had screamed his name, as if somehow she could have warned her stepbrother.

Matthew Hart had killed Thurold. There seemed some sort of symmetry at play—Ravenne had killed Alice, Thurold had avenged her and Matthew had avenged Ravenne. A tallying, a setting aright. But how could it be right to kill Thurold?

Matthew swiveled in his saddle to view King Richard, surrounded by rebels. He was being remiss in his duty, squandering precious moments, yet he could not leave Margery until she understood. He groped for the proper words, all the while knowing comfort was beyond his powers.

"I must return, Meg, but I will come for you. Are you and Serill at the Shop?"

Margery's only response was to shake her head. She wanted to say that she was glad that Ravenne was dead, but was she really? It all seemed so... irrelevant... so inconsequential. But not to Thurold. She prayed he'd died happy knowing he'd gained his revenge. What had he said about death? She curled her fingers in his hair, his head resting in her lap, while trying to remember. That death was a tiny thing? Hardly worth bothering about? But why couldn't it have been someone else who had killed Thurold?

"You knew Ravenne deserved to die..."

"Aye, and I curse the fates that brought us to this moment. But he was one of mine, Meg, kin as well as lord. No matter my private feelings, I had no choice."

"I know." Margery closed her eyes, fighting back a fresh wave of pain. Matthew had acted out of instinct and duty. How could that be wrong? Anything else would have been alien to his nature. He was a warrior with a warrior's thoughts and attitudes; she could not have expected him to be otherwise. Just as she could not have expected Thurold to be other than what he was. Had they four been predestined to end here, their fates forever entwined? As written in *Beowulf*, "Fate goes ever as fate must?"

Wat Tyler moaned again. A trio of yeomen, muttering something about "priests" and "tending wounds," lifted Tyler by his shoulders and feet and carried him carefully in the direction of St. Bartholomew's.

Matthew cocked his head, listening. From the direction of Cow Cross Street came a sound like marching feet. William Walworth and the volunteers, returning to dispatch the rebels.

Matthew again looked in the direction of His Grace, then to the men retreating with Tyler, and those who remained clustered around Margery. Their expressions carried equal measures of hostility and anxiety, and Matthew knew why.

You sense it as well, that you have lost your war, heaven help you all.

"If you will wait," Matthew said to Margery, "I'll help you carry your brother away. I will see that he has a decent burial. Until then, please, remove yourself. Do not be out here exposed." He touched spurs to his horse's flank, calling as he rode away, "Wait for me, Meg. I will return quick as I can."

Margery also heard the noise. Like hoof beats, louder with each passing moment. She must get Thurold away before the lords took their revenge, which would most likely include mutilating his body.

With Matthew's leaving, most of those around Margery began hurrying away, intent on reaching the warrens that made up so much of London in order to disappear, God willing, without harm.

"Please. Help me hide my brother," she called after them.

A bulky figure emerged from the shadows near St. Bartholomew's Hospital and hurried to her, robes flapping around his thick calves.

"Be gone from here, Dame Margery," John Ball said. "I will take Thurold and bury him in a secret place, where they'll ne'er be able to find him."

She craned her neck to gaze up at him. "What are you doing here? I thought you were long gone from London."

John Ball responded with a shrug. He had been at the beginning; he had returned to view the end. What more was there to be said?

"Thurold is my brother. I will wash his body and tend to him. I do not want him buried in some place where I'll never even know."

Bending over, he shifted Thurold away from Margery and gathered him in his arms.

Margery stood, aware of the wetness of her gown, not needing daylight to know that she was bathed in her stepbrother's blood.

They faced each other, Thurold little bigger than a boy lolling against John's massive chest.

"How could you have been so stupid as to believe you could really triumph over them?" she whispered.

"Because we are right."

As if that meant anything. John knew King Richard's promises contained no more substance than smoke in the wind. He also knew that, while he would carry his friend's body, at least, to safety, England contained no surcease for him or the rest. They would all be flushed from their hiding places and hunted down like hares. They would be torn to pieces by the hounds.

"I am speaking with ghosts who do not even know they are gone," Margery said wearily. "No one will see you or hear your pleas.'Tis past, John Ball. You are all dead men. Dead men like my brother."

~

EVER A MAN OF ACTION, William Walworth returned to the city at top speed where he sent criers to—incorrectly—inform Londoners that their king had fallen into enemy hands. Up to four thousand, weapons in hand and bearing the banners of London's wards, rushed toward Aldgate. Led by the mercenary, Robert Knolles, two bodies of citizens approached—one along Cow Cross Street, the second through St. John's Street. Almost negligently, Londoners and their leaders encircled the startled peasants like sheep in a pen.

King Richard, however, did not seek revenge. "They have not harmed me. I brought them here, and I'll not have the innocent suffer with the guilty." He ordered the rebels to disperse, but he promised he would attend to their grievances.

Understanding that their cause was lost, many rebels fell on their knees, thanking the king for his goodness and clemency. Others slunk noiselessly away, back toward their homes, hoping to avoid the vengeance they were sure was coming.

Seeing the danger for King Richard had truly passed, Matthew Hart raced back to Smithfield, hoping to find Margery. Upon approaching St. Bartholomew's, he saw William Walworth, who had dragged Wat Tyler from the chamber of the Master of St. Bartholomew's where his wounds were being tended, out into the square. As Matthew passed, Walworth signaled for his man to behead Tyler.

Matthew guided his horse away from that macabre tableau, toward

Smithfield Hospital. It was dark and he was so tired, but he questioned everyone he met about Margery's whereabouts.

"She and another carried someone off. I canna say where," a man dressed as a merchant answered in response to his question.

But no one else could offer any clues. He would seek her out tomorrow. He did not yet dare ride through London's streets alone, but tomorrow... somehow he would set things right.

WILLIAM WALWORTH PRESENTED a grisly souvenir to King Richard—Wat Tyler's severed head on a pike.

"Take it to London Bridge," His Grace ordered, as calmly as when he'd addressed the rebels. "Put it up in place of Archbishop Sudbury's."

Richard knighted William Walworth and the squire who had run through Wat Tyler. Then, leading his triumphant knights, His Grace returned to London and his mother, who had remained at the Wardrobe, frantically awaiting word.

"Rejoice and praise God," King Richard said, as the Queen Mother embraced him. "For today I have recovered my heritage that was lost, and the realm of England."

CHAPTER 24

The Kingdom
Summer, 1381

> Man beware and be no fool:
> Think upon the axe and of the tool!
> The stool was hard, the axe was sharp,
> In the fourth year of King Richard.

*R*etribution was swift and relentless. How could this be when His Grace had seemed so magnanimous, so understanding throughout the revolt? Any rebels caught were executed. Many were beheaded by the widows of the merchants they had killed. Hundreds were held without bail in overflowing jails and dungeons. Legal niceties such as due process or trials were ignored. Gibbets glutted England's highways and byways and hanged men glutted the gibbets—seven thousand by the end of the bloodletting. Armored knights crowded the roads, on their way to smash pockets of resistance or to administer their own brand of military justice. As the troops thundered past, common folk trembled in their fields or hid in their cottages or fled deeper into the forests after the example of that legendary outlaw, Robin Hood.

On June 22, a corrupt lawyer from Cornwall, Sir Robert Tresilian, replaced Bury St. Edmund's murdered Chief Justice John Cavendish in that part of East Anglia. Tresilian led what was described as a "bloody assize" against the rebels, torturing them into giving up names of suspects and then contriving to have the resultant charges presented as felonies rather than the less serious trespasses. Tresilian's favorite punishment was hanging; his second, hanging, drawing, and quartering. When a first jury refused to find against the peasant leaders who'd laid waste to Bury St. Edmunds Abbey, Tresilian selected a second and then a third, warning this last batch of jurors that if they failed to abide by his will—meaning blanket executions—they themselves would be put to death.

It was here in East Anglia that the closest thing to an actual battle took place between the Great Rising rebels and King Richard's men.

Henry Despenser, Bishop of Norwich, had been nicknamed the Fighting Bishop because of his participation in the French wars. Henry Despenser's ancestry—as was typical among the tangled skein of nobility, marriages and alliances—could be traced back to his great-grandfather, Hugh Despenser, who had been one of Edward II's favorites, and who had been hanged, drawn and quartered after King Edward's queen had knocked her feckless husband from England's throne.

The Fighting Bishop was incensed by Gerald Listler, a moderately wealthy dyer who some had taken to calling "King of the Commons." Listler and his band of followers had ravaged Norwich, which was not only one of England's largest and most important cities, but part of Henry Despenser's bishopric. In addition to murdering several prominent citizens, Listler's rebels had destroyed the property and possessions of poll tax collectors and other city officials, including legal records, court rolls and taxation documents.

With John Ball the only other rebel leader remaining free, Bishop Despenser was determined to make an example out of the King of the Commons, who was holed up in the North Walsham area, a half-day's ride away. In turn, Geoffrey Listler, seeking recruits in order to face a much better armed foe, had sent riders through nearby villages. Enough men responded to technically be called an "army," though few had any fighting or tactical experience. The men did their best to prepare by digging a military ditch around their camp. They then reinforced the ditch with tables, shutters and gates, all held together with wooden stakes, and barricaded the rear with carts and carriages.

One did not need the skills of a diviner to foretell the outcome.

The chronicler, Thomas Walsingham, described Henry Despenser as a "wild boar gnashing its teeth." And that he was. After calling his trumpeters and buglers to sound, the Fighting Bishop seized a lance and led his knights in a charge which soon had the rebels fleeing in the carts that had been placed to the rear of their camp, or on foot or horseback across East Anglia's streams and rivers and fens.

The King of the Commons was easily captured. Forgoing a trial, Bishop Despenser sentenced Geoffrey Listler to a traitor's death. Since Henry Despenser was still a member of the clergy, he did hear the unfortunate dyer's confession before beheading him. Then Listler's body was cut into four pieces with the last quarter nailed up outside his cottage in the picturesque market town of Framlingham.

"As a reminder to all who pass," growled the Fighting Bishop. "This is what happens to false kings."

Those rebels who weren't killed or captured hid until the bishop and his men retreated to Norwich.

Including a black-haired, black-eyed blacksmith who tied his long mane behind his neck with a leather thong.

"THE POPULACE SHUDDERED at the spectacle of so many gibbeted bodies exposed to the light of day... Despite all the retribution thus visited on the guilty the severity of the royal displeasure seemed to be no way mitigated but rather to be directed with increased harshness towards the punishment of offenders... it was widely thought that in the circumstances the king's generous nature ought to exercise leniency rather than vindictiveness..." ~Westminster Chronicles

In July, 1381, King Richard, allowing himself to be persuaded by his royal uncles and England's great landowners, annulled the charters he had issued at Miles End. Richard claimed the privileges had been made under duress and therefore counted for nothing.

In mid-July, John Ball, who had fled into the Midlands, was captured at Coventry where he'd been hiding in a ruin. Ball was brought in chains to St. Albans, thirty miles north of London, where he awaited King Richard's version of justice.

During that time, Matthew Hart had surrounded his son with some of his most battle seasoned retainers and had Serill safely removed to Cumbria. Margery had agreed with Matthew's decision, though she had declined his imprecations for her to ride with Serill. John Ball, who had rescued her from Ravennesfield, who had taught her to read and write, who had buried her stepbrother for her, merited the presence of at least one friend at his execution.

Margery remembered when her time had been due with Serill, before her labor pains had become too great and John Ball had been shooed from her lying-in chamber, when he'd sat beside her, reading aloud from that book by Roger Bacon, that Franciscan Friar who predicted such future wonders. A world that seemed enchanted, and so very different from the horror of present-day England.

Was the rebellion's outcome preordained? Since God had created all the vices and virtues, had He then shaped man's nature to strive for dominance, to keep one above the other? Had God, who had appointed kings to rule, also decreed that the few must always rule over the many? It seemed so. Otherwise, it would not be so.

But just as God had created the ruler and the ruled, He also must have planted the yearning for equality in men like Thurold and John Ball. Otherwise, *that* would not be so. Or mayhap that longing wasn't from God, but simply another symptom of man's sinful nature, or the whisperings and proddings of Satan, stirring up man's anger and discontent at their station in life.

But Jesus had spoken lovingly of the poor. In the Beatitudes He'd preached:

"Blessed are the poor in spirit, for theirs is the kingdom of heaven...

Blessed are those who mourn, for they shall be comforted... Blessed are those who hunger and thirst for righteousness, for they shall be satisfied...

Blessed are those who have been persecuted for the sake of righteousness, for theirs is the kingdom of heaven..."

John Ball and Thurold had certainly been persecuted for the sake of righteousness, when all they'd sought was a life with *enough*, not too much, in which they had the right to say, "Yea" and "Nay" and enjoy the same liberty as their lords. Surely their desire did not contradict Christ's words. If it did, then their lives and the lives of all those who came before and after, all those who expressed the belief that "we are all one and the same," "that everything shall be in common," who fought so valiantly to bring such ideals into being would have been for naught.

And that Margery would not accept.

MARGERY SAT near the back of the chamber. Hundreds of former rebels had already disavowed any sympathy or even knowledge of their erstwhile leader, and the few here today hoped their presence would be public proof of their allegiance, not to John Ball, but to King Richard.

Matthew Hart, along with some of England's greatest magnates who had traveled to St. Albans exclusively to view the hedge-priest's extermination, arrayed himself close to the front. Since that day in Smithfield, Margery and her lover had rarely seen each other, at least to converse. He had his duties, of course—always duty—though she did not begrudge him that. Margery's ability to judge him over Thurold or related events seemed to have been suspended. Perhaps she was simply numb.

She still had no idea what she would do after John Ball's execution. Follow Matthew to Cumbria, as if nothing had occurred? Return to London? What? The entire world was upended, as it had been during the Death, but she had not really pondered the possibilities beyond the fact that 'twas *her* duty to say good-bye to her friend.

During the proceedings, the corrupt Judge Tresilian lingered over each of John Ball's charges. King Richard sat beside the judge, alert and seemingly engaged, as if the outcome had not already been predetermined. Margery studied England's sovereign.

You look so beautiful, so pure and innocent. Such perfectly formed lips, still as plump and red as a child's. And such clear eyes. Ah, but your heart, 'tis as treacherous as a viper's, she thought, though without acrimony. *You lied so prettily to the commons, and now you will gain revenge on a good man.* She knew with blinding certainty that Englishmen and women would rue the day when Richard II had been crowned king.

After a vitriolic summation, Judge Tresilian—who in less than a decade's time would be begging the man beside him to spare his own neck—handed down John Ball's sentence in his gratingly high-pitched voice. "As a traitor of the realm, you will be taken out on the morrow, and you shall be hanged, drawn, and quartered. May God have mercy on your soul."

"Oh, my friend," Margery whispered.

She was in a position to see little more than John Ball's profile and his back. The hedge-priest's posture did not change; he remained standing tall and straight. Tears stung Margery's eyes. *How can I ever witness what they are going to do to you?* As John was being led from the chamber, he glanced at her in passing. A slight smile touched his lips, as if he were telling her that he was well.

The lords left their benches for the exit. When Matthew approached he hesitated before walking over to Margery. He appeared so very weary, the lines alongside his mouth and eyes unusually prominent.

"Ah, Meg." He looked as if he would embrace her, but then held back."'Tis dangerous for you to be here, to call attention to yourself. Will you not stay at the inn until this is over and then we will be able to... at least decide..." He stumbled to a finish. "About... plans."

At Matthew's request, Margery was staying at an inn outside St. Albans guarded by a pair of Hart retainers. No personal servants, however, for all had known John Ball and, though it made no logical sense, Margery felt as if keeping even a few away might give her friend a measure of dignity and respect that he would otherwise be denied.

"I will leave after my friend is dead," she said. "Not before. He deserves that much."

Matthew nodded, and after one last searching look into her eyes, followed the others.

On the following day, July 15, Judge Tresilian allowed John Ball to speak.

John calmly addressed his accusers. "I am guilty of all your charges. I did lead the rebellion. I did send seditious letters around the countryside, calling my flock to unite. I do not apologize for my acts, or seek pardon from anyone. I have naught to ask forgiveness for."

As John finished his simple statement, Margery noticed the admiration on the faces of several lords. Without sword or armor to protect him, John Ball would go to his death as bravely as any of them. No matter how foreign his beliefs, the barons were impressed by such courage. Margery's gaze swung to her lover, trying to decipher his reaction.

But Matthew Hurt merely looked sad.

JOHN BALL'S demise was as savage as Margery had feared, but still she kept her word. As was customary, the executioner had hanged John, only to cut him down before he'd expired so he would still feel the executioner's blade as his stomach was slit open and his entrails drawn forth. Throughout, John had made very little noise, or so it seemed, for sometimes it was hard to hear. While the crowd was small it was raucous, as if jeers and cheers might hide the now dangerous reality that many of them had also committed treason. But beyond those few, the usual holiday atmosphere was missing. Some, like Margery, could not hide their disgust or horror, and returned to their homes with heads down and shoulders slumped.

I am glad Thurold did not live long enough to view the end of his hero, or the hopes and dreams of the commons. I am glad he died still believing, at least a bit, in King Richard.

After John Ball was declared dead, his head was removed. Later it would be placed on a pike atop London Bridge while the quarters of his body would be sent to four different towns.

The crowd began dispersing; Margery drifted aimlessly among them.

'Tis all over then.

John Ball and Thurold, two who counted among the most important in her life, were dead. As she walked she noticed that her legs were surprisingly steady and that her mind was blank, that if she was feeling anything, she could not describe it. She paused, inhaled deeply and closed her eyes.

Then it happened.

She heard a voice. It might have been Thurold's or John Ball's or God's or the Devil's or simply her imagination, she couldn't tell. Or whether it was inside or outside her skull. Nor could she describe its tone. Mocking or triumphant or simply making a statement, as one would comment on the weather or the time of day?

The voice said, so very clearly, *"As if you can kill an idea!"*

With the words reverberating in her mind, Margery absently crossed the precincts of St. Alban's Abbey toward the massive cathedral. Although it was nearing Vespers, the emerald lawns were nearly deserted, as if this final act of bloodletting had left everyone exhausted or eager to hide their faces in shame.

Not even sure why she was here, Margery entered the ambulatory of St. Alban's Cathedral just as the Benedictine monks began chanting. She sank onto one of the benches intermittently placed along the walls and peered through the gloom to the altar. Its white cloth shimmered in the candle flame; the monks, swathed in their black capes and hoods, stirred the darkness with their rich voices. Praising God.

Folding her hands in her lap, Margery watched.

Does God even hear? she wondered. *He certainly did not seem to listen to the pleas of the commons or to John Ball. Was it His plan that*

John be tortured and cut in quarters, and that the commons should be crushed like gillyflowers beneath their lords' boots?

She pondered these matters, but without emotion. Mayhap because they did not seem as real as had been that whisper: *"As if you can kill an idea!"*

Margery leaned her head and back against the cold stones. The monks' hymns must have lulled her because she fell into a half dreaming, half waking state, with that curious refrain drifting in and out of her consciousness, when she felt a hand on her shoulder.

She dragged herself back and looked up.

"I am sorry for your friend," Matthew said simply.

She blinked. Her lover didn't seem quite real either. She felt as though she were sleepwalking, even after he pulled her gently to her feet.

"I know things are wrong in England," Matthew said softly, as if continuing a previous conversation. "It saddened me to witness the hedge-priest's death, for he was an honorable man, in his own fashion. I know that he, your brother, all of them had some proper grievances. Such problems should be addressed, but in *this* England that may be impossible. I tell you true that it sits poorly on me that His Grace has so blithely gone back on his word. But what can I do? I am only one man—one man who is so weary, and so finished with it all."

Margery licked her lips. She wanted to tell Matthew not to worry, that everything was fine, that what they fretted about and imbued with such importance was just a stitch or two in an immense tapestry. It was not only death that was such a tiny, inconsequential thing...

"Sometimes I think England is truly a house divided," Matthew continued. In the darkness, she could hardly see his face, though his body language mirrored his lamentation. It had been a very long month, eviscerating the dreams of English men and women as brutally as the executioner had eviscerated John Ball's body.

"Our bishops mistrust both us and Parliament, thinking we threaten their material interests; our merchants think we threaten their civic privileges and monopolies, and the commons mistrust everything and everyone. Without trust as a foundation, mayhap 'tis just a matter of time before it all crashes down upon our heads."

"Aye," Margery murmured, standing to face him. "Though we cannot know. We are not soothsayers, are we?"

But Roger Bacon had been and he had predicted a preposterous future. As preposterous as the promise implicit in those mysterious words that had come to her?

Flames from St. Alban's altar candles flickered far in the distance. Light from a rising moon filtered through the stained glass windows to illumine the rows of monks chanting the versicles and their response. The monk's voices whispered round the shadowed columns, the tombs of the dead, the gilded and painted statues, before drifting to the raftered ceiling. Hard to imagine the barbarity that had just been perpetrated beyond these walls upon one of their own. Margery hoped that John Ball was included in their prayers. She would have to pay for masses for both him and Thurold and even for Fulco the Smithy, in case he had already joined them...

Margery raised her head to Matthew. "I love you so much it makes my heart ache," she whispered. Though that wasn't quite true. Margery loved him so much that it made her heart happy, just as that arcane whisper brought her, if not happiness, at least acceptance. She brushed away a strand of hair that had fallen over Matthew's forehead and allowed her palm to rest against his cheek, the roughness of his beard. Forty-four years old, two years younger than when his Prince Edward had died, and she was not so very far behind.

The remainder of their days, under the best of circumstances, could not be long. And must not be wasted.

"'Tis such a very ancient war, Meg. I do not know that it will ever end." Matthew placed his hand over hers, resting upon his cheek. "It is peaceful in Cumbria. Will you yet go with me?"

The monks had begun singing a final hymn.

Margery's lips curved in a smile. Odd that Matthew would fear he must convince her of their shared destiny, just because of Thurold and John Ball and... just because...

Margery need not travel to Cumbria to find the peace she felt now

—a peace that would surely fade as all emotions did. But she would hold onto it and nurture it as she would her herbs and flowers. And she would remember the whisper that she chose to view as a promise. Remember and hold onto it as surely as she would hold onto Matthew.

"As if you can kill an idea!"

Lacing her fingers in between her lover's, Margery and Matthew exited St. Alban's.

The End

LORDS AMONG THE RUINS

THE KNIGHTS OF ENGLAND SERIES,
BOOK FIVE

Something nagged at Matthew Hart. As he watched Fulco the Smithy recite *Robin Hood and the Monk*, an image kept flitting through Matthew's mind, one he couldn't hold on to. What was it? Something... dark... something...

There it was, just a glimmering.

And then it slipped beyond his grasp.

The smithy stood in the center of Cumbria's Great Hall, legs planted, movements minimal. He possessed a certain stillness that Matthew recognized from a lifetime of mingling with fellow warriors. A concentrated stillness that, without warning—or upon command—could explode into violence. Matthew wondered whether Fulco had participated in any of England's *chevauchees*. Perhaps as a mercenary? Or as one of the blacksmiths who had been such an integral part of Edward III's war machine, repairing weapons and armor, shoeing pack and cart and war horses?

Suddenly he remembered: where he'd first seen Fulco the Smithy.

Twilight. Chaos. Dead bodies in the courtyard. Heads on spikes. Fires in outbuildings. Shouting to the milling rebels, "Have you seen a woman and a boy?"

Bury St. Edmund's Abbey.

The Peasants' Revolt.

Fulco grabbing his horse's reins. Piercing black eyes raised to Matthew's. "Your lady and son escaped on horseback. They be London bound."

How had a stranger known his family's identities, or their where-abouts? In the aftermath of those terrible times, he and Margery had chosen not to re-visit the parts of their past that stirred the most unhappiness.

What secrets might his Meg be keeping?

"I took a lover," she'd once taunted.

That night as they lay in bed with Margery's head on his chest, his arms looped around her, Matthew said, "Tell me something."

"Aye." Margery tried to keep the wariness from her voice, tried to pretend that nothing had changed—when everything had.

"This Fulco the Smithy. I've seen the way he looks at you."

Margery pushed up so that she could better view her husband's face against the pillows. With only the faintest light from a slivered moon to ease the darkness, she felt somewhat protected from his scrutiny, though her nerves were afire. Which would never do. She must behave precisely as if she were innocent.

I am innocent!

"I've spent no time in the smithy's company. And surely you are imagining his interest." She ran a finger across his lips and said in a hopefully teasing tone, "My love, are you jealous? I'm flattered."

Matthew caught her hand. "And I see how you react to him."

Margery's throat tightened. She felt as if she could not breathe. As if she were indeed guilty.

"You're mistaken. I am courteous to everyone." She scooted back down to once more rest her cheek on Matthew's chest. So that he could not probe her expression for truths best kept hidden.

Matthew's heart thumped, strong and rhythmic, against her ear. Not as it would if he were angry. She slipped an arm across his abdomen. "Let us not waste time on such silliness."

"You told me once you'd taken a lover," he said, rubbing a tendril of her hair between his fingertips. "Was he the one?"

Oh! What should she say? She loved Matthew so very dearly. Before their marriage he'd shared everything, the horrors of the campaigns, the horrors of his actions, the holocaust that had been Limoges. He'd laid bare his soul as if to a confessor. But Matthew had not been seeking absolution. He'd merely wanted to face his past, shine the light on the hidden places, expose his shame to the air in order to heal. "This is who I truly am," he had been saying. "Will you love me now that you know? And if you don't, I will survive."

He asked so little of her in return.

To answer this one simple question.

"Was Fulco the Smithy your lover, Meg?"

It was on the tip of her tongue to tell him the truth about that ancient relationship. But what then would happen? Their peace, the quiet joy of their love had been hard won. They'd buried so much pain; must it be exorcised again?

Margery struggled up and faced her beloved. "My heart," she breathed. She forced herself to look into his eyes in a simulacrum of innocence. "No. Never."

And in that moment it seemed so.

Matthew smiled, pulled her close... and pretended to believe her.

Lords Among the Ruins
Available in eBook and Print

ALSO BY MARY ELLEN JOHNSON

The Knights of England Series

The Lion and the Leopard

A Knight There Was

Within A Forest Dark

A Child Upon the Throne

Lords Among the Ruins

ABOUT THE AUTHOR

Mary Ellen Johnson's writing career was sparked by her passion for Medieval England. Her first novel, *The Lion and the Leopard*, which took place during the doomed reign of Edward II, was followed by *The Landlord's Black-Eyed Daughter*, a historical novel based on the Alfred Noyes poem, "The Highwayman." (Published under the pseudonym, Mary Ellen Dennis.) *Landlord* was chosen as one of the top 100 historical romances of 2013.

In 1992, Mary Ellen's life took a 20 year detour when she became involved in a local murder. Later she championed the fifteen-year-old, Jacob Ind, who killed his abusive parents and chronicled that event in *The Murder of Jacob*. As the Executive Director of the Pendulum Foundation, a non-profit that serves kids serving life in prison. she has been featured in *Rolling Stone*, on the documentaries, PBS Frontline's *When Kids Get Life* and *Lost for Life*, as well as countless radio, TV and print outlets around the world.

As Mary Ellen's goal of sentencing reform nears its successful completion, she has happily returned her attention to her first love, novel writing, and her favorite time period. Her five book series, *Knights of England*, will follow the fortunes of the characters (and their progeny) introduced in *The Lion and the Leopard* through the

Black Death, the reign of that most gloriously medieval of monarchs, Edward III, the Peasants Revolt of 1381 (with issues of class and inequality that remain relevant) and ending with the tragic death—or was it murder??—of Richard II. A tumultuous and exciting century as seen through the eyes of characters, both historical and fictional, who Mary Ellen hopes you will find as engaging, frustrating, complex and unforgettable as she does!

www.MaryEllenJohnsonAuthor.com

 facebook.com/mejauthor